Also by Jenni Fletcher

Married to Her Enemy
The Convenient Felstone Marriage
Besieged and Betrothed

Discover more at millsandboon.co.uk.

CAPTAIN AMBERTON'S INHERITED BRIDE

Jenni Fletcher

MILLS & BOON

First Published in Great Britain 2018
by Mills & Boon, an imprint of HarperCollins*Publishers*
1 London Bridge Street, London, SE1 9GF

© 2018 Jenni Fletcher

ISBN: 978-0-263-93278-2

Printed and bound in Spain
by CPI, Barcelona

For Rachel and Phil. Congratulations!
Also for Therese, my writing bestie.

Prologue

Amberton Castle, North Yorkshire—1862

'There's no way out, Lance. I'm trapped.'

Captain Lancelot 'Lance' Amberton turned his attention away from a particularly attractive redhead on the dance floor and fixed his twin brother with a speculative stare. From the tone of his voice it was obvious he wasn't talking about the ballroom. He'd listened to Arthur's railing against their father's domineering behaviour a hundred times before, but the new note of despondency was unsettling enough that he almost missed the footman passing by with a fresh tray of drinks. Almost.

'It's your own fault.' He darted a hand out, swiping the tumbler of brandy he knew was destined for their father. 'You shouldn't be so damned responsible all of the time. Do something shocking. Try saying no to him once in a while.'

'Easier said than done.' Arthur's eyes, the same rich amber shade as his own, looked woebegone. 'It's not as if we can both run away and join the army.'

'I had to run away.' Lance tossed back a lock of dark chestnut hair. 'He would have thrown me out if I hadn't.'

'That's not true.'

'It is and you know it. Father and I have done nothing but argue ever since Mother died. We get on far better at opposite ends of the country.'

'I just wish you'd told me what you were planning.'

'So you could have done the *right* thing and told him?'

Arthur dropped his eyes guiltily. 'He would have bought you a commission if you'd asked.'

'That's not the point. I didn't want to owe him anything. I had the money Mother left us and I wanted to choose my own regiment. Father would have kept me in the local militia just to keep an eye on me.'

'He's still glad to have you back here tonight.'

'So he can show off his ne'er-do-well son in uniform, you mean?'

Lance threw a scornful glance around the ballroom. As pleased as he was to see Arthur again, his family home held little appeal any more. After just two days' leave, he was already itching to get back to his regiment. There were rumours that they were about to be posted abroad and he couldn't wait to put Yorkshire behind him.

'Don't put yourself down.' Arthur gave him a sympathetic look. 'You're a captain in the Fusiliers at twenty-two and doing pretty well by all accounts. That's something to be proud of.'

'I'm glad someone in the family's noticed.'

'He's noticed. He's proud of you, too, in his way.'

Lance gave a snort of derision. 'That makes a change. It's just a good thing I'm rejoining my regiment next week or we'd be back at each other's throats—and this time I'm armed.'

'Well, I've missed you these past six months. I've even missed the arguing. His lectures have got ten times worse since you left. He talks about duty and responsibility from the moment I get up until the moment I go to bed, which is early to escape. He tells me where to go, what to wear, who to talk to, even what to say. It's exhausting.'

'I've noticed.'

'I don't know how much longer I can stand it. I wish I had your stamina for fighting, but I don't. I'm just…tired.'

Lance took another swig of brandy, trying to

think of something reassuring to say and failing. Arthur had always been the thinker, the rational, peaceful son, whereas he… He was too much like their father, attacking first and asking questions later. All he knew was how to fight.

'Well, don't let it bother you tonight.' He clapped a hand on Arthur's shoulder in an attempt to lighten the mood. 'There's enough pretty girls here to entertain both of us. Let's have some fun.'

'Father doesn't approve of fun, you ought to know that by now, and I don't want to hear another rant about how not to behave.'

'That's easy. Just watch me.'

'What did you think I meant?' Arthur threw him a look that was part reproof, part appeal. 'Just don't do anything scandalous like at the Kendalls' last year. He'll never forgive you if you ruin his ball.'

'I've no intention of ruining anything. And as for the scandal, as you call it, I barely touched Olivia Kendall. No more than she wanted me to anyway.'

'She was engaged! If it had been anyone but me who'd found you on the terrace…'

'Who ruined my evening, you mean?'

'That, too, but just try behaving for once, Lance, please. As much as I'd like for you to distract Father's attention, I've got enough to deal with this evening.'

'It's only a ball, Arthur.'

'It's not *only* a ball.' Arthur sighed heavily. 'Haven't you wondered why Father decided to throw such a big event all of a sudden?'

'No.' Though come to think of it, it *was* odd, especially considering the parlous state of the estate's finances. The oak-panelled ballroom was usually opened up only once a year, for the spring ball their father considered his social duty, but tonight he seemed in uncharacteristically lavish mood. The room had rarely looked so splendid, with white and red bouquets of cut flowers adorning every available surface and a floor so highly polished it resembled glass, glittering with the light of a hundred candles suspended in crystal chandeliers above.

'Well, I did. I thought he was planning something, but I never expected...' Arthur drew in a deep breath. 'Look, I'm not supposed to tell you, but Father called me to his study this afternoon. He wants me to marry Jeremy Harper's daughter.'

'Harper the shipbuilder?' Lance almost spat out his mouthful of brandy. 'That miserable old curmudgeon? Since when does he have a daughter?'

'Since she was born eighteen years ago.'

'I didn't even know he was married.'

'He's not. His wife died a few years before Mother. Don't you pay attention to anything?'

'Not things like that, no.'

'Lance…'

'Oh, don't look at me like that. You know I prefer to swim in the shallows.'

'No, you like to swim out of your depth and not think about it.'

'What's the difference?'

Arthur shook his head remonstratively. 'The difference is that one day you might want to stand up in the water and not be able to. You ought to look under the surface once in a while.'

'Duly noted. I'll read the obituaries tomorrow.'

'That's not what I meant.'

'I know, but it's the best I can do.' Lance tossed back the last of his brandy and deposited the glass on a passing tray. 'So what's she like, your new bride?'

'Her name's Violet and she's not my bride, not yet anyway. I've no idea what she looks like, never mind the rest, and nobody else seems to know either. Harper's kept her locked away in that redbrick mausoleum he calls a house her whole life. So far as I know this is the first time she's been out in society.'

'Well, if she's anything like Harper…' Lance

started to laugh and then stopped himself. 'Sorry. But at least you know she'll be obedient. She couldn't not be, growing up with him. That can't have been easy.'

'True,' Arthur conceded. 'I've never understood how Father could be friends with that old tyrant.'

'Something to do with money, I expect. She'll be as rich as Croesus some day. But you know if you're supposed to be meeting your *prospective* bride, you ought to take your eyes off Lydia Webster. You've been acting like a lovesick puppy all evening.'

'Is it that obvious?' Arthur's cheekbones suffused with colour.

'Only to me and everyone else in the room.'

'I can't help it, Lance. She's the most exquisite creature I've ever laid eyes on. I'm in love.'

'With Lydia Webster?' Lance took a second glance across the ballroom to make sure they were talking about the same woman. 'She's a flirt and a gold-digger, and a pretty shameless one, too. She'd throw you over the moment she found out about our family finances, or lack of them, I should say. Better take your chances with Miss Harper.'

'Don't!' Arthur's face displayed a rare flash of temper. 'Don't speak of her like that.'

'I'm only trying to stop you making a mistake.'

'No, you're treating me the same way Father does, as if I can't think for myself. Well, I can and I ought to be allowed to choose my own bride.'

'You're right, you should. So tell Father that. Refuse to marry Miss Harper.'

Arthur's expression turned sullen. 'I don't hear you saying no to a woman very often.'

'I don't need to. I'm not the heir. No one wants to ensnare the feckless younger brother.'

Not that it stopped them wanting to do other things, he thought cynically... Cordelia Braithwaite for one had been throwing beckoning glances in his direction all evening, ever since her husband had abandoned her for the card room. Not to mention the pretty, and currently partnerless, redhead. Even if he *had* just promised to behave, some opportunities were too good to miss. As soon as he finished consoling his brother, he'd start taking advantage of them.

'Only younger by ten minutes.' Arthur sounded bitter. 'Sometimes I wish we could just change places. Then you could tell Father for me.'

'Wouldn't work, I'm afraid. I'd never be able to look as responsible or intelligent as you. Ten minutes makes all the difference, apparently.'

'Then maybe you're right.' Arthur's dolorous

tone shifted suddenly. 'Maybe it *is* time I stood up to him.'

'That's the spirit.'

'I just need to be blunt.'

'Absolutely.'

'I'll tell him I have my own plans.'

'Exactly.'

'I'll say… Wait!' Arthur's hand shot out and gripped his shoulder. 'There she is.'

'Who?'

'Violet Harper!'

Lance turned casually towards the doorway, though it took him a few moments to actually locate the subject of their conversation. Standing between their two fathers, she was the tiniest, most unusual-looking woman he'd ever seen, nothing at all like he would have expected, an innocent daisy between two bristly thistles. Dressed all in white, she looked more like a fairy-tale creature than a woman, seeming to give off an almost translucent glow in the candlelight. Even her hair was pale, a shade of shimmering, silvery blonde that fell in a perfectly straight line to her waist. It gave her an oddly top-heavy appearance, though the top of her head barely skimmed the shoulders of their father, whose six-foot frame both he and Arthur had inherited. How would one kiss such a woman without getting backache, he wondered, not to mention other things? Not that he'd shirk such a challenge…

'It could be worse.' He nudged Arthur none too subtly in the ribs.

'What, your behaviour?'

'Very funny. I mean Father's choice of bride. She looks like a kitten.' He grinned. 'I want to pat her on the head.'

'You marry her, then.'

'Shall we go and suggest it? I'd like to see Father's face if we did. Harper's, too. They'd both have apoplexies on the spot.'

'Maybe we ought to suggest it, then.'

'She's pretty.'

'Do you think so?'

'Unusual. I like unusual.'

'You would. Have you ever met a woman you didn't like?'

Lance shrugged, unabashed. It was true, he wasn't biased towards any one type of woman. He liked variety—the more of it the better—though there was something particularly intriguing about Miss Harper, something that piqued his interest more than he would have expected. He let his gaze roam over her face and figure appreciatively. Her tiny size and distinctive colouring made her appear strangely ethereal, as if she were in the room and yet apart from it somehow.

He couldn't think of another way to explain it, but the duality only increased her appeal.

The longer he looked, the more he noticed other contradictions about her. Pint-sized though she was, her hips and breasts were disproportionately wide and generous, quite distractingly so, in fact. Her facial features were large, too, her eyes in particular seeming to take up half of her face, their intense blueness striking even from a distance. And as for her lips—he found himself running his tongue along his own instinctively—surely they were the most sensuous-looking pair he'd ever laid eyes on. Plump and voluptuous, like a bow he wanted to pluck on.

He took a flute of champagne from a passing footman and gulped it down quickly, taken aback by the strength of his attraction to her. If it hadn't been for the obligation of marriage, he might have felt jealous of his own brother.

'I wonder what she thinks about marrying you.' He dragged his gaze away finally.

'She doesn't know anything about it.'

'What?'

Arthur turned his back pointedly towards the doorway. 'The whole thing's bizarre, but Father and Harper have already drawn up papers. According to their agreement, I'm only to marry her after Harper dies. He married late, so who knows how old he is now. We're engaged, but she's not to be told anything until after the funeral. Then we get married, I get his fortune and she gets a title.'

'Doesn't she get a say in the matter?'

'Apparently neither of us does.'

'What if Harper lives another twenty years? He looks like he'll go on for ever.'

'There's probably a clause to cover that, too. No doubt Father expects me to produce an heir and I don't suppose he'll be willing to wait that long.'

'Then maybe there's a way out after all.' Lance lifted an eyebrow as Harper let go of her arm, passing her across to their father as if at some kind of prearranged signal. 'You just have to keep the old ghoul alive.'

'It's still morbid.'

'What else do you expect from those two?'

Arthur shook his head contemptuously. 'You know Father's only throwing this ball to impress him. He just assumes I'll go along with their scheme. He treats me like a dog sometimes.'

'Then bite back.' Lance found his gaze drawn inexorably back towards her. 'Do you really think he's kept her locked up her whole life? There *is* a kind of fairy-tale quality about her. Just look at that hair…'

'It's white.'

'It's silver.'

'If she's old enough to be engaged, then she ought to be wearing it up.'

'Maybe he won't let her. In any case, here they come. Prepare to be charming.'

'I don't want to be—'

Arthur fell silent as their father appeared at his shoulder, Miss Harper's elbow grasped firmly in one hand.

'Father.' Lance smiled innocently as Arthur made a stiff bow. 'Won't you introduce us to your charming companion?'

'I was just about to.' Their father regarded him suspiciously for a moment. 'Miss Harper, these are my sons, the Honourable Arthur Amberton and...' there was a brief, but noticeable pause '... Captain Lancelot Amberton.'

'The not-quite-so-Honourable.'

Lance flashed his most charming smile and reached for her hand, brushing his lips along the delicate line of her knuckles. Up close, her eyes were an iridescent shade of blue, he noticed, lighter in the middle and darker towards the edges, surrounded by a thick black line that served to make them look even bigger.

'Charmed to meet you, Miss Harper.'

'Oh...thank you.' She dropped into a wavering curtsy, darting a quick glance across the room to where her father stood watching.

'Miss Harper...' his own father shot him a

warning look '…is here to accompany Arthur into supper.'

'I am?' She looked up quickly, her voice slightly breathless-sounding, as if she were surprised to find herself the subject of so much attention.

'Yes, my dear. Your father's given his permission.'

'He has?' This time she sounded positively shocked.

'I'm afraid that's impossible, sir.' Arthur spoke up at last. 'I've already promised to escort Miss Webster into supper. My apologies, Miss Harper.'

'Then you must *un*-promise Miss Webster.' A look of surprise crossed their father's features. 'I've agreed that you'll escort Miss Harper.'

'Then perhaps you ought to have informed me of your wishes earlier, Father. Or at least asked. I've no wish to be ungallant.'

'*This* is ungallant!'

'Perhaps I might escort Miss Harper into supper?' Lance interrupted smoothly. 'Keep her in the family, so to speak?'

'You can stay out of it!' Their father's face was starting to take on a familiar puce colour.

'As you wish. I was only trying to help.'

'We all know very well how you help, sir!'

Their father gave a sudden jolt, as if he'd just

realised what he'd said and who was listening, though he seemed unable to think of a way to remedy the situation, his jaw quivering with a combination of frustrated rage and embarrassment.

'In any case, my offer stands, Miss Harper.' Lance broke the ensuing awkward silence, regarding his father with amusement. 'Though I might not be able to offer such scintillating conversation as my brother here. As you can tell, you'd be in danger of him talking your ear off.'

'Arthur.' Their father's tone was threatening. 'A word.'

Lance gave his brother a supportive look as the two men stepped to one side, leaving him alone with his distinctly embarrassed-looking companion. At least her cheeks had some colour now, he thought sardonically, having turned a vibrant shade of luminous pink, as if she were even more mortified by their situation than his father.

'I didn't mean to cause any trouble.' Her voice was so quiet he found himself leaning forward to catch it.

'And you haven't.' He took a step to one side, attempting to block her view of his father and brother arguing. 'We aren't happy in our family unless we're butting heads.'

'Your brother doesn't look very happy.' Her

tiny brow wrinkled as she peered around him. 'He looks very unhappy.'

Lance twisted his head with a frown. That was true. As much as he hated to admit it, Arthur did look unhappy. His shoulders were slumped forward as if he were wearing some kind of heavy garment that he couldn't shrug off or put down. Not that there was anything that *he* could do about that—nothing except tell him to stand up to their father and he did that often enough— but Miss Harper was more observant than he'd expected. If he wasn't careful, she'd force him to be serious.

'If he's made a promise to Miss Webster, then he ought to take her in to supper.' She looked back at him, wide-eyed. 'I don't understand why your father's being so insistent.'

He shrugged in what he hoped was a con- vincingly offhand manner. 'Our fathers are old friends. I suppose they want the two of you to get to know each other.'

'But not you?'

'No.' He couldn't repress a smile. 'I'm afraid my reputation precedes me.'

'Reputation for what?'

He opened his mouth and then closed it again, fighting the impulse to laugh. He wasn't often rendered speechless, but in this case he had no idea how to answer. Was she really so innocent that she didn't know what he meant? He was tempted to tell her, even more so to show her, but he could already sense her father's disapproving stare from the other side of the ballroom. It wouldn't be long before the old man made his way round to interrupt them and he felt reluctant to let her go quite so soon.

'Shall we have a dance before supper?' He extended one arm with a flourish.

'Dance?' She looked as if he'd just suggested something indecent. 'Oh, no, I couldn't.'

'Why not?' He made a pretence of looking around. 'This is a ball, if I'm not mistaken.'

'I'm just not very good. That is, I've had lessons, but only with women and never in public. I really don't think that I could.'

'You mean you've never danced with a man before?'

'No. My father says—'

'But this is perfect! You have to start some time.'

He grabbed hold of her hand impetuously, ignoring her father's furious glare as he pulled her on to the floor. The idea of being her first anything was strangely appealing, even if it was only a dance, and there was no harm in getting to know his potential sister-in-law. It wasn't as if he was flirting with her, no more than came naturally anyway, and it wasn't like Arthur would care—or even notice. Judging by the heated discussion taking place on the edge of the dance floor, his brother had chosen the most public of venues to finally make a stand. It didn't look as if that was going to end any time soon. In which case, the longer he distracted the subject of that discussion, the better. It was almost selfless of him really...

'No!' She dug her heels in and tore her hand away abruptly.

'Miss Harper?'

He swung round in surprise. She looked defiant all of a sudden, like a cat arching her back, flashing her eyes and hissing at him. The effect was as impressive as it was disarming, and he felt a dawning sense of respect. Apparently she wasn't as obedient as he'd assumed, wouldn't be charmed or cajoled or bullied on to the dance floor. There were claws behind that small, soft-looking facade. Damned if that didn't make her even more attractive!

'I apologise for my forthrightness, Miss Harper.' He bowed in an attempt to look suitably chastised. 'I can only blame overenthusiasm.'

'I told you, I'm not good enough to dance.'

'But I am, though I say so myself. I haven't dropped anyone for a good half hour.' He moved back towards her, putting a hand over his heart with mock solemnity. 'But I promise I won't let *you* fall. If you'll do me the honour of accepting this dance, that is?'

Her eyes widened slightly, as if she wasn't sure how to react, and he found himself willing her to say yes. Out of the corner of his eye he could see her father bearing down on them, coming to drag her away most likely, and by the slight tilt of her head he had the distinct impression she'd just noticed him, too. To Lance's surprise, the sight seemed to decide her. After a moment's hesitation, she took his arm, following him out into the middle of the dance floor.

The orchestra struck up a tune and he smiled with satisfaction. It was a polka, a livelier dance than the waltz, but still one that allowed him to face her, to place one hand on her shoulder blade while he clasped her gloved fingers in the other.

'My father told me not to dance with anyone except your brother.' She tensed as his hand skimmed across the small of her back.

'Then you're more rebellious than I thought, Miss Harper.'

'I'm not rebellious at all.' Her expression shifted subtly. 'Though sometimes I think I'd like to be.'

'Indeed? Then you've come to the right man. I'd be more than happy to help.'

'Oh.' Her brow furrowed with a look of confusion. 'Thank you.'

He bit back a laugh, flirting by habit, though in truth, he was surprised by the variety of ideas that sprang to mind, none of which were remotely suitable in relation to his brother's future wife. Over the top of her head he could see Cordelia Braithwaite pouting at him, though the sight left him cold. For some inexplicable reason, he preferred the unworldly, unusual Miss Harper.

'The music's very fast.' She sounded nervous.

'Just follow my lead.'

He squeezed her fingers reassuringly as he led them off, sweeping her in a series of increasingly wide circles around the dance floor. She stumbled slightly at first, but quickly caught up with the rhythm, gradually relaxing in his arms as she adapted to the lively pace of the music. Contrary to what he'd expected, it was surprisingly easy to dance with her. He didn't have any backache at all. She was so light that he found himself actually lifting her off her feet with every hop, her natural poise making her float like a feather in his arms.

'I didn't peg you for a liar, Miss Harper.' He arched an eyebrow accusingly.

'What do you mean?' She looked startled again.

'You said you weren't a good dancer. You're a natural.'

Her whole face seemed to light up as she

smiled. 'I do enjoy it. We have a ballroom at home, though we've never had a ball.'

'What a waste.'

'Sometimes I dance there by myself.'

'Without music?'

'I sing.' She bit her lip suddenly as if regretting the admission. 'I suppose that sounds ridiculous.'

'On the contrary, I'm sure you make quite a charming picture. I'd like to see *and* hear it.'

She smiled again and he tightened his grip on her shoulder, amused and intrigued in equal measure. He'd never visited the Harpers' mansion in Whitby, though it was rumoured to be immense and as chilling in appearance as its owner was in reality. The daughter really was straight out of a fairy tale. At this point he wouldn't have been surprised to learn that she'd grown up in an ivory tower.

'This is your first ball, I understand?'

She nodded enthusiastically. 'It's my first anything. I've never seen so many people in one place. The ladies all look so beautiful.'

'I suppose so.' He glanced around, though the rest of the room seemed to have lost some of its lustre. All the other women looked drab by comparison.

'Would you introduce me to some of them?'

'The ladies?' He raised both eyebrows this time. 'Don't you know anyone?'

'The only people I know here are my father and yours, and now you. I don't have many acquaintances.'

'Not even in Whitby?'

'No.' She looked vaguely apologetic. 'My father doesn't like to make calls and he doesn't approve of me going out on my own.'

'Indeed?' He felt a flicker of anger towards her father. Had she really been a prisoner, then? And yet she spoke matter-of-factly, as if she didn't expect anything else. 'In that case I'd be glad to make some introductions. Then perhaps you could encourage your father to throw his own ball? So that you can dance in your own house, I mean.'

'Father?' Her laugh sounded like a bell tinkling. 'I can't imagine that ever happening.'

'Not even for your coming out?' He felt a sudden impulse to test her, to see if she suspected anything of their fathers' scheming. 'I'm sure you'd find plenty of suitors.'

The silvery glow that had seemed to envelop her faded, as if a shadow had just fallen over her face. 'My father doesn't approve of suitors.'

'Maybe not, but after tonight I'm sure there'll be plenty of young men eager to renew your acquaintance.'

'Eager for my father's money, you mean?'

He almost tripped over his feet, taken aback by her bluntness. It was an unfortunate truth that in the eyes of the world her fortune would constitute her most attractive feature. She was too unusual looking to be called beautiful—he wouldn't be surprised if his father actually saw coins when he looked at her—but such things weren't usually spoken about out loud.

'I see.' Something of his thoughts must have shown on his face because an expression of hurt swept over hers. 'I think I'd like to stop dancing now.'

He blinked, surprised for the second time in less than a minute. Never in his life had a woman asked to stop dancing with him before. Most wanted to do a lot more than that. He couldn't have been any more surprised if she'd slapped him across the cheek.

'Miss Harper, if I've offended you then I apologise.'

'You haven't.' She stopped stock-still in the middle of the dance floor, every part of her body turning rigid at once. 'I know what I am.'

'What you are?' He made a brief gesture of apology as the couple behind them polkaed straight into his back.

'Yes! And I refuse to stand here and be mocked for it.'

'What…?'

He didn't get any further as she twisted away from him, pushing her way through the dancers as he stared speechlessly after her. What on earth had he said to cause such an extreme reaction? That she might have suitors? Women liked to be told they'd have suitors, didn't they? And yet she'd seemed to think he'd been laughing at her, as if the very idea were a joke—as if *she* were a joke. Why the hell would she think that?

He started after her, taking a different path through the throng. He had to fix it, whatever it was that he'd done. If his father were really so determined to have her as a daughter-in-law, then he didn't want to make a bad situation any worse—although he didn't want to upset her either, he realised. The look of hurt on her face had elicited an unexpected feeling of guilt. It wasn't an emotion he was accustomed to, had actually taken him a few moments to identify, and he wanted to be rid of it as quickly as possible.

'Miss Harper.' He intercepted her before she could reach her father. 'I wasn't mocking you. I was only trying to make conversation.'

'Well, I didn't find it amusing.'

'Then blame my shoddy manners.' He put an arm out as she tried to dodge past him. 'I was too forward, but for what it's worth, I think you might have any number of eager suitors. There aren't many women I'd run across a ballroom for.'

She lifted her chin, meeting his gaze with a dignity that managed to make him feel even more guilty. 'I'm not devoid of intelligence, Captain Amberton. My father's told me not to think about marriage and I don't. He's warned me that any suitors would only be after my fortune.'

'But that's preposterous!' He felt a spontaneous burst of temper. What kind of father would say such a vile thing, as if she had no attractions of her own? She had more than enough, in his eyes anyway, not that it was his place to say so. That was supposed to be his brother's job. Where *was* Arthur anyway? There were enough people looking in their direction now, but no sign of his brother among them.

Her eyes flashed. 'My father wants what's best for me. He's trying to protect me.'

'He's a liar!'

'Indeed, sir?'

Lance clenched his jaw, stifling an oath at the sound of her father's voice behind him. So much for behaving himself. Somehow he'd managed to cause a scene and insult one of his father's oldest friends into the bargain. Not that he felt particularly sorry. On the contrary, now that he'd started a scandal, he saw little point in stopping.

He turned around, looking the older man

square in the eye. 'If you've told your daughter that no man would want to marry her for herself then, yes, sir, you're a liar.'

'What I say to my daughter is no business of yours.' Harper's beady eyes narrowed malevolently. 'And I'll thank you to keep your distance in future. She won't be dancing with a reprobate like you again.'

'Better a reprobate than a liar.'

'Captain Amberton!' Miss Harper pushed herself between them, though her tiny height did nothing to obstruct either one of their views. 'You've no right to insult my father!'

'I do when he insults you.'

'I've only told her the truth.' Harper jutted his chin out as if daring him to take a swing at it. 'Or are you saying that *you'd* marry her without my money?'

'What?' He said the word at the same moment she did, though it was impossible to tell which of them sounded the most horrified.

'I asked if you'd marry her for herself? Since you take such a keen interest.'

Lance dropped his gaze to her face, but she was already looking away, arms folded around her waist as if she were trying to make herself look as small and unobtrusive as possible. *Would* he marry her? No. Of course not. He had absolutely no intention of shackling himself to any woman, no matter how attractive or intriguing he found her, though he could hardly say so without causing her further embarrassment. Better that than an engagement, however…

'I'm about to return to my regiment, sir.' He gave the first excuse that came into his head. 'I've no provision for a wife.'

'Ha!' Harper's face contorted with a look of malicious glee. 'I thought not.'

Somehow Lance resisted the urge to grab the older man by the lapels and throw him headfirst through the nearest window. What on earth was the matter with him? Every eye in the room was turned towards them, every ear honed to hear every word—even the orchestra had stopped playing to listen—and yet Harper seemed so determined to win their argument that he had no qualms about humiliating his daughter in public. Just how much of a monster was he?

'What's going on?' His father burst upon them suddenly, trailing a defeated-looking Arthur behind him. 'Lance, I told you to behave yourself.'

'I *was* behaving myself.'

He ran a hand through his hair, torn between exasperation and dull fury. How exactly had he found himself in this position, between two livid fathers, a silent brother and a tiny kitten of a woman who looked as though she wished the ground would open up and swallow her? Why the hell was *he* the one defending her?

'He called me a liar.' Harper's tone was indignant.

'And you called me a reprobate.' Lance shot him a savage look. 'I believe that makes us even.'

'Apologise!' His father's voice was a hiss, bristling with rage. 'Apologise to our guest right now.'

'Don't you want to hear my side of the story?'

'Your side of the story is always the same. He called you a reprobate because that's what you are. Now apologise or get out of my house this instant!'

'Stop!' It was Miss Harper who interrupted this time. 'Please stop. It was all my fault. I overreacted, I'm sure.'

'I doubt that, my dear.' His father didn't even bother to look at her. 'You mustn't distress yourself.'

'But you mustn't do this! Not because of me. It's too awful.'

'It's no more than he deserves. This is the last straw, Lance.'

'For you, too, Father.' He didn't wait another moment, turning his back and cutting a swathe through the dancers as he stormed towards the door. 'Don't expect me to set foot in this house ever again!'

'Good!' His father's voice reverberated around the ballroom. 'Because I wouldn't let you in! You're no son of mine any more!'

Lance stopped in the doorway, opening his mouth to hurl one final parting shot, then closing it again as he caught sight of his brother. Arthur was standing off to one side, a picture of such abject misery that he was half tempted to march back across the room and drag him away with him, too. But he was going back to his regiment and Arthur...well, Arthur was going to marry Violet Harper.

He took one last look at her face, at her big blue eyes made even bigger with shock. She was right about one thing. This *was* all her fault. If she hadn't been so damned oversensitive, then he wouldn't have had to run after her to apologise, wouldn't have run into her father or stood up for her either, not that she'd thanked him for that! His lip curled contemptuously. From now on, he'd stick with the Cordelia Braithwaites of the world. Women like Violet Harper were more trouble than they were worth.

He turned away, mentally consigning his father, Harper and the whole room, Arthur excepted, to the deepest, darkest region of Hades. As for Violet Harper, future sister-in-law or not, he earnestly hoped he never set eyes on her again.

Chapter One

❦

March 1867—five years later

The snow started to fall around midday.

Violet tugged at the hood of her thin grey, woefully inadequate cloak and tipped her head back, sticking her tongue out to catch a flake on its tip. It melted at once, sending an icy trickle sliding down the back of her throat. Snow. She'd never been out in it before, had only ever watched it fall through a windowpane, and the new experience was invigorating.

Nothing, not even bad weather, could dampen her spirits today. She ought to be frightened, sitting in the back of a rickety old cart rattling its way high over the moors, running away from her home, her few friends and everything else she'd ever known, but instead she felt exhilarated. Even the barren heather-and-gorse-filled wilderness didn't intimidate her this morning, as it always had from a distance. Today it looked free and unconfined and alive, the way that she finally felt inside. In the space of a few hours, she'd travelled further than she ever had in the whole of her twenty-three years previously, not just in distance, but in herself, too. At long last, she'd taken charge of her own future, refusing to be the old, shrinking Violet any longer. For the first time in her life, she felt proud of herself.

Not a bad accomplishment for her wedding day.

'The mine's just over that ridge!' the driver's boy called back to her. 'Don't worry about the weather, miss. We've ridden through worse.'

She gave him a dazzling smile and settled back against the crates bearing supplies up to the miners at Rosedale. The driver had promised to take her on to Helmsley afterwards, though she could only imagine what he and his boy must be thinking of her. Her friend Ianthe had vouched for them, both for their characters as well as their ability to keep a secret, but they must surely still be wondering why a lone gentlewoman would arrange to meet them at dawn on the outskirts of Whitby as if she were fleeing the clutches of some evil tyrant.

Which in one sense, she supposed, she was.

She'd been planning her escape for the past

week, almost from the moment Mr Rowlinson
had taken her aside after her father's funeral,
saying he preferred to communicate the terms of
the will in private. It hadn't taken her long to understand why. The lawyer had been apologetic as
he'd read, watching her anxiously over the metal
rim of his spectacles, though no amount of sympathetic looks could have mitigated the shock
of those words. Looking back she felt strangely
detached from the scene, as if it had been someone else sitting in her chair like some kind of
black-clad statue, frozen in horror as her father
bequeathed her in marriage to the heir of Amberton Castle.

Bequeathed!

In that moment she'd felt something harden
inside her, as if all her feelings of grief and loss
had crystallised into something else, something
colder and darker. She didn't know what the
emotion was, if it even was an emotion at all. It
felt more like the absence of one, an emptiness
at the very centre of her being, as if her ability
to feel anything had been suspended.

She remembered laughing. She must have
sounded hysterical because Mr Rowlinson had
rushed to pour her a glass of brandy and, for the
first time in her life, she'd accepted. Her father
had never allowed her to touch any kind of alco-

hol, but she'd wanted to drink the whole bottle just to spite him.

A few sips had put paid to that idea, making her cough and splutter and her head spin even more as she'd tried to understand how her father could have done such a thing to her. After so many years of obedience, of living her life in the shadows, tolerating his abuse and his insults, how could he have arranged a marriage without even telling her—let alone asking her? Just when she'd thought she might finally be free.

She ought to have known that he wouldn't let her go so easily. He'd never allowed her to make any decisions of her own and now it seemed he intended to keep on controlling her life even after his death. The terms of the will were so strict that even Mr Rowlinson had faltered in reading them. Unconventional as it was to hold a wedding so soon after a funeral, her father's words were as uncompromising and unyielding as ever. Unless she married the man of his choosing within one month of his burial, she would be disinherited, would lose her home and her fortune to a distant cousin in Lancashire. In short, she would be penniless.

Unless she did as she was told.

Her spinning thoughts had rushed back to the ball at Amberton Castle five years before, the one and only such event she'd ever attended. At least the will finally explained why her father had been so uncharacteristically keen for her to spend time with Arthur Amberton, not just at the ball, but on the monthly visits he'd made with his own father since.

She'd been vaguely suspicious, especially when her father had started to drop hints about her future, even once going so far as to actually say he'd arranged a marriage for her, though she'd eventually concluded that it was some kind of cruel joke. After all, he was the one who'd always told her how small and unattractive she was, how only a fortune hunter would pretend to want her, how she was better off without a husband. It hadn't made any sense that he would ever want her to marry.

Besides which, there had never been anything in Arthur Amberton's behaviour to suggest that he was remotely interested in her. He'd always looked as depressed on his visits as he had the first time they'd met at the ball. Their few conversations had been stilted and uncomfortable, their fathers watching over them like a pair of severe-looking owls. He'd never as much as hinted at a secret engagement, if he'd even known of it, though if he had, he couldn't have made it any more obvious that he didn't want to marry her. No more than she'd wanted to marry him.

Though even he would have been preferable to the alternative...

She pulled her hood tight around her face, oppressed by a wave of sadness. Arthur Amberton had been lost at sea seven months before, sailing his small boat along the North Yorkshire coast on a calm, late summer's day. He'd gone out alone, without telling anyone where he was going, and his boat had been discovered by a fishing vessel the next day, intact and undamaged, though Arthur himself had been nowhere to be found. There'd been numerous theories—that he'd hit his head and fallen overboard, that he'd been attacked, that he'd gone for a swim and developed cramp—though no one had wanted to mention the obvious answer, that he'd taken his own life rather than live with his despair a day longer. Rather than marry her.

Ironically, she'd been the one who'd insisted on keeping the news from her father. He'd been bedridden already by that point and she hadn't wanted to distress him any further. She'd been half-afraid that Henry Amberton, Arthur's father, might make an appearance, but the following day had brought further bad news. The father had suffered a fatal heart attack on being told about the empty boat. Father and son had died within twenty-four hours of each other, leaving a different heir to the estate.

Captain Lancelot Edward Amberton, the new Viscount Scorborough.

The very thought of him made her shudder, evoking the same feeling of stomach-churning embarrassment she'd felt at their first encounter. She'd been hopelessly naive, actually enjoying his company to begin with. She'd been excited and nervous about her first ball, all too vividly aware of the strange looks and whispered comments she knew her tiny size and extreme paleness attracted, but Captain Amberton had seemed not to notice.

He'd been confident, friendly and open, unlike any man she'd ever met before, seeming to embody the very freedom the ball represented. He'd come to her rescue when his father and brother had been arguing, encouraging her to talk when she felt tongue-tied and putting her at ease when she'd been too afraid to dance. She'd actually defied her father by dancing with him and she couldn't deny how attractive she'd found him, far more so than his brother despite their being identical twins, with his carelessly swept-back chestnut hair, his broad, muscular frame, and the roguish glint in his eye that had made her want to smile, too. When he'd held her in his arms she'd felt a new and distinctly alarming sensation, a tremulous fluttering low in her abdomen, that had made her feel giddy and excited and awkward all at the same time.

That was *before* she'd realised he'd been laughing at her, mocking her about the possibility of suitors, as if she'd ever have any. She'd felt self-conscious enough at the start of the evening, but then she'd earnestly wished herself back in the isolation of her own bedroom.

Despite that humiliation, however, worse still had been the scene that had followed. Confusingly, he'd seemed to be standing up for her at first, though she'd felt compelled to defend her own father. The moment when he'd said he wouldn't want to marry her had been one of the worst of her life. She could hardly have expected any other answer, but the words had still felt like a knife to the heart.

Yet his subsequent banishment had seemed like her fault somehow. Too late, she'd tried to say something to help, but she hadn't been able to stop it. He'd stormed away and the look he'd given her from the doorway had been anything but friendly. It had seemed more like he hated her.

Her father had taken her aside afterwards, forbidding her to mention the name Lancelot Amberton in his hearing ever again, and she'd overheard enough of the subsequent gossip to understand why. What she'd thought was a hint of scandal about him was in fact the whole truth. He was exactly what her father had called him, a reprobate. A drunkard, a gambler, a notorious ladies' man—and now the man that she was supposed to marry!

Never in a thousand years would her father have intended to leave her at the mercy of such a man, but he'd made one significant mistake in writing his will. He hadn't specified a name, simply stating the heir to the Amberton estate— and the new heir was Lance.

She refused to even consider the possibility of marriage to him. He'd returned to Yorkshire a few months before, invalided out of the army a bare month after the deaths of his brother and father with a bullet wound to the leg, or so she'd heard, though he hadn't been seen in Whitby at all. It was rumoured that he'd become a recluse, never venturing further than the walls of Amberton Castle.

He hadn't attended her father's funeral either, hadn't sent any flowers, nor so much as a card of sympathy. The only communication had come two days afterwards through Mr Rowlinson—a brief note to say that he intended to honour the terms of their fathers' agreement, that he would meet and marry her exactly one week later, at ten o'clock on the tenth day of March, 1867.

So she'd run away. He was the last man on

earth she wanted to see, let alone to marry, and yet she was very much afraid that if she stayed then she would. After a lifetime of obedience, she wasn't sure exactly how to assert herself, and Lancelot Amberton had struck her as the kind of man who knew exactly how to get what he wanted. And he wanted her fortune—that much she was sure of. It was the only possible motive he could have for wanting to marry her.

In which case, she'd decided, all she needed to do was hide and wait for the terms of her father's will to expire. Captain Amberton might make efforts to find her during that time, but once the month lapsed, he'd lose interest and she'd be safe. It would leave her almost penniless, all except for a small legacy left by her mother, but it would mean freedom, and surely even a life of poverty would be better than him.

She'd confided her plans to her dearest friend in the world, Ianthe Felstone, and whilst she hadn't approved, she *had* understood. After some initial reluctance they'd plotted her escape together.

Ianthe had arranged for Violet to join the supply run that left her husband Robert's warehouse every two weeks for the Rosedale mines. Then she'd volunteered to go to Whitby station on the morning of the wedding, draped in a heavy black veil to catch the train to Pickering as a decoy. Even her eccentric Aunt Sophoria had been roped in. Ianthe had flatly refused to let her travel without a chaperon, so it was Sophoria that Violet was going to meet in Helmsley, from where they intended to travel to York.

Nervous as she was, the thought of visiting such a large city with all its museums and art galleries and parks was thrilling. She'd resolved to make the most of her time there because afterwards...

In all honesty, she had no idea about what she'd do afterwards, but she'd think of something. She'd escape first and think about the future later. She could be a governess or a companion, if anyone would take her, but there was one thing she was absolutely determined about, that she would never live under the control of any man, not ever, *ever* again. She wouldn't be told what to do, nor how to think about herself or anything else either. From now on, she'd be free.

She clenched her fists at the thought, then loosened them again quickly as the cart lurched forward suddenly and then down, giving an ear-splitting creak as it dropped to one side so force-fully that she toppled with it, banging her head against one of the crates. For a few seconds, the world seemed to spin and blur, the whirling snowflakes above turning rainbow-coloured, before she focused again on the boy's face peering down at her.

'Are you all right, miss?'

Tentatively, she reached a hand to her temples. She felt slightly dazed, but otherwise unharmed. That was a relief. She wouldn't get very far injured.

'I think so.' She took his proffered hand and clambered inelegantly over the front of the trap. 'What happened?'

'Pothole. One of the wheels has come loose from the axle.'

'Can you fix it?' She felt a flutter of panic at the thought of turning back.

'Aye.' The driver was crouched down beside the cart, examining the undercarriage. 'We just need to get out of this hole first.'

'Can I help?'

'A tiny thing like you?' He shook his head dismissively. 'But if you want to be useful, lead the horses on a bit and hold them there.'

Violet grasped hold of the leather bridles, stifling a sense of resentment as she walked the animals on a few paces, dragging the cart back on to flat terrain. She was used to people commenting on her small size, but it wasn't as if the driver's lad was much bigger than her. She wasn't completely useless, no matter what everyone around her seemed to think. There was more that she could do, she was sure of it, if only someone would give her the chance.

'Right, then.' The driver wiped a hand over his brow. 'Now we just need to lift the frame and... Who's that, then?'

Her heart almost jumped out of her chest at the words. The moorland road was rarely used these days, not since the railway had replaced the old stagecoach, and they hadn't passed any other vehicles that morning. Not that there was any cause for alarm, surely. At this moment, Captain Amberton was most likely in pursuit of the steam train or, failing that, riding along the coast road towards Newcastle. Still...

Her nerves tightened as she peered around the edge of the trap, back along the road towards two bay-coloured horses just cresting the top of the rise behind them, one of them bearing a chestnut-haired man wrapped in a long, black greatcoat.

No! She whipped her head back again. It couldn't be him. The riders were still too far away for her to be certain, but surely it couldn't be. How could he possibly have found her? Even if he'd somehow discovered that she hadn't caught the train, there was no way he could have guessed the direction in which she was travelling, never mind with whom... Was there?

'Looks like they're in a hurry.' The driver

stepped out into the road to hail them. 'But maybe they'll lend a hand.'

'Wait!'

She tried to call out, but her voice seemed to have abandoned her, emerging as a fierce whisper rather than a call. It was too late anyway. The riders were already slowing to a halt, drawing rein just a few feet away from the trap. Quickly, she pushed her way between the two horses, glad for once of the short height that allowed her to hide more easily. With any luck they wouldn't notice her, but even if they did, she still had her hood pulled over her hair. If she kept her head down, they wouldn't be able to see her face, would hopefully assume she was another boy. She might still escape as long as she didn't draw attention to herself—*if* it was him.

'Might we be of assistance?'

Her heart plummeted. It *was* him. Captain Amberton, or her pursuer, as she now thought of him. Even after five years, there was surely no mistaking that voice, rich and deep, though without the hint of laughter that had seemed to accompany almost everything he'd said to her at the ball. It sounded positively stern now as he conversed with the driver, saying something about the wheel, although the blood was gushing so loudly in her ears that she couldn't make out the individual words. The tension was unbearable. She peered out again, desperately hoping that her imagination was running away with her and that she'd made a mistake...

She hadn't. She stifled a gasp. Somehow whilst he'd been just a distant idea, a reclusive villain who she hadn't seen in five years, her plan to escape had seemed plausible, likely even. Now he was standing so close, she wondered how she could ever have thought she might fool him.

She'd forgotten how physically imposing he was, tall and broad-shouldered with an intimidating male presence she could sense even from her hiding place. He looked just as handsome as he had the first time they'd met, though his face appeared leaner and edgier, too, as if the soft angles had all been chiselled away and made more pronounced. A dark moustache and swathe of stubble gave him the rugged look of a man who didn't care what anyone else thought of him either, a man who might plausibly do anything and could, too.

He dismounted in front of her, wincing slightly as he swung his right leg over his saddle, though by the way the muscles bunched in his jaw, she had the distinct impression he was trying not to show any pain. For a moment, he simply hovered in the air, holding himself up with his arms, before dropping to the ground with an abrupt thud. His companion dismounted at the same time, though he didn't offer any assistance, she noticed, taking up a position to one side almost as if he were making a point of not doing so.

She held her breath as her pursuer made his way towards the cart, placing his weight on his left leg and limping with the right. Apparently his injury, whatever it was, had been even worse than the gossips had reported. After five months at home, the damage appeared to be permanent. She felt a flicker of pity, quickly repressed, though surely it was possible to pity him and still not want to marry him? After all, her objections had nothing to do with his leg.

He nodded to his companion and the pair of them braced themselves against the side of the trap, lifting it up with their bare hands.

'Can you get the wheel back on?' He spoke to the driver again.

'Aye, I reckon so.' The driver set to work at once, pushing the wheel back over the axle and hammering the pin swiftly into place before standing up again with a look of satisfaction. 'There, that should hold for now. My thanks.'

'You're welcome.' Her pursuer gestured towards the road. 'You're travelling up to Rosedale?'

'Yes, sir. Supposed to be going on to Helmsley as well, though it looks like the weather's closing in.'

Violet looked up at the sky in alarm. The boy had said they were used to driving in this weather, but there was no denying that the snow was getting heavier, gathering in piles now where before it had seemed to melt into the ground. What would that mean for her escape?

'Then you'd better hurry.' Her pursuer gave a curt nod. 'I'm glad we could be of assistance.'

He turned away and she let out a sigh of relief, hardly able to believe the closeness of her escape. He was leaving! He hadn't seen her! Even if she was going to be delayed up at Rosedale, she was still free...

'Miss Harper?'

She jumped halfway into the air at the sound of her own name, heart pounding like a heavy drum in her chest, so hard she thought she might develop bruises on her ribs. She leaned out slightly, but her pursuer was facing in the opposite direction, still walking away from her. He hadn't so much as turned his head to call out. If it hadn't been for all the other faces looking in her direction, she might have thought she'd imagined it, but clearly she hadn't. How had he known she was there? He'd shown no sign of being remotely aware of her presence.

'Miss Harper?' He sounded more insistent this time.

'Yes?' Her voice was little more than a squeak.

'We're leaving.'

The habit of obedience was so strong that for a moment she almost followed after him. She actually stepped out into the open before she stopped herself, seized with a fierce rush of indignation. How dare he summon her as if she were one of his soldiers, as if he thought he could just issue commands and she ought to do what he said! Just like her father! Well, she didn't have to go with him. She was a free woman—in principle anyway. She could do what she ought to have done in the first place and simply refuse. She'd say that she didn't want to marry him, not under any circumstances. How hard could it be to assert herself?

She stepped out from her hiding place and on to the track, keeping her hood lowered over her face so that he couldn't see how nervous she felt.

'No.'

He stopped at once, turning to greet her with a look that managed to be both jaw-droppingly handsome and icily menacing at the same time. There was no hint of emotion, as if he were deliberately presenting a blank canvas, and yet the undercurrent of tension was palpable.

'It's a pleasure to see you again, too, Miss Harper.'

She felt a shiver run the full length of her body. How could a man who'd seemed so warmly charming the first time they'd met now be so glacially chilling? She barely recognised him. There was an edge of danger about him now, as if he were restraining more than his temper. Her nerves quailed beneath the force of that formidable dark stare, but she didn't respond, didn't curtsy or so much as bend her head. She had the discomforting feeling that if she moved at all, then she might lose her resolve and give in. She already felt a powerful impulse to walk forward, as if he were drawing her towards him through sheer force of will.

He lifted an eyebrow slowly, though if he was concerned by her lack of response he didn't show it.

'I apologise for not having visited you before our appointment this morning, but I regret to say I've been indisposed.' He didn't sound apologetic at all.

'You didn't come to my father's funeral,' she accused him, finding her voice at last, though it sounded pitifully small in comparison.

'Simply because I prefer not to add hypocrisy to the long list of my faults. I doubt he would have wanted me there and I was only informed about the terms of his will after the funeral.' He shrugged. 'However, I'm here now and willing to proceed.'

Willing to proceed? She sucked in a breath at the insulting tone of his words. He made it sound as if he were doing her a favour. As if the only reason she'd run away was because he hadn't visited her before the wedding, as if it were simply a case of wounded pride and not abject loathing—as if she'd ever want to marry a reprobate like him!

She lifted her chin disdainfully. 'You're mistaken if you think I was offended by your absence, sir. I've no wish to keep our appointment at all.'

'Indeed?' His jaw tightened. 'Then what, may I ask, are your plans?'

'I'm going to Rosedale.'

'To pursue a career in mining, perhaps?'

'That's none of your concern.'

'On the contrary. Your father's will was rather explicit on that point. He made me responsible for you.'

'I can take care of myself!'

'Really?' The eyebrow lifted even higher. 'Have you ever done so before?'

'No.' She stiffened at the insinuation. 'But that doesn't mean I can't.'

'True, though apparently your father thought otherwise. He made me your protector.'

'He meant your brother, not you!'

Amber eyes blazed with some powerful emotion, quickly repressed. 'None the less, it's me that you've got. Your father wanted an Amberton to look after you and I appear to be the only one left.'

She felt a burst of anger so overpowering that her body started to shake with the force of it, as though she'd been holding her temper for so long that she felt about ready to burst. Words seemed to erupt out of her suddenly, pouring out in a fierce torrent that she seemed unable to either stop or curtail.

'My father never cared whether I was looked after or not! He only wanted me to look after him. He wanted to control me. He *still* wants to. That's why he gave me to you!'

She clamped a hand over her mouth at the end of her tirade, looking around in embarrassment, but the others weren't looking at her any more. At some point they'd moved off to one side, turning their backs to stare out at the moors as if it were a pleasant day for enjoying the view and not the start of a blizzard, leaving her effectively alone with Captain Amberton.

'I don't want to marry you.' She pulled her

hand away again, saying the words with as much conviction as she could muster.

'No more than I want to marry you. But since neither of us was offered a choice, I suggest that we make the best of it.'

'I'm going to Rosedale.' Maybe if she kept on saying it, then he would accept it, too...

'Not in this weather or in that cart. Given the circumstances, it would be unwise to put any further strain on the axle. Wouldn't you agree, Driver?'

'Oh...aye.' The man looked over his shoulder with an apologetic expression. 'I'm sorry, miss, but we won't make it to Helmsley now. We might be stuck at t'mines for a bit making repairs and it's no fit place for a lady.'

'There you are.' Her pursuer's expression was glacial. 'It seems you've no choice. You'll have to come back to Whitby with me after all.'

She held his stare resentfully. It was true, she had no choice. Even if it weren't snowing, it was too far to walk to Helmsley and, as usual, no one was paying any attention to what she wanted. Besides, she had the strong suspicion that her pursuer wasn't going to take no for an answer. If she kept on refusing, he'd probably throw her over his saddle anyway.

She gestured towards a carpet bag on the back

of the cart, trying to feign an appearance of composure. 'My bag.'

'Is that all you've brought?' He glanced towards it and frowned.

'Yes. Since I was going to be disinherited, it seemed wrong to take more than was rightfully mine.'

'And those are *all* your belongings?'

'Yes.'

'How very honest of you.' He sounded less than impressed, jerking his head at his companion. 'Martin will bring your bag. Now might I suggest we get moving before the snow gets any worse?'

She walked stiffly towards him, unable to delay any longer, looking between him and his horse with an almost equal sense of trepidation. From a distance, she'd hoped that the scale of the animal might have been deceptive, but up close it was even bigger than she'd feared, so tall that the top of her head barely came level with the saddle.

She stopped beside it, lowering her voice with embarrassment. 'I can't ride.'

'Of course you can't.' He let out a small sigh. 'Just put your foot into the stirrup and pull yourself up. I won't let you fall.'

She tensed instantly. *I won't let you fall...*
He'd said those words to her before, five years

ago when he'd asked her to dance. She knew them by heart, had spent hours reliving every humiliating moment of that evening, wishing she'd never followed him out on to the dance floor. That had been her first taste of freedom, or so she'd thought at the time, the only time since her long-ago childhood when she'd felt happy and carefree. Whirling around in his arms, she'd felt as if she'd been breaking out of her prison at last—before reality had set in with a vengeance.

His casual mockery had made her feel even worse than she had before. She'd made a fool of herself in front of everyone, dancing with a reprobate who'd only encouraged her to rebel for his own amusement, so that he could mock her more easily. And now he was mocking her and her attempt at rebellion again, as if she were just a child who couldn't take care of herself. He'd already said as much. It seemed that every time she tried to assert herself, he ruined it somehow.

She gritted her teeth at the thought. Well, this time she wasn't going to let him. She wasn't going to be small and helpless any more. He might have thwarted her escape attempt, but that was the only victory she'd allow him. She'd go back to Whitby, but she would never marry him, no matter how much he tried to convince or intimidate her. She loathed him.

'You look cold.'

'What?' His words jolted her back to the present.

'I said that you look cold.' He sounded impatient.

'No,' she lied. 'Not at all.'

She pulled her cloak tighter around her shoulders defensively. It was the warmest garment she owned, though still sadly lacking. Her father had never allowed her to spend much time out of doors so she'd never had need of very warm clothes, but she certainly wasn't going to tell Captain Amberton that. He'd only take it as further evidence that she wasn't able to take care of herself.

'Here.' He shrugged himself out of his greatcoat and draped it around her shoulders.

'You'll be freezing!' She gestured at his jacket sleeves in protest.

'I've been living in Canada. I'm used to it.'

'But you're injured!'

'Then we're fortunate my injury isn't one that's affected by cold.' He heaved another sigh. 'Now can you mount before we all freeze to death? I believe you've inconvenienced these men, not to mention myself, long enough.'

She glared at him, cheeks flaring despite the cold. Inconvenienced. He couldn't have said it any more clearly. That was all she was to him, an inconvenient woman with a convenient fortune. That was why he'd pursued her—for the money, not her. She jammed her foot in the stirrup angrily, hoisting herself up into the saddle, then gasped in shock as his fingers wrapped around her ankle, wrenching it loose again.

'What are you doing?' Her breath caught in her throat at his touch. No man had ever seen, let alone touched, her leg before!

'I'd like to ride, too.' He looked up at her scathingly. 'Or do you think I should walk?'

'Of course not.'

'Good. Because if it's propriety you're worried about, I'd remind you that we *are* engaged. If it hadn't been for this little escapade, we'd be married already.'

He mounted behind her, uttering a small grunt as he swung his injured leg over the horse's back. She shifted forward quickly, trying to keep their bodies from touching, though the curve of the leather saddle made that impossible. His thighs were already wrapped tight around hers, her bottom pressed against his... She closed her eyes in mortification.

'Comfortable?'

'No!' By the tone of his voice she could tell he was mocking her again.

'Then let's get this over with, shall we?' He reached around her, imprisoning her within the circle of his arms as he grasped hold of the reins and gave them a decisive flick.

Violet fumed inwardly, her fear of the horse all but forgotten. She had no qualms about accepting his greatcoat now. On the contrary, she hoped he *was* cold. It would serve him right, not just for ruining her plans, but for making her feel such a fool as well. A tiny, naive, helpless fool. Just as her father had always said—just as he'd always made her feel, too!

She looked past her captor's shoulder, blinking back tears of frustration as she watched the cart recede into the distance, obscured by a shifting, lace-like curtain of snow. How had her plans failed so badly? How had he found her? She wasn't about to deign to ask him, no more than she was actually going to cry in front of him, but she still wanted to know, even if it didn't matter any more. Her escape plan had failed and now he was taking her...

She straightened up with a jolt. Where *was* he taking her? This wasn't the road the cart had followed that morning. It wasn't a road at all. It was the moorland itself, the wild and boggy terrain she'd always been warned about. She spun around in alarm, only to find her captor's companion, or manservant as he seemed to be, riding alongside, though whoever he was, he still hadn't uttered a word. Where were *they* taking her?

'You said we were going back to Whitby.' She tried to keep the panic out of her voice.

'I lied.' Her captor's tone was implacable. 'Although I'm sure Martin here would enjoy standing guard outside your house, it's far easier to keep an eye on you at Amberton Castle.'

'You think I'll try to run away again?'

'Won't you?'

Yes. She didn't say the word aloud, though now more than ever the answer was obvious. She was riding over the moors with a man she despised, back to the scene of her hurt and humiliation five years ago, a place she'd hoped never to visit again. Of course she was going to try to run away. As soon as she could.

'That's what I thought.' His mouth set in a hard, firm line. 'I'm taking you back to Amberton Castle, Miss Harper, your new home.'

Chapter Two

Lance looked down at the woollen lapels of his greatcoat and muttered one of his most colourful soldiers' oaths. From his companion's audible gasp, he could tell that she recognised the inflection, if not the exact meaning of the words. Somehow he doubted she'd ever heard such language before, but he wasn't in the mood to be polite. He was in the mood to swear like a trooper and invent a few more words besides. His leg hurt, his head ached and his temper was close to breaking point. The rest of him was freezing and it was all her fault.

'Shouldn't we keep to the road?'

She sounded anxious and he felt a vindictive sense of satisfaction. Good. If she was worried, then it was revenge for all the trouble she'd caused him that morning.

'I've heard the moors are dangerous.' She tried again when he didn't answer.

'You've heard right.'

He gave a twisted smile. In fact, they were following a trail, an old farm track known only to locals, though it was admittedly hard to tell in the snow. Not that he'd any intention of reassuring her. If she was frightened of the moors, then so much the better. They might deter her from making another misguided escape attempt—something she was clearly already considering, if her earlier silence was anything to go by.

Besides, he didn't want conversation, especially with a woman who'd done her damnedest to humiliate him that morning. He'd arrived at his own wedding to find it all but deserted except for one decidedly anxious-looking lawyer. Mr Rowlinson had gone to collect the bride only to find that she'd run away some time during the night. He'd wrung his hands as he'd told him, looking and sounding far more distressed by her absence than Lance did. But then *he* hadn't been distressed. He'd been livid. It wasn't as if he'd wanted the marriage either, but at least he'd been prepared to honour the terms of their fathers' agreement. He'd been determined to do the right thing for once in his life, more fool him, and he'd be damned before any woman was going to stop him!

'I saw her just yesterday,' Rowlinson had babbled. 'She told me she'd made all the necessary arrangements.'

'What arrangements?' The words had caught his attention. He'd been the one who'd arranged the time and venue. What had she had to arrange? 'What did she say exactly?'

'Just that she knew what she had to do. I thought she was talking about the will.'

'She didn't say she'd be here?'

'Not specifically, no.'

He'd stormed away, seething with anger. Whatever arrangements Miss Harper had made, they clearly hadn't been for their wedding. The idea that she might run away had never even occurred to him. He'd never imagined that she'd have either the nerve or the spirit for it, but any burgeoning admiration he might have felt had been overwhelmed by anger. She'd jilted him without even seeing him first, as if the idea of marriage to him was so abhorrent that she'd rather flee and be penniless than so much as look at him. As if his injured leg was so objectionable to her!

The insult was too great to be borne. Bad enough that he couldn't walk more than a hundred paces without needing to rest. He wasn't going to let some minuscule mouse of a woman make a fool of him, too! Her running away only made him doubly determined to go ahead.

Not that it had been easy to find her. She'd done an impressive job of leaving clues, but he'd learned enough about tracking in Canada to recognise a false trail when he saw one. She hadn't taken the train, that much he'd been certain of, and to his relief no merchant vessels had left Whitby harbour that morning. After a few pointed enquiries, he'd finally taken a gamble on the moorland road, riding so furiously that Martin had eventually told him to slow down or risk laming his horse. Since his former batman only spoke when it was absolutely necessary to do so, he'd listened, then done his best to calm down and look at the situation objectively.

In retrospect, he supposed he hadn't helped his own cause. He ought to have visited her as soon as he'd found out about the will. He'd intended to, but then his injury had flared up again, putting riding out of the question for a few days. He ought to have ordered the carriage and suffered the bumpy roads anyway, but his mind had shied away from that idea. If he were honest, his injury had been a good excuse. He hadn't wanted to see her again. No matter how intriguing he'd found her at the ball five years ago, any attraction had long since crystallised into resentment. Aside from the way she'd taken offence—the reasons for which he still wasn't able to fathom—that night was inextricably bound up with too many other painful memories.

That had been the last time that he'd seen either his father or Arthur, the night that he'd been banished from his home for ever, and it had all been her fault! If she hadn't been so ridiculously oversensitive over a perfectly innocent comment about suitors, then he might never have got into an argument with his father in the first place, might have made it through the whole week of his leave without any fighting at all! Then he might have listened to Arthur, really listened, might have found a way to help him, too...

So he'd kept away from Miss Violet Harper, reluctant to face any reminder of that night, the very worst of his life until seven months ago, hoping that his mind might somehow adapt to the idea of seeing her again. It hadn't. Whatever his first impressions had been, they'd long since been replaced by the image of an ice maiden with white hair and piercing blue eyes, cold and casually destructive—Arthur's unwanted bride, now his.

And now he'd found her, in the midst of a snowstorm of all things! He'd hoped that reality wouldn't match up to his fears, but the instant he'd glimpsed her—her skirts anyway, just visible beneath the horse's flanks—he'd felt all the emotions he'd striven so hard to forget come rushing back to the surface. He'd been glad that the wheel of the cart had come loose. It had given him a task to do, something to distract his mind while he'd wrestled with a near-overwhelming feeling of grief. Anger had come next, as he'd known it would, followed by guilt. Most of all guilt. Which led back to anger again.

At last he'd steeled himself to confront her. Not that he'd been able to see much of her, with her hood pulled so low over her face as to make it well nigh invisible. Only her distinctive size had given her identity away, not to mention her voice, that same breathless purr he remembered, the one he'd found so alluring until she'd shown her true colours.

He'd striven to keep a rein on his temper. So much so that his jaw was now aching from the effort. He'd remained calm even when she'd mentioned Arthur, even when she'd flatly stated that she didn't want to marry him—as if he wanted to marry her! The thought was just as abhorrent now as it had been when Rowlinson had informed him about the terms of the will, but it was still his father's agreement, one he couldn't renege on without condemning her to a life of poverty, and he couldn't do that, no matter how much he was tempted to walk away. He'd been made responsible for her and there was one unlooked-for benefit after all. He might not want the woman, but the money... The money he could definitely do something with.

He was relieved when the trail descended at last into a valley and the imposing, snow-capped turrets of Amberton Castle appeared out of the wintry vista ahead of them. In an ironical twist that had surprised him more than anyone, his father had never actually got around to legally disinheriting him, so that after his death both the title and lands had come to him, informally at least. Returning to claim them, however, had been the hardest thing he'd ever done. After declaring that he'd never set foot in the place again, he'd never thought to return, had initially done so only because he'd had nowhere else to go.

The situation was further complicated by the fact that Arthur's body had never been found. Without proof of his brother's demise, the title and estate were effectively frozen, his to look after, but not to legally possess for a period of seven years. Under normal circumstances, his marriage to Violet would never have gone ahead until the legal situation was resolved, but the time limit on her father's will made it imperative that it did so. He'd already procured a special licence. She had to marry him within one month, whether he were the heir to Amberton Castle or not.

Despite its many negative associations, however, he'd retained a genuine affection for the house itself. Probably because it had been built with his mother's money and according to her own medieval-inspired designs. She'd been the one who'd insisted on turrets and crenellations and even a few faux arrow slits, all intended to make a thirty-five-year-old building look as if it had stood for centuries. She'd even called it a castle.

That part at least his father had approved of. Anything to bolster the family name, to make the world believe that the Ambertons were still a force to be reckoned with, not just the burnt-out, impoverished end of an ancient family, even if their depleted fortunes were entirely due to the fact that his father had never actually *done* anything.

Back in their heyday, Ambertons had been soldiers and adventurers, men who'd won their fortunes and titles through action. His father, by contrast, had been content to sit in his study, watching the last of his wife's money trickle away rather than sully his hands with anything so distasteful as work or, even worse, trade. He'd never let Arthur do anything either. It was no wonder his brother had been depressed, he thought bitterly, trapped inside the house like some kind of museum exhibit. Arthur had never been rebellious enough to defy their father and when he'd asked Lance for help…

He forced the memory away, although the bitter sting of it remained. He didn't want to think about Arthur, but he was going to honour his family's promise anyway. He wouldn't have chosen to shackle himself to Miss Harper either, not by a long chalk, but he was going to go ahead with the marriage, for all the same cynical reasons as his father, and simply *because* his father had wanted it. At long last, he was going to be the son his father had wanted him to be, with one notable difference. He wasn't going to simply exist on the money and do nothing. He was going to restore the family fortunes, no matter what anyone might think of an Amberton going into business.

He'd already made a start with his new mining venture, but with the Harper fortune he could achieve even more, could build a blast furnace to go with the new tunnels that had already been dug so that his iron wouldn't have to be transported for smelting. He could start his own works on the site, provide employment for people in the estate villages, as well as schools, new houses and maybe even a hospital, too. He could revitalise the whole Amberton estate and Violet Harper could pay for it. There was a kind of poetic justice to the idea. Since the rift with his father had been largely her fault, it seemed only appropriate that she ought to pay.

They rode into the courtyard and he felt an intense sense of relief. What had started as a mild blizzard was rapidly turning into a full-blown snowstorm and he felt as if the cold had seeped into his very bones, making them freeze from the inside out.

'Bring her in.'

He addressed the words to Martin as he dismounted and limped towards the front door without so much as a backward glance. Even if he *had* wanted to help her, which in his present state of mind he didn't, his leg was causing him far too much pain to do anything about it. What he wanted—no, what he *needed*—was a drink and the stronger the better.

He barged through the front door and headed straight for the drawing room, snatching up a decanter of brandy and gulping straight from the bottle, revelling in the warmth of the liquid as it scoured the back of his throat.

'Captain Amberton?'

He lowered the bottle again, wiping his mouth on his sleeve at the sound of his housekeeper's prim voice at his shoulder. Clearly his trials with the opposite sex weren't yet over with today and Mrs Gargrave was a perpetual trial. He wouldn't have been surprised to learn that his father had trained her specifically to annoy him. Her strait-laced and perpetually disapproving manner were eerily reminiscent of the old man, not to mention her habit of creeping up silently behind him.

'Yes?' He didn't bother to hide his bad temper.

'I came to offer my congratulations on your nuptials, sir. Cook has prepared a celebratory luncheon if you'd like to adjourn to the dining room?'

'No.' He took another swig from the bottle. 'She's not my wife and she can damned well starve for all I care.'

'Captain!' The housekeeper's stiff posture turned more rigid than a guardsman's. 'I've asked you to moderate your language before.'

'So you have and, as usual, I apologise. But as I just mentioned, she's not my wife.'

'Then might I enquire what the young lady is doing here? If you're not married, then it's highly improper for her to be visiting on her own.'

'She's not visiting either. She's moving in early.'

'But she doesn't have a chaperon. It's not seemly.'

'I can't see what difference it makes if I intend to marry her anyway.'

'People will talk.'

'People already talk. I wouldn't have thought there was much more they could say.'

'I won't be party to any licentiousness. I thought I made that clear when you came home and I agreed to carry on with my duties.'

Lance took another swig of brandy deliberately to provoke her. Mrs Gargrave's habit of implying that he'd begged her to stay was yet another irritation in his life. Frankly he would have been happy to see the back of her, but she'd been there for so long that he doubted she had anywhere else to go. He'd never heard her mention any family and his conscience had prevented him from simply dismissing her. That and the fact that she was an excellent housekeeper—when she wasn't lecturing him, that was.

'You made it crystal-clear, Mrs Gargrave. At great length, too, as I recall, though I don't believe I've given you any cause for complaint.'

'Until now.'

'The worst thing I've done so far is threaten not to give her luncheon. I haven't exactly ravished her on the hall table.' He flashed a sardonic smile. 'Not yet anyway.'

'Captain!'

'But since you object so strenuously, you have my permission to drive her back to Whitby in the snow yourself if you wish. You'll probably freeze to death, but at least your virtues will be intact.' His smile widened insincerely. 'Just be sure to hurry before the roads become completely impassable.'

The housekeeper made an indignant sucking sound, pursing her lips so tightly they looked in danger of turning blue. 'I suppose, under the circumstances... In that case I'll take her up to the blue room.'

'Damned if you will!'

'Captain Amberton!'

This time he didn't apologise. This time he raised the bottle to his lips and drained what was left of the liquid in one long draught. The blue room had been his mother's chamber, adjacent to the master bedroom that had belonged to his father, though he hadn't summoned the nerve to enter either since his return. He'd avoided the family quarters altogether, to Mrs Gargrave's frequently expressed disapproval, selecting one of the guest chambers to sleep in instead. He'd intended for his wife to share that, for a while at least, but since they weren't yet officially married, he supposed for propriety's sake he ought to make alternative arrangements. After what had happened that morning, however, his mother's chamber was the very last room she could use.

But he knew exactly which one she could.

'Captain?'

Mrs Gargrave gaped open-mouthed as he stormed past her and back out to the hallway. His mother had designed the entrance to resemble a medieval great hall, with wooden beams across a high ceiling, oak floorboards and a matching oak table in the centre, a selection of antlers and coats-of-arms around the walls, and a perpetually crackling fireplace, in front of which Miss Harper now stood warming her hands.

She'd removed his greatcoat, he noticed, though not that ridiculously flimsy cloak. She hadn't even pulled the hood back from her head. Was she ever going to take the damned thing off? He'd barely caught a glimpse of her face and what he *had* seen had been cast deep in shadow, as if she were trying to hide from him on top of everything else. The thought, aggravated by brandy, made him suddenly furious.

'Come with me.' He seized her hand as he limped past.

'Where?' She almost tripped over her skirts as she spun after him. 'Your housekeeper said…'

'My housekeeper had no business saying anything.'

He tightened his grip on her fingers as he mounted the staircase. There was no carpet here either, so that the hard tread of his footsteps echoed loudly around the cavernous hallway. Generally, he preferred to climb stairs on his own, or at least without an audience, but he was too angry now to care what she thought of him or his leg. If she was offended by his infirmity, then the sooner she got used to it, the better.

'Where are we going?'

She tugged against him as they reached the half landing, but he held tight, hauling her up the right-hand branch of the staircase and down a wood-panelled corridor.

'You can't hold me here against my will!'

She sounded more defiant than frightened and he felt an unwonted flicker of admiration. He would have expected most women to burst into tears by now.

'I'm offering you hospitality in a snowstorm, Miss Harper. Or would you prefer to be out on the moors by yourself?'

'Better than being trapped here with a beast like you!'

He gritted his teeth. Was that how she thought of him, then, as a beast? Admittedly he wasn't behaving much like a gentleman, but if that were the case then he'd show her just how much of a beast he could be!

'Then let's say I'm protecting you from yourself.'

He hauled her towards the furthermost door at the end of the corridor and took a rusty iron key from a hook on the wall, pushing it into the lock and twisting it around with a loud scraping sound. He doubted that the door had been opened more than a handful of times in the past ten years. The octagonal tower had been his mother's sitting room, though after her death his father had covered the furniture in dust sheets and never set foot inside again. No one had found any use for it since, but for some reason it seemed particularly suited to Miss Harper. Hadn't he once thought she belonged in a fairy-tale tower?

The lock clicked at last and he turned the handle, ramming one shoulder up against the door as an icy draught whistled past them.

'Make yourself at home.' He released her hand finally and gestured inside. 'I'm sure you'd like a rest after your busy morning.'

'In here?' She sounded shocked and he felt a moment of misgiving. In truth, the place looked even more cold and cheerless than he'd expected.

'In here.' He hardened his heart mercilessly. 'I think you'll still find it preferable to the mines at Rosedale.'

'But…' She took a tentative step forward and then twisted her head sharply, sniffing the air as she did so.

'You're drunk!'

He caught a flash of sapphire from beneath her hood and let his temper get the better of him, lifting a hand and wrenching it back to reveal a pair of enormous blue eyes in a small, outraged-looking face. He stiffened in surprise. It was the same face, even the same expression she'd been wearing when they'd argued five years ago, as if time had stopped and she hadn't aged a day. He'd thought of her first as a kitten, then as an ice maiden, and yet he seemed to have remembered every detail of her face perfectly, as if they'd been imprinted on his memory. There'd been enough women, too many women, in his life before and since, and yet hers was the face he remembered... How was it possible for her to have changed so little, while he felt as though he'd aged decades?

'I've been drinking,' he corrected her. 'That doesn't make me drunk.'

'Really?' She gave him a look that would have made Mrs Gargrave proud.

'I take it that your father never drank in the daytime?'

'He never drank at all.'

'Of course.' He adopted what he hoped was a suitably scathing expression. 'I forgot what a paragon of virtue he was, but I'm afraid you'll need to lower your standards here. I drink every day. Sometimes for breakfast.'

Her chin jutted upwards. 'It's not something to boast about.'

'I'm simply stating a fact. You'll need to get used to it when we're married.'

'I won't marry you! It doesn't matter how long you keep me here, I won't change my mind. I don't want to marry anyone, especially not a man like you!'

'And what kind of man would that be exactly?' He advanced a step towards her, expecting her to retreat, but she only lifted her chin higher.

'You have to ask?'

'Indulge me, Miss Harper. Educate me, if you will.' He lowered his face down to hers, so close that they were almost touching, daring her to answer. 'Tell me just what it is that you find so very repellent?'

'Everything! You're a drunk and a gambler and...' her cheeks flushed slightly '...a libertine!'

He drew back in surprise, a retort fading on his lips. That hadn't been what he'd expected, not at all.

'Are you saying that it's my *character* you object to?'

'Of course!' She blinked. 'What else would it be?'

He glanced pointedly down at his leg. What else indeed? He'd been so wrapped up in his resentment of *her* character that he'd never stopped to wonder what she thought of *his*. He'd simply assumed that she found his injury distasteful. In which case...

'Then I'm curious to know why you have such a low opinion of me. Because of what happened at the ball? I believe that both of our fathers called me a reprobate.'

'Partly.' Her eyelashes fluttered perceptibly when he mentioned the ball. 'And I've heard rumours.'

'Gossip, Miss Harper? I wouldn't have thought you one to indulge in that particular vice.'

'I don't, but I've still heard stories. Or are you saying they aren't true?'

'On the contrary, I'm sure they're all true and worse besides. I doubt the whole truth would bear repeating in polite circles, especially to young ladies.'

'Are you proud of your reputation, then?'

'No, but I have so few other distinctions.'

Her eyes widened with a look of consternation. 'I'll *never* marry you!'

'Then I admire your resolve, but you might think differently when you've had a little time to reconsider.' He moved away from her, pulling the door shut behind him. 'I trust you'll be comfortable here.'

'Wait!' She caught at the edge of the door before it closed. 'I have a friend. I need to send word that I'm all right or she'll be worried.'

'An accomplice?' He half opened the door again, still blocking the way out with his body.

'Was that why you were going to Helmsley, to meet her?'

'No. That is…not her.'

He narrowed his gaze suspiciously. Did she have two accomplices, then? Her evasiveness suggested that one of them was a man—a lover? That was the most likely answer, though the idea of her having another suitor hadn't crossed his mind until now. He didn't like it.

'If I could just send a message…please?'

He gave an unsympathetic snort. If she'd been going to meet a lover, then he had absolutely no intention of setting the man's mind at rest so easily. If whoever it was wanted to marry her, then he ought to have come and confronted him man to man, not plotted an elopement behind his back.

'No.'

'But…'

'No!' His voice sounded even fiercer than he'd intended. 'If you think that I'm going to send anyone out in this weather, then you're even more of a little fool than I thought!'

She drew in a sharp breath at the insult, though she still didn't flinch, staring back at him instead with an expression of intense loathing.

'Then I'll wait here until the storm clears. After that, you've no right to keep me.'

'You're absolutely right, I don't. Though I

doubt the storm will clear by tonight and unless you want to leave in the dark then I'm afraid you're stuck here with me, a renowned libertine, and without, as my housekeeper so delicately pointed out, a chaperon. Whatever your plans for the future, I hope they don't depend on your keeping a good reputation.'

Her defiant expression crumpled into one of horror. 'But that's monstrous! No one would ever employ me if they knew. You wouldn't be so cruel!'

'Didn't you pay any attention to all that gossip? If you had, then you'd know very well that I would.' He smiled mirthlessly. 'Welcome to Amberton Castle, Miss Harper. I hope that you have a good night.'

Chapter Three

'Miss Harper?'

Violet frowned in her sleep. The voice in her dream seemed to be coming from a distance, but she had no idea what it was doing there. It was a woman's voice, though she didn't recognise it, repeating her name over and over, though that made no sense either. In her dream, she was out alone on the moors, desperately trying to find shelter as towers of snow piled up higher and deeper around her, imprisoning her behind their thick, white, impenetrable walls. She was lost and afraid, without any hope of rescue…

'Miss Harper?'

A hand touched her shoulder this time and she jolted awake with a start.

'Where am I?' She looked around, but whoever had woken her was holding their candle directly in front of her face and all she could see was a bright orange glow.

'Amberton Castle.' It was the voice from her dream, though it sounded distinctly less than welcoming. 'I'm Mrs Gargrave, the house-keeper.'

'Oh…yes, of course. I remember.'

She sat up, squinting into the candlelight. Had she really fallen asleep? After pacing the room for what seemed like an eternity, she'd eventually curled up beneath a dustsheet on one of the old armchairs, though she hadn't expected to sleep. Between the encroaching cold and the fading light, she hadn't thought it possible to sleep in such an eerie-looking icebox of a room, but clearly she had. After all the anticipation and tension of the past few days, she must have been more tired than she'd realised. Judging by the darkness, not to mention the ache in her neck, she must have been there for a few hours, too.

'We spoke in the hall earlier, I think? You said you'd arranged luncheon.'

'I *had*.' There was an indignant-sounding sniff. 'Cook prepared a special meal to celebrate your marriage. Against master's orders, I might add, but we wanted to welcome you properly. It's all ruined now, though.'

'Oh.' She wasn't sure what to say. It wasn't as if she'd intended to get herself locked in a tower. 'I'm sorry. I didn't mean…'

'In any case, your room's almost ready.'

'My room?' She scrambled quickly to her feet, dimly making out the features of a gaunt-looking woman in late middle age. 'I thought Captain Amberton said this was my room.'

'He's had a change of heart.'

Heart? Somehow she doubted that. He'd have to grow a heart before he could change it and it was hard to imagine the brute who'd locked her up having any kind of conscience. Still, whatever the reason for her release, she wasn't going to dispute it.

'I'm relieved to hear that. I was afraid I was going to be trapped here all night.'

'It's a disgrace!' The housekeeper gave another loud sniff. 'There was a time when this house was renowned for its hospitality. When his mother was alive things were done properly, but it's been nothing but decline ever since. I don't know why I stay sometimes…'

'But I'm sure my new room will be very comfortable.' Violet gestured towards the door encouragingly. Mrs Gargrave seemed to be warming to her subject and if she was going to listen, then she preferred to do it some place warmer. 'Shall we?'

'Aye. Very well.' The housekeeper looked disappointed to be interrupted mid-flow. 'This way.'

Violet followed her gratefully out of the tower, relieved to find herself back in the wood-panelled corridor. It seemed to stretch the full length of the house, with at least ten doors on one side and a long banister and yet more stairs on the other. Mrs Gargrave led her towards them and then up to another landing, almost identical to the one below.

'I see they didn't exaggerate, then.' The housekeeper threw a quick glance over her shoulder as they approached one of the doors.

'I'm sorry?'

'About your height. You're even smaller than they said.'

Violet faltered mid-step. Just for once she wished she could meet someone who didn't feel the need to either stare or make some comment about her height when they met her, as if she were somehow unaware of it, like a child to be critiqued and belittled, not a woman with feelings. There was only one person who'd ever treated her as if he hadn't noticed and she was in no mood to think charitably of *him*. As for everyone else, she'd had enough. She'd spent her whole life being judged for her height and she wasn't going to tolerate it any longer. It wasn't as if she could do anything about it.

'I may be small, Mrs Gargrave, but at least I have the manners not to comment on somebody else's appearance. If I didn't, I might say you look like you've swallowed a lemon.'

The shoulders in front of her stiffened perceptibly. 'Well, I'm sure I didn't mean any offence,
but you can't pretend it's not noticeable.'

'I wouldn't try to pretend. Neither can I grow
any more.'

'Aye, well.' There was a third sniff. 'Here's
your room, then.'

Violet approached the door with a new and
invigorating feeling of triumph. There! At least
she'd stood up for herself that time, just as she'd
tried to stand up for herself earlier. She wasn't
going to be criticised by Mrs Gargrave any more
than she was going to be intimidated by Captain Amberton, though she didn't exactly feel
as if she'd bested him. On the contrary, she'd
got herself locked in a tower. For all his talk of
protecting her, deep down he was no better than
her father, assuming that she'd simply do what
she was told.

At least he'd finally relented and let her out
again. That was one small victory. Now she just
had to stand firm and keep on refusing to marry
him. Her capture was a setback, not the end to
her hopes of freedom. Even if her reputation was
ruined, she could still find her own way in the
world. Once he realised that she wasn't going to
give in then he'd *have* to let her go. Either that or
the month would expire. Not that she'd be there
for so long, surely. Once Ianthe found out where

she was then she and her husband Robert would come to her rescue for certain… She only hoped it wouldn't take them too long.

She was so engrossed in her thoughts that it took her a moment to realise that she was inside a new room, a cosy, candlelit chamber decorated in tones of cream and pale yellow, with a few solitary sticks of furniture and a large bay window overlooking what she presumed was the back of the house. A fire was already roaring in the grate, illuminating a curtained and canopied four-poster bed, where a maid was busily turning down the covers.

'This is my bedroom?' Violet looked around in amazement, half suspecting it to be some kind of trick. It was hard to imagine a greater contrast to the room she'd just left. Or to her old bedroom in Whitby for that matter. 'It's lovely.'

'I won't have it said that we don't know how to look after guests.' The housekeeper folded her arms emphatically. 'No matter how badly the master behaves. Or anyone else, for that matter.'

'It's all ready, Mrs Gargrave.' The maid, a curly-haired girl in her teens, bobbed a curtsy in front of them.

'Very good, Eliza. Now I expect that Miss Harper would like some tea. Isn't that so, Miss Harper?'

'Very much, thank you, but might I ask, where is Captain Amberton?'

'In the drawing room, though I doubt he's in any fit state to be seen. He usually isn't in the evenings. Martin, that's his manservant, looks after him.'

'Is that the man who was with him earlier?'

'Aye. He came back from Canada with him. Some kind of retainer from the army, apparently, though he keeps pretty much to himself. He deals with the worst of the captain's behaviour, though he won't have a word said against him.'

'Why not?'

'You'd have to ask him. Or the master, though I wouldn't advise it, not tonight. You'd do best to keep to your room, miss.'

'You mean he's been drinking?' Violet wrinkled her brow in distaste. 'I thought he had earlier.'

'Aye, well.' The housekeeper's expression wavered slightly, as if she were about to say something and then changed her mind. 'As to that, I couldn't say. He's the master and an Amberton, whatever else he is. I won't be accused of disloyalty, no matter how much he deserves it. Now, as you can see, I've unpacked your bag.'

'Thank you…' Violet glanced across to the dresser '…but I've no intention of staying here beyond tonight.'

The older woman drew herself upright, sucking in a long breath as if she were trying to lift her ribcage as high as possible. 'I was told the wedding was still going ahead.'

'Then I'm afraid you've been misinformed. I've no intention of marrying anyone, especially not Captain Amberton. I intend to return to Whitby as soon as possible.'

'Without a chaperon again, I suppose?'

Violet regarded the housekeeper steadily. Judging by her tone, Mrs Gargrave held her at least partially responsible for her own situation. Well, the old Violet might have accepted that, might have shrunk inside herself at the implied accusation. The new Violet wasn't going to shrink from anything any more.

'Why do I get the feeling you don't approve of me, Mrs Gargrave?'

'It's not my place to have an opinion.'

'Really?' She lifted an eyebrow sceptically. She had the distinct impression that the housekeeper had a great deal of opinions, most of them negative. 'But if I wanted to know? If I asked you what you thought of me?'

'Very well, then, since you asked, I don't approve of any woman who flouts her father's wishes and runs away from home on her own. It's a disgrace! In my day, girls did as they were told.'

'I see. Then it might interest you to know that I've spent twenty-three years doing almost everything I was told.'

'That's as may be…'

'I went out once a week in my father's company. I had no other family, very few acquaintance and even fewer friends. I was told what to do, where to go, what to wear and even what to eat. Now I believe I've earned the right to make a few decisions of my own, including who I do or don't want to marry.'

'It's still not right for an unmarried woman to stay in a house with an unmarried man on her own.'

'Maybe not, but that was hardly by choice. I was brought here against my will by a man who insists that I marry him despite my repeated refusals. I would have thought you'd be more shocked by that than my so-called disobedience.'

'Well.' Mrs Gargrave pulled her shoulders back. 'Like I said, it's none of my business. I've told him what I think of his behaviour, for all the good it'll do, and now I've told you what I think of yours. In my book you're as bad as each other. I've done my part to make you comfortable and I won't have it said that I didn't. The rest is between the two of you. I shan't be dragged into anything sordid.'

'How charitable of you, Mrs Gargrave.' Violet felt seized with the unlikely desire to laugh. The housekeeper's flinty expression clearly suggested that she thought her some kind of harlot. It was the first time in her life she'd been criticised for loose morals and the feeling was strangely liberating. 'As long as your conscience is clear.'

They were prevented from saying anything more as the door opened again and Eliza came back into the room bearing a tray laden with tea and sandwiches.

'There now.' The housekeeper gave one last resounding sniff as the maid deposited the tray on a table. 'If there's anything else you need, ring the bell. Eliza here will see to you. Goodnight, Miss Harper.'

'Goodnight, Mrs Gargrave.' Violet inclined her head with exaggerated politeness. 'I'm very grateful. To you, too, Eliza.'

She stood, smiling and motionless until the door closed behind them, then scurried across to the tea tray, tucking into the sandwiches and gulping the tea down with relish. She hadn't eaten anything all day and her empty stomach had been making gurgling sounds all the way upstairs.

Satiated at last, she made her way to the nightstand, poured some water into a basin and scrubbed her face and neck vigorously. That felt better. Strangely enough, she didn't feel the least bit tired any more. Quite the opposite, she felt restored and reinvigorated, and now she was free she had absolutely no intention of staying where she was told, no matter what Mrs Gargrave suggested. As long as she avoided the drawing room, what better time to explore the house than when everyone else was in bed? It might be useful to work out an escape route.

Before she did anything, however, it was best to be prepared. Quickly, she rummaged in the dresser for her shawl and wrapped it around her shoulders on top of her other clothes. She still hadn't removed her cloak and she didn't intend to just yet. She wouldn't put it past Captain Amberton to lock her up again if he found her and this time she intended to stay warm, even if it meant wearing all her clothes at once. Finally she picked up a candle and opened the door, listening at the crack for a few seconds before stealing out into the corridor.

The house seemed to echo with silence as she crept along the landing, down the first flight of stairs and back to the main staircase. Heart beating erratically, she waited at the top of the banisters for a few moments, straining her ears, but there were no sounds, not as much as a faint murmur of voices in the background.

A tingle of apprehension ran down her spine. If she hadn't know better, she would have thought the entire place abandoned. In the near darkness, it looked full of mysterious shapes and shadows that made her want to rush headlong back to the safety of her room, but that was what the old, timid Violet would do. The new Violet steeled her nerve instead and made her way determinedly down the staircase to the front door. As she'd expected, it was locked.

She turned around, resting the back of her head against the wood as she surveyed the great hall. The fire in the grate was low, so that only half of the room was illuminated, the rest of it shrouded in an eerie, uncanny gloom.

Or was it? She took a few steps forward, screwing her eyes up to be certain. There was one other source of light, a thin orange glow emanating from beneath one of the doors that led off from the hall. It was the room Captain Amberton had stormed out of earlier, just before he'd dragged her upstairs. Was that the drawing room? She put her candle down on the central table and tiptoed towards it, pressing her ear against the wood. Silence. Was he inside? Mrs Gargrave had said so, but then it was possible that he'd gone to bed in the meantime. Failing that, he might have fallen asleep. She felt a sudden overpowering urge to find out, to see the inside of the monster's lair, if not the monster himself.

Cautiously she wrapped her fingers around the door handle and twisted, ignoring the voice of common sense that told her to walk, if not run, away as she opened the door and peered nervously around the edge, letting out a breath of relief as she did so. The room appeared to be empty, though it was nothing at all like she would have expected, far more inviting than a monster's lair, albeit with a distinctly masculine feel, with walls of gleaming mahogany wood, half-a-dozen burgundy leather armchairs, two green-velvet sofas and deep crimson-coloured rugs and curtains.

Intrigued, she took a few steps inside. The fashion for trinkets seemed to have completely passed the room by. There were no extraneous ornaments, nor as much as a lace doily in sight, just two large sideboards on which stood an impressive selection of bottles, empty glasses and books. The only decorations were a few paintings dotted around the walls, mostly of horses, and one landscape, a view of Whitby Bay, hanging over the still furiously roaring fire.

That was when she caught sight of him, sprawled in an armchair by the fireside, one booted foot propped up on a stool with the other stretched out in front of him, his chiselled features half-obscured by the sweeping locks of his unkempt dark hair. She froze instantly, afraid that he might have heard her, though by the regular rise and fall of his chest, he was fast asleep.

She waited a few moments to be sure before moving closer, slowly and steadily, hardly able to believe her own daring. For some reason, she wanted a closer look. Now that his anger had dissipated, temporarily at least, he looked strikingly handsome again, although the effect was somewhat spoiled by the pungent aroma of cigar smoke and whisky that filled the air around him.

Her foot bumped against an empty decanter lying beside his chair and she frowned down into his face. It was still recognisably that of the charming young officer she'd met five years before, only slightly more weatherbeaten, with lines etched into his forehead and between his thick brows that she didn't remember—too many, as if his burdens had increased tenfold since then. But then, a lot had happened in the meantime. His banishment, the loss of his father and brother, his injury… Were they lines of dissipation or of grief?

'Ah, Miss Harper.' His voice was so low it was almost a growl. 'My reluctant fiancée. Taking a good look?'

Chapter Four

$\diamond\!\!\sim\!\!\sim\!\!\sim\!\!\diamond$

Violet leapt backwards, stifling a cry of surprise as a pair of bloodshot, golden-brown eyes sprang open.

'I thought you were asleep.' She pressed a hand to her chest, trying to calm her frantically pounding heartbeat.

'Sleeping lightly is one of the first things you learn in the army. That, and to know when you're being watched. Or hunted.'

'Hunting would imply that I wanted to capture you.' She tossed her head resentfully. 'And I've already told you that I don't.'

'It might also suggest a desire for revenge. There's a suit of armour around here somewhere. I thought you might have borrowed a weapon.'

'Unfortunately I didn't notice. Maybe next time.'

There was a brooding silence while they regarded each other, the wood in the fireplace crackling and spitting as if it were trying to break the tension between them. She tensed one leg, ready to flee if he made a lunge, but he didn't look as if he had the energy to move, let alone manhandle her again. His posture looked indolent, almost as if he were about to go back to sleep, although she had the unnerving impression that he was of aware of everything she was thinking.

Then he grinned, revealing a row of gleaming white teeth, and she let herself relax slightly. At least his temper seemed to be under control, even if his smile looked even more dangerous somehow...

'Did you come to thank me for letting you out?'

'To thank you?' From the tone of his voice she could tell he was taunting her, though she still couldn't help spluttering with outrage. 'You were the one who locked me in!'

'For your own good.'

'What part of dragging me upstairs and locking me in a freezing cold tower was for my own good?'

He shrugged. 'The dragging part and the cold I apologise for. The rest was to stop you acting like a child.'

'I am not a child!'

'You ran away across the moors without any

thought or long-term plan for the future. I'd call that pretty childish.'

'I *had* a plan.' She hoped he couldn't tell she was lying. 'I've just no intention of sharing it with you.'

'If you want me to let you go, then I'd suggest that you do.'

She gritted her teeth, trying to control her own temper this time. She almost wished he *were* angry again. His smilingly indifferent tone was doubly infuriating. 'You've no right to make any demands. Or do you think that locking me up is some sign of maturity?'

'No, it's a sign of too much brandy. Though in my defence, I was acting under intense provocation. I'd had a particularly trying morning.'

'*You* did?'

He laughed, tossing his hair back to reveal almost ludicrously sculpted cheekbones. 'I trust that you prefer your new quarters?'

She glared back at him. 'I do, though I believe the credit belongs to Mrs Gargrave.'

'My fearsome housekeeper, yes. Has she warned you to barricade your door tonight?'

'No.' She hesitated, then couldn't resist asking, 'Why would she?'

'Why?' There was a distinctly wicked glint in his eye as he answered. 'Because I doubt there's any depravity she thinks I wouldn't stoop to, molesting virgins in their sleep among them. I'd be quite curious to know what she imagines actually, but I assure you you're perfectly safe in this house. As I explained earlier, my intentions are entirely honourable.'

She swallowed nervously, trying to hide her shock at his casual tone. How could he talk about molesting virgins so brazenly?

'Honourable or not, I've already given you my answer. And if you think that letting me out of a locked room is enough to persuade me to marry you, then you're very much mistaken.'

'I don't. It only occurred to me that it might prove difficult to marry a block of ice. It's a strange kind of wooing, I know, but the whole idea of marriage is new to me. How is a man supposed to propose?'

'I've no idea. All I can tell you is that however you do it, my answer will be the same.'

He gave another infuriating laugh. 'Do you know, I always suspected you had claws, Miss Harper. I just didn't realise they were quite so sharp.'

She blinked in surprise. What did *that* mean? Since when had anyone suspected her of being anything other than a timid and obedient daughter? Not that it was relevant now, but still it seemed—felt—like a compliment, as if he'd seen something in her that no one else had.

She pushed the thought away and pulled her shoulders back, trying to look as resolute as possible.

'I won't marry you, Captain Amberton, no matter what the cost to my reputation. You might as well let me go.'

'You're absolutely right. And since you asked so nicely, you're free to leave.'

'Really?' She gave a small start. 'Do you mean it?'

'By all means. You can leave this very moment with no hard feelings.'

'Just like that?'

'Just like that. Though, of course, I can't provide any kind of transport in this weather and it's five miles to Whitby, but feel free.' He leaned back in his chair with a sleepy expression. 'By the by, have you looked outside this evening?'

'No.' She walked quickly to one of the windows and wrenched back the curtains, heart sinking as she looked out.

'It's a full moon, I believe.' He gave an exaggerated yawn. 'That should be enough to see by.'

Violet tightened her knuckles over the edge of the windowsill. The storm had passed, but the moon was bright enough for her to see the good four feet of snow heaped up on the terrace outside, all but obscuring her view of the garden.

She couldn't have been imprisoned any more effectively if she'd still been locked in the tower.

'I hope you packed some sturdier boots than the ones you were wearing this morning.' His voice was a languid drawl. 'If you still want to leave, that is?'

'More than ever!' She swung around furiously. 'Just as soon as it's light.'

'As you wish. In which case...' he reached down and scooped the empty decanter up off the floor '...why don't we get to know each other in the meantime? There's a bottle of whisky on the sideboard. Care to join me?'

'No, thank you.'

'Ah...' He heaved his foot off the stool with a sigh. 'I forgot that you disapprove.'

'I do.' She put out a hand to stall him. 'But since it's impossible for me to disapprove of you any *more*, I'll fetch you a drink.'

'Taking pity on an injured man?'

She didn't answer as she stalked across to the sideboard and poured some dark amber liquid into a fresh glass, holding it out at arm's length so that he had to lean forward to reach it.

'Thank you, Miss Harper.' His fingers brushed lightly against hers for a second before she snatched them away. 'I suppose it's best that you keep a clear head. You've a long walk ahead of you in the morning.'

She narrowed her eyes resentfully. 'Don't think that I won't.'

'I wouldn't dream of naysaying you, but why don't you sit down for a while first? I won't bite, no matter what Mrs Gargrave says. I feel like I'm being interrogated with you standing there.'

'I prefer to stand.'

He let out a long sigh. 'Forgive my manners, Miss Harper, but would you please be so kind as to sit down?'

She hesitated for another moment and then perched warily on the edge of the velvet sofa opposite. It felt wonderfully soft and inviting, not to mention so cosy in front of the fire that she was almost tempted to relax her guard and curl her legs up beneath her. Almost. But he seemed to be watching her, eyes aglow with a look of such strange and sudden intensity that she felt her temperature start to rise.

'That's better.' He dropped his gaze after a few seconds and nodded. 'I'm glad we understand each other at last, Miss Harper.'

'Do we?'

'A little, I think. This morning I acted on the presumption that there was a certain...aspect about me that you found objectionable. Immodest as it sounds, the thought of it being my character never occurred to me.'

'I don't understand. What did you think my objection was?'

'Honestly? I assumed that some women might resent shackling themselves to a man with only one working leg.'

'But that's horrible!' She shot to her feet again in outrage. 'I would never think such a thing!'

'You called me a beast.'

'I meant you, not your leg!'

There was a momentary silence before he threw back his head and roared with laughter.

'What is it?' She stared at him in bewilderment. She'd never been so deliberately, unpardonably rude to anyone in her whole life and he was laughing? 'What's so funny?'

'Just that you find my character so objectionable. I applaud your good judgement.' He rubbed a hand across his face as if he were trying to control his own mirth. 'Although it might reassure you to know that we've something in common. I wouldn't want to marry me either.'

'So you don't mind what I said?'

'Not at all. I perfectly agree with your estimation, though I'm curious to know what exactly you've heard about me? It must have been perfectly scandalous.'

She folded her hands primly. 'I told you before.'

'Gambling and women again?'

'They aren't things I care to repeat.'

'Then I'll take that as a yes. Although, with all due respect, that gossip refers to the past. A man can change, can't he?'

'He can, though I find it hard to believe from a beast who locked me up in a tower.'

'Good point.' He took a mouthful of whisky and then peered dolefully into the cup. 'I had hoped for a full measure.'

'I'll get you another if you answer a question.'

'Just one?' His eyes glittered with amusement. 'I suppose that's fair. What would you like to know? Ask anything you like.'

She hesitated thoughtfully. What *did* she want to know? She had so many questions that she hardly knew where to start, but if she was going to find another way to escape, then she supposed she ought to find out what had gone wrong the first time…

'I'd like to know how you found me this morning.'

'How did I know you hadn't taken the train, you mean? Let's just say that next time you choose an accomplice you ought to find one the same height. The stationmaster remembered a woman in a black veil, but he also recalled her being reasonably tall. Whereas you, Miss Harper, are quite…' his gaze roamed leisurely over her body, down to her ankles and back up again '…distinctive.'

Distinctive. She dropped back on to the sofa with a thud. That was better than small, she supposed, though in essence it meant the same thing. Strange, unusual, odd-looking, the same words she'd been hearing her whole life. Except that no one else had ever looked at her in the way Captain Amberton just had, without criticism or disapproval, but with… She hardly knew what with, only that whatever it was made her feel too hot suddenly, with a quivering sensation deep in her chest. No, lower than that, in her stomach, something between a tingle and an ache. It was the same way he'd looked at her five years before, the way that had made her feel, albeit briefly, like a woman and not just an object of curiosity. Before she'd realised he'd only been laughing at her.

She shifted away from the fire, willing the feeling to subside. 'What about Rosedale? How did you know I was going there?'

'I didn't, but Mr Rowlinson happened to mention your friendship with Ianthe Felstone. I guessed that you might have used one of her husband's connections.'

'It's still only a minor supply route. How did you find out about it?'

'I asked her husband. He thought it might be the likeliest possibility.'

'*Robert* told you?' She couldn't hide her dismay.

'Robert?' His gaze darkened slightly. 'Yes, I'm afraid *Robert* did, though in his defence, he was trying to help you. Apparently he didn't think running away was in your best interests either. But then, I presume you already knew that or you would have included him in your plans, too?'

She lifted her chin, annoyed that he'd guessed correctly. 'It wasn't something I could explain to a man. I knew Ianthe would understand.'

'But to encourage a wife to keep secrets from her husband? Tsk, tsk, Miss Harper. You know he was quite offended by the suggestion of his wife's involvement at first, though once I explained the circumstances, he seemed to agree it was likely. It should be an entertaining evening in the Felstone household tonight.'

'It's not funny!' She felt a stab of guilt. Robert would forgive Ianthe anything, she knew, but any rift between them would still be her fault. Maybe she shouldn't have asked for help after all, but she'd needed to talk to someone.

'I wouldn't worry.' He sounded nonchalant. 'Every marriage needs a bit of drama now and again, or so I've heard.'

'I forgot how much you enjoy arguing.' She shot him an irate look and then shook her head despondently. 'All that planning…'

'I take it that running away wasn't a spur-of-the-moment decision, then?'

'No. I made up my mind as soon as I heard the terms of the will.'

'Ah.' His expression sobered. 'So your father didn't tell you about the arrangement before? I wondered about that.'

'You mean you already knew?' She sat bolt upright again in surprise. 'Since when?'

He held out his empty glass. 'I believe that you said one question. If you want me to answer another, then you'll need to alleviate my thirst.'

'All right.'

She took the glass and refilled it quickly, feeling his gaze on her back the whole time. The awareness unnerved her, making her hands tremble slightly as she poured. What on earth was the matter with her? More precisely, what was the matter with her body? It seemed to be acting independently of her mind. She didn't want to be so aware of him and yet every part of her seemed to be on the alert. Another thing she resented him for!

'Here you are.'

'Thank you, Miss Harper.'

He raised the glass, though his eyes remained

fixed on hers. They were an intense shade of amber, she noticed, the same colour as the liquid in his glass, as if each was reflecting the other. Quickly, she retreated back to the sofa.

'To answer your question, then—' he peered at her over the rim '—I knew that our fathers had come to an agreement about you marrying Arthur, though I never knew the exact details of the will. I certainly never imagined it would apply to me, too. I believe we discovered the truth about that on the same day. I took the news marginally better, of course, but it was still quite a shock, I assure you.'

'So you knew a while ago?'

'Yes.'

'At the ball?'

'That was the night I found out.'

'And your brother?' She sat very still, forcing the question past dry lips. 'Did he know about it then, too?'

'Yes.' He paused briefly before continuing. 'He was the one who told me.'

'Oh.' She closed her eyes, head spinning with all the implications of his words. If Arthur had known about the marriage agreement at the ball, then surely it explained his strange behaviour towards her. In which case, his despair must have had something to do with marrying her, too... As if the idea of it had been so truly appalling.

As if she were as strange and unattractive as she'd always been told.

'So he knew all along...' She forced her eyelids open again, struck with a deep sense of despondency. 'Why did you have to come after me? Why can't you just let me go?'

'Isn't it obvious?'

Yes. Her stomach plummeted. Of course it was obvious. It was just as her father had said, the only reason any man would want to marry her...

'Because of the money?'

'Because of the money.' He repeated the words softly. 'My father agreed to this bizarre arrangement because the estate needed money. It still does.'

'So you're just as mercenary as he was?' She didn't bother to hide her contempt, but he only shrugged.

'I prefer to think of myself as pragmatic. As I'm sure you've heard, my career as a soldier recently came to an abrupt and unfortunately irreversible end. I returned home without any means to support myself and to find my inheritance close to ruin. Your fortune presented itself at a most opportune juncture.'

'So that's all I am, then, an opportunity?'

He leaned forward, resting his forearms on his knees. 'I'll do you the courtesy of not sugarcoating the truth, Miss Harper. My father threw me out of this house, if you recall, without so much as a penny. He told me to make my own way in the world and I was glad, even eager, to do so. Unfortunately, as it transpired, my way was the wrong way. I made a mess of everything and now there's no way for me to put it right. There's no way for me to reconcile with my family either, but I still feel the need to make amends to my father, to save the estate if I can.'

'I don't care about your estate.'

'But your father did. He was just as mercenary as mine, only in his case he was appropriating the land and title. He might have intended for you to marry Arthur, but I'm the one that you've got.'

'*That* was a mistake. He would never have wanted me to marry you. He detested you.'

'Then I'm curious to know why he didn't alter his will?'

'I'm sure he would have if he'd known.'

His face paled visibly. 'He didn't know about Arthur?'

'No. He was sick when it happened so I never told him. If I had…'

'If you had, then neither of us would be in this situation.' A muscle jumped in his jaw. 'But it still doesn't change anything. We're both of us bound by the terms of the will. You can either marry me or be destitute. I admit that the bargain works in my favour, but for the sake of my conscience, as well as my bank balance, I'd prefer that you choose the former.'

'If you had a conscience, then you'd let me go.' She wasn't going to sugar-coat the truth either. 'How many times do I have to say that I don't want to marry you? You're a drunk!'

'Oh, come now, Miss Harper, is that really the best you can do? You called me a libertine earlier. I quite liked that. Besides…' he lifted the glass to his lips again '…the alcohol's largely medicinal. It dulls the pain.'

'In your leg?'

'In my past.' He smiled sardonically. 'You might not like me sober.'

'I don't like you now.'

'Then you'll be pleased to hear that once I've fulfilled my side of the bargain, I wholly intend to drink myself into oblivion.'

She frowned, taken aback by the note of conviction in his voice. 'What do you mean?'

'Just that, like you, I've no particular fondness for my company either. Only alcohol makes it bearable. Once I've fulfilled my father's wishes, I fully intend to spend as little time sober as possible.'

'But that's abominable!'

'Is it? I rather thought you might be heartened

by the idea. In all likelihood you'll be rid of me in a few years.'

'And that's supposed to make me *want* to marry you?'

'I thought that it might. Then you'd have everything without the inconvenience of a husband you dislike.'

'Detest, not dislike!'

'I believe we've established that, and believe me, Miss Harper, of all the women in the world, you were the last I ever wanted to marry.'

She flinched. No matter how much she despised him, the insult still hurt as much as it had at the ball. She stood up, trying to hold on to some scrap of dignity.

'There's no need to tell me that. You made your opinion perfectly obvious five years ago.'

'Did I? I remember being quite taken with you at the time.'

'What?' Her legs trembled as if he'd just knocked her feet out from under her.

'I found you quite intriguing, if I recall correctly.'

'You made fun of me!'

'In your opinion, although I assure you, I wasn't.'

She stared into his eyes uncertainly. He looked sincere, for once, as if he truly meant what he was saying, but surely he didn't. He couldn't…

'So when you said I might have suitors, you meant it?'

'Of course. I never did understand why you were so sensitive.'

'I thought… That is, my father…'

She let the words trail away. If he was telling the truth, then it cast her own behaviour at the ball into a very different light. If she'd simply overreacted, then everything that had followed had been her fault.

'But that means…'

'That my being denounced as a reprobate and banished by my father was based on a misunderstanding?' Amber eyes flickered with golden sparks in the firelight. 'Yes. Ironically I was actually behaving myself that night, though I find it hard to see the funny side.'

She opened her mouth and then closed it again. What could she say? If his banishment *had* been her fault, then how could she ever apologise enough?

'I never intended for any of that to happen.'

'And yet it did.' His gaze narrowed perceptibly. 'Ungentlemanly as it sounds, as much as I was intrigued by you to begin with, I had a very different opinion by the end of the evening. I believe I came as close to hating you as I ever have anyone. You see, my brother tried to tell me something important that night and I didn't listen. I didn't go to his aid when he confronted my father either. I danced with you instead. If I hadn't, then I might have been able to help him. I might have prevented him from drowning himself.'

She felt a roiling sensation in her stomach as if she were about to be sick. No one else had ever uttered the suspicion out loud, that Arthur Amberton's death had been anything other than an accident. Clearly his brother thought otherwise.

'So you think it was my fault, what happened?'

'At the ball, yes. To Arthur, not entirely. There's plenty of blame to go around, but you weren't quite the innocent bystander either.' He raised his glass in the air as if he were making a toast. 'But I do believe that you owe me a debt, Miss Harper. The very least you can do to repay it is marry me.'

Chapter Five

Lance raked his hands through his hair and staggered to his feet, keeling slightly as the floor pitched like the deck of a ship beneath his feet. How much had he drunk? He grimaced at the sight of another empty bottle on the sideboard. Too much, then. He was well aware that Mrs Gargrave watered it down, but the back of his throat still felt as though it had been scraped raw with sandpaper.

Had he slept? He felt marginally less exhausted than he had when he'd sat down, though refreshed was too much to hope for. He hadn't slept well in six months and there was no reason to expect he'd start doing so now. He must simply have dozed at some point.

Something had happened the previous night though, something to do with Miss Harper... His drink-addled brain seemed to be trying to tell him something, as if whatever it was, was important. Had she been there in the room or had he dreamt it? He stared intently at the sofa as if it might give him the answer, fragments of conversation coming back to him, fuzzy and yet vivid enough that they must have been real. They'd talked about her escape, about the will, about the money, about—he moaned out loud—Arthur.

Now he remembered. She'd dashed out of the room on the verge of tears after he'd practically accused her of causing Arthur's death, looking even more distraught than when he'd locked her in the tower, and he hadn't been so drunk that he hadn't felt a sting of remorse. The accusation had been cruel as well as unjust, but it was easier to lash out than face his own part in it. Easier, too, to keep on drinking afterwards than go and apologise.

He reached into his breast pocket and drew out the letter, the last one he'd ever received from his brother, the one that should have brought him home from Canada on the next available ship, but that he'd never answered and kept locked in a trunk instead, as if doing so would make its unwanted contents go away. He'd kept it with him ever since he'd received word of his father's and Arthur's deaths, over his heart like some kind of bandage, partly as a reminder of the amends he owed to his family, partly as a form of self-punishment, to remind him of how worthless a specimen of manhood he was by comparison.

He'd proven that again last night. He'd spent years blaming Violet Harper for his banishment, yet when he'd finally said the words aloud, they'd sounded utterly ludicrous. Of course she wasn't to blame. She hadn't intended to cause the rift with his father. That had been coming for a long time. She'd simply been the catalyst. He'd always been the cause.

As for what he'd said about Arthur, he had to apologise and the sooner the better. As much as he wanted her money, he should never have implied anything so vile, especially when the blame sat so squarely on his own shoulders. He forced himself to look down at the letter, at his brother's faded and increasingly illegible handwriting begging him to come home, to help him stand up to their father, to save him. And why hadn't he? Because he'd been too busy with a woman, that was why, with his own major's pretty and bored young wife. He'd stooped as low as he could go, and he'd paid for it. But so had Arthur.

'Good morning, sir.' Martin entered the room, wearing his usual taciturn expression.

'Good morning.' He tucked the letter away again. 'What time is it?'

'Eight o'clock, sir. The maids are waiting to come in and clean up.'

'Are they too frightened to come in and tell me themselves?'

'Probably.' Martin stood to attention and Lance sighed inwardly. Touching though his former batman's devotion was, there were times when he wished he'd simply go back to the army and leave him alone. He might have saved the man's life once, but he'd only done what anyone else would have under similar circumstances. He didn't deserve such loyalty.

'Miss Harper's in the breakfast room, sir.'

'Already?'

Lance lifted both eyebrows in surprise. It only seemed like a few minutes since she'd left him, though at least that meant she wasn't crying on her bed in despair. That made him feel slightly better.

'In that case, I'd better join her.'

Martin cleared his throat. 'All due respect, sir, but you might want to shave and clean up a bit first. You don't want to scare her.'

'Is that so?' He rubbed a hand along his jaw, finding enough stubble there to qualify as a beard. Hadn't he shaved for his wedding yesterday? He couldn't remember, but apparently not. No doubt he looked as bad as he felt, but he still had to apologise first.

'Then I'll just say good morning. Meet me upstairs in ten minutes, will you? Bring a razor.'

He made his way unsteadily to the breakfast room. Martin was right, she was already there, sitting neatly at the table, her pale face and white hair contrasting starkly with her black day gown. *Black.* He groaned inwardly. He'd been so angry yesterday that he'd forgotten she was in mourning for her father. As if she needed another reason to hate him.

'Miss Harper.' He propped one shoulder against the doorjamb for support.

'Captain Amberton.' She glanced up briefly, her shoulders tensing at the sound of his voice, though her outward expression remained calm.

He stood there in silence for a few moments, the ticking of the grandfather clock in the hall sounding deafeningly loud as he wondered what to say next. She wasn't crying this morning. Quite the opposite, she looked tranquil and self-contained, as if nothing he'd said the previous night had bothered her at all. He had to admire her fortitude, even if the dark rings around her eyes gave her away.

'I trust you slept well, Miss Harper?'

'Quite well. I suppose there's no need to ask how you feel.'

'I'm used to it.' He looked around the room and then gestured towards her plate. It was piled high with what looked like a mountain of toast. 'Is that all they've given you?'

'It's plenty.' She smeared marmalade on to the uppermost slice.

'Only toast?' He frowned. His cook had long since given up providing any kind of breakfast for him, but Miss Harper ought to be a different matter.

'At least it's not burnt.'

His frown deepened at the implication. 'Any particular reason, or do I strike you as the kind of man who serves his guests burnt food?'

'You strike me as the kind of man who might do any number of things, but apparently we're not very popular in the kitchens. According to Mrs Gargrave your kitchen staff prepared a special meal to celebrate our wedding yesterday.'

'And then were forced to eat it themselves?' He rolled his eyes. 'That's still no reason to starve you today. Is there anything else you'd like? Eggs, bacon?'

'No, thank you, I've already told Mrs Gargrave that this is sufficient. I like toast.'

'So I see.'

He watched as she took a large bite. Despite her age, she was still wearing her hair down, just as she had the first time he'd seen her, though it looked even longer now. It looked, quite frankly, overwhelming, swamping her tiny figure and shrinking her already small face. Did she like it like that, he wondered, or had she simply never tried putting it up? Only her large features stopped her face from being totally overpowered.

Not that it wasn't attractive, he conceded. It was really quite lustrous, thick and shining and smooth like a mirror. Even so, he preferred to look at her face. There was a smudge of marmalade at the side of her mouth and he felt a sudden powerful urge to reach over and wipe it away. No, not wipe—*lick*. He wanted to lick it away. He blinked a few times, distracted by such an errant thought. He oughtn't to reach out and do anything. If he tried, he'd probably keel over. The floor was still pitching slightly. And why on earth would he want to lick her, of all women, anyway?

'How many pieces of toast have you had?' He forced his attention back to the subject.

'Four, maybe five.'

'Preparing for your walk back to Whitby?'

The muscles in her jaw tightened instantly. 'The snow's still too deep. I checked.'

'Then at least I get to enjoy your company for a while longer.'

He pulled out a chair and levered himself down carefully. The atmosphere between them felt as thick as the fog in his head. He really ought to go upstairs and get cleaned up, but he wanted to clear the air first. Arthur was the very last subject he wanted to talk about, especially sober, but he needed to clear his conscience of one burden at least.

She peered at him askance for a moment and then nudged the toast rack in his direction. 'Would you like some?'

'No.' He winced as the smell hit his nostrils. 'Thank you, but I only have coffee in the mornings. When I'm awake in the mornings, that is.'

'Just coffee?'

'You sound like Mrs Gargrave. She finds my habits equally deplorable.'

'Maybe she has a point.'

'Maybe she does.'

He poured himself a steaming cup and downed the too-hot liquid in one painful draught, trying to find the words to begin.

'About last night…'

She pushed her chair back as if she'd just remembered something important elsewhere. 'I'd rather not discuss it.'

'Then just listen.' He raised a hand in appeal. 'What I said about Arthur was unforgivable. It was an appalling accusation and I'm sorry. I didn't mean it.'

'Yes, you did.' She looked him straight in the eye and he sighed.

'Yes, I did. At least, I thought I did. You see, I've spent the past six months thinking about what happened to Arthur, trying to blame everyone except myself. It's far easier that way, I've found. I thought that if I blamed you for my banishment, then it would justify my keeping away, for abandoning him when he needed me, but the truth is, I failed him. It's easy to blame someone you think you'll never see and I never expected our paths to cross again, Miss Harper, not until I was told about your father's will. When I met you again yesterday it forced me to confront some of the things I've been trying hard not to think about. I'm not proud of how I acted or what I said, but believe me, what happened to Arthur wasn't your fault.'

'Not totally, perhaps.' She lowered herself back into her chair slowly. 'But it was still true, what you said. If I hadn't started that argument at the ball, then you might never have been sent away. You might have been able to help him.'

'You didn't start that argument, you only finished it. My father and I had been arguing for ten years. He was bound to throw me out some time, and as for Arthur, I might have had all the time in the world and still not listened to him. He was always telling me to be serious, but I thought I could go through life avoiding it. I actually managed quite well for twenty-six years.'

'Your brother was unhappy the first time I met him.' She picked up another piece of toast and stared at it. 'He only seemed to get worse every time since, but I didn't understand why. I was upset when I heard what had happened to him, but I never thought…' She swallowed, as if she were struggling to go on. 'It was only when Mr Rowlinson told me about our fathers' agreement that I realised his death hadn't been an accident, that he'd drowned himself because of it. It was my fault in that regard.'

'No.' He held himself very still. She looked so anguished that he felt a powerful impulse to wrap his arms around her and comfort her. To seek comfort from her, too, he realised with a jolt, as if she might somehow alleviate his own guilt as well. What the hell?

She looked directly at him, fixing him with a defiant, overbright stare. 'You said he knew about their agreement at the ball. That means he knew the whole time.'

'Yes, but…'

'So he didn't want to marry me, did he?'

'No.' There was no point in lying when she already knew the truth. 'But it wasn't your fault. You didn't know about any of it.'

'I wish that he'd told me. If I'd known then, perhaps we could have stood up to our fathers together.'

'I doubt it would have made any difference.

Neither of them ever listened to what any of us actually wanted.'

'No.' She gave a wan smile. 'I suppose not.'

'It wasn't personal, Miss Harper.'

'It felt personal.'

'He was in love with somebody else.'

'The whole time?' She sounded appalled. 'But that's awful.'

'Even more so when you consider the woman.' He shook his head in disgust. 'Lydia Webster. Arthur mentioned her to me at the ball, but I thought it was just a passing infatuation. I should have known him better than that. Just over a year and a half ago he wrote to me, saying that they were in love but that our father refused to permit the marriage. A few months later, he wrote again, begging me to come home. A few weeks after that he went sailing. I've no idea what happened between him and Miss Webster, but after I came home, I took it upon myself to seek her out. Foolishly I thought she might have been upset by events.'

'Wasn't she?'

'We had tea and didn't mention his name once. She told me about her recent marriage to a lawyer from Scarborough. She got married one month after Arthur drowned. I think we can conclude she wasn't heartbroken.'

'But you think that was why he was depressed,

because he couldn't marry her himself? And that was why he…'

'Drowned himself?' He forced himself to utter the words. 'Part of the reason, yes. I prefer your method of running away, Miss Harper.'

'He must have been desperate.'

'Yes.'

He regarded her sombrely across the table. Arthur *had* been desperate, that much should have been obvious from his letter, but then so had she been—so desperate that she'd preferred to run away and be penniless rather than marry him. The realisation made him uncomfortable. He'd been so obsessed with the idea of punishing her and rebuilding the estate that he hadn't stopped to consider her feelings, nor the possibility that she might feel guilty about Arthur's death, too.

He started to reach a hand across the table and then pulled it back again. She wouldn't want comfort from a man like him, only practical reassurance.

'I promise you, Miss Harper, none of it was your fault. You and Arthur were the only innocent parties in this whole damned business.'

'Last night you said I was indebted to you.'

'Last night I was drunk. And wrong. There's no debt and there's been enough suffering because of this blasted agreement.'

Her eyes locked with his. 'You mean *you* think that it's wrong?'

'I think it was a terrible thing to do. Even if it does work in my favour.'

She tipped her head to one side, as if she were trying to understand something. 'But don't you feel trapped as well? Isn't there someone else that you'd prefer to marry?'

'No.' He bit back a smile. 'I'm not exactly the marrying kind.'

'But you'll marry me for the money?'

'Yes, to be blunt. Forgive me, Miss Harper, I don't say it to upset you. I say it because I want to be honest. I want the money, but I want you to be content, too. I don't want you to become desperate like Arthur. I have enough on my conscience.'

She inhaled sharply. 'I would never do what he did!'

'I'm glad to hear it. But what I'm trying to say is that I don't want to force you. I wasn't there for Arthur, but I am here for you. I want to do the right thing for once in my life. I know I've acted badly so far—worse than that, even. You were right to call me a beast. I behaved like one. I understand that you don't want to marry me, but tell me this, what *do* you want?'

She stared at him open-mouthed, apparently struck dumb by the question.

'Miss Harper?' he prodded her. 'If you tell me, then I might be able to provide it.'

'I don't understand.' She looked genuinely confused. 'What do you mean?'

'You said that you had some kind of plan when you ran away. I presume it was something you wanted a great deal since you were prepared to risk penury for it?' He leaned back in his chair, steepling his fingers in front of him. 'Or was it someone rather than something? Is there someone else *you'd* prefer to marry?'

'You mean a man?'

'That would generally be the case, yes.'

'No!'

He cocked an eyebrow, surprised by a feeling of relief. Any other woman and he might have thought she protested too much, but Miss Harper appeared genuinely shocked. Still, he wanted to be sure...

'You said you were meeting someone in Helmsley.'

'That was Ianthe's Aunt Sophoria.' Her brow creased suddenly. 'She'll be worried about me.'

'Will she still be there?'

'We reserved a room at the inn for last night. After that we were going to take the train to York, but I expect she'll have gone back to Pickering by now.'

'Then I'll send Martin with a message as soon

as he thinks he can get through. If anyone can weather these conditions, it's him.'

'But last night you said...'

'Last night I was a beast, remember? Today I hope I'm a man again—and not so bad that I'd let your friends worry about you.'

'Thank you.' Her frown eased gradually. 'And I didn't have a plan, not exactly. It was more of an idea. I wanted to see York.'

'Just see it? Haven't you been before?'

'I've never been anywhere. My father said I was too delicate to travel. He thought it wouldn't be good for me.'

'So why York?'

'I wanted to walk around the city walls.'

He stared at her for a moment incredulously. 'Are you saying that you were willing to lose your inheritance just to walk around some old walls?'

'Yes.' She seemed nonplussed by his reaction. 'My mother had a book about them. I used to look at the pictures when I was little. I've always wanted to go.'

'Indeed.' He didn't know whether to laugh or be offended. 'You must have heard some *very* interesting stories about me, Miss Harper. I've always flattered myself that I was more attractive than crumbling stone.'

'I didn't mean it like that. It's not the wall

itself—more the idea of it. The freedom to do something I want to do. That's what I want, freedom.'

'Freedom.' He repeated the word thoughtfully. Just how little of it had she had that she was prepared to risk so much to get it? His memory skittered back to the first time he'd seen her, when he'd thought she must have been raised in a tower—a fairy-tale prison like the one he'd put her in last night. How ironic that the only thing she wanted was the one thing he'd already taken away.

But perhaps it wasn't too late. She seemed to have accepted his apology and they were already on better terms than yesterday. She hadn't said that she hated him that morning yet—that was progress—and he'd meant what he'd told her. As much as he wanted her money, he wanted her to be content, too. For some reason, that seemed particularly important now. Perhaps he could still put things right between them and persuade her to marry him after all...

'How about a tour of the house first? We have some very attractive walls here, too.' He flashed his most charming smile, one that rarely failed to convince any woman to do anything, although Miss Harper seemed more interested in her breakfast.

'All right.'

'Good.' He tried again, but she was too engrossed in spreading a fresh layer of marmalade over her toast to notice. 'I might as well show you around since we're snowed in together.'

'I suppose so.' She looked up again at last, her expression oblivious and resolute. 'But only until the snows clears. After that, I'm leaving.'

Chapter Six

'Cutting it a bit close, aren't you?' Lance winced as the blade scraped across his cheek.

Martin harrumphed, though his hand didn't falter. 'You need a haircut, too.'

'There's no time.'

Another harrumph. 'You ought to try to look like a gentleman even when you don't act like one. You'll never get her to marry you otherwise.'

Lance blinked in surprise. It wasn't like his taciturn retainer to comment on either his appearance or his behaviour, no matter how bad either of them were.

'I doubt I'll get her to marry me anyway. It appears I'm losing my touch with women. It's me she objects to, not my leg.'

Though the realisation of that fact made him feel strangely buoyant. As furious as he'd been at the insult to his injured limb, the insult to his character didn't bother him even half as much. He could perfectly understand her objections to that. Now that he'd stopped blaming her for the past he could even start to see their situation from her perspective, too. He didn't resent her any more. On the contrary, after their conversation at breakfast, he felt strangely close to her, but he supposed Martin was right. If he wanted her to marry him, then he really ought to start behaving more like a gentleman.

'She's more intelligent than the rest, then.' Martin put the blade aside.

'So it would seem.'

Lance wiped a towel over his face and then pulled on a pair of breeches, fresh white shirt and cravat. Now that he'd had a bath and a shave, he felt impatient to get downstairs, as if he were actually eager to see her again.

He'd made a bad start with Miss Harper— in all honesty, it was hard to imagine a worse one—but now he felt determined to woo her for real. It would be a challenge, but even that idea was exhilarating. He already felt less oppressed than he had when he'd woken up that morning. If he could convince her to marry him, then he could expand his mining venture in earnest. He'd already invested the money he'd made soldiering, but her father's fortune would make all the difference.

'There.' He tied his cravat with a flourish. 'Gentlemanly enough for you?'

'Better than usual.'

'Remind me why I keep you around, will you?'

'Because no one else would put up with you.' Martin grunted. 'Tell her she looks nice. Women like that.'

Lance spun around in astonishment. 'Are you offering me tips on how to deal with the opposite sex, Martin?'

'It was just a suggestion, sir.'

'Good, because if there's one thing I know...'

'Begging your pardon, sir, but she's not like the rest.'

'Is that so?' He was beginning to feel faintly irritated. 'Because of her alleged intelligence, or is there something else that makes her different?'

'I just don't think she's the kind of woman to play games, sir. Or cheat on her husband either.'

Lance clenched his jaw at the words. Martin had made his disapproval about the major's wife obvious from the start, though he'd remained at his side when the storm had broken. He'd even removed the bullet.

'I don't want to seduce her, Martin, I only want to marry her. From what I've observed the two impulses are quite different.'

'Not always, sir.'

'Really?' Irritation was turning to downright annoyance. 'And you're speaking from experience, I suppose? Are you married, Martin?'

'Was married, sir. She died twelve years ago. Cholera.'

'Oh.' He froze with his arms halfway into a black-superfine jacket. 'I had no idea. I'm sorry, Martin.'

'It was a long time ago, sir.'

'I'm still sorry.' He put a hand on the other man's shoulder. 'From now on you have my permission to give as much advice as you see fit. Feel free to beat it into me if necessary.'

'I wouldn't dream of it, sir. I never saw you lose a fight yet.'

'Never?' He made a cynical face, but Martin's expression didn't alter.

'You didn't lose that one, sir. You did the right thing.'

Lance squeezed his shoulder and then limped his way down the stairs. In their five years together, Martin had never once mentioned a woman, and definitely not a wife, though he'd known about every tawdry indiscretion of his master's. How little attention had he been paying to the man who'd served him so loyally? As if he needed any more proof of his own self-centredness? Perhaps Miss Harper *was* more intelligent than the rest after all. Perhaps she'd been right to run away from a man like him…

She was waiting in the hallway when he arrived, sitting by the fireplace with her hands folded neatly in her lap, a model of self-contained calm and tranquillity. Considering the situation, he had to admire her poise, but then he was starting to admire a lot of things about her. He was starting to remember what he'd seen in her the first time…

'I don't understand this.' She caught sight of him and pointed to a crest above the fireplace. 'It says 1832.'

'That's when the house was built.'

'This house?' She got to her feet and looked around as if she were seeing the hall with new eyes. 'But it looks so old. I thought it must be Tudor at least.'

'It's supposed to. They even weathered the stone to make it look older. My mother was a voracious reader of Sir Walter Scott. Though I believe her favourite writer was Malory.'

'Arthurian legends?' She burst into a smile as her gaze settled on the largest and most central piece of furniture. 'You have a round table!'

'My mother's version of it, yes.' He watched her changing expression with interest. There it was again, the effect he'd noticed the first time they'd met, the radiant silvery shimmer that seemed to envelop her whole being when she smiled. Only the effect seemed even more powerful this time.

'And you're Lancelot!' She spun towards him gleefully.

'I'm afraid so.' He made a face. 'Just don't expect me to answer to it. Most people call me Lance. You can, too, if you want.'

She didn't acknowledge the offer. 'It could have been worse. Wasn't there a Sir Lamorak?'

'And Bedivere.'

'And Bors.'

'Imagine if I'd had more brothers.' He quirked an eyebrow. 'I suppose calling you Violet is out of the question, then? Or shall I call you Guinevere instead?'

'I remember your mother.' She appeared not to notice his question either, looking thoughtful instead. 'She visited our house sometimes with your father when I was a child. She was kind to me.'

'She was a kind person.'

'She even brought me a doll once. I think she'd noticed I didn't have many toys. I played with it for years... I was very sorry when she died.'

He cleared his throat. How had they got on to this topic? He was supposed to be wooing her, for pity's sake, but she seemed determined to be serious.

'She caught a chill that turned into a fever.' He tried to keep his voice matter-of-fact. 'Two weeks later, she was dead.'

'I'm sorry. My mother had some kind of fever, too, I think.'

'You don't know?'

'No.' Her brow creased slightly. 'I was never quite sure what happened. My father used to tell people she died when I was born, but I remember her. She was there, and then she was just... gone. He rarely spoke about her and no one else was allowed to either. After a while, it seemed strange to ask.'

'So nobody told you anything?'

'No. I was only young when it happened so I don't remember much. I can hardly remember what she looked like. I wish I could.'

'Like you.'

Her eyes shot to his, lit up with a glimmer of hope. 'How do you know? Did you meet her?'

'No, but I've seen your father. You look nothing like him, I'm relieved to say.'

'Oh.' A faint blush spread over her cheeks. 'But still strange.'

'Strange?'

'My appearance, I mean. I know that I look... different.'

'From?'

'From everyone else.'

'The implication being that it's a bad thing?'

Her blush deepened. 'People make comments. They say I'm too small and too pale and that my features are too big and my eyes are like saucers.'

'People say all that?'

'Some people.'

'Ah.' He frowned. Her father, then, most likely, although he could imagine that there had been other tactless comments over the years. Was that how she thought of herself as well? Was that why she'd been so oversensitive to his words at the ball? He'd assumed that she was shy, but he'd never considered that she might be insecure about her looks as well. Why would he have when he'd been so enchanted by them? But now her glowing cheeks and evasive gaze suggested a deep well of hurt.

'Then we make a perfect couple, Miss Harper.' He held out an arm, trying to lighten the mood. 'As you know, people make comments about me all the time, mostly because they have nothing better to do. Now, are you ready for your tour?'

She looked faintly relieved as she threaded a hand through his arm and followed him through the long line of reception rooms. The drawing room and breakfast room she already knew, but there was also the dining room, a music room, the day parlour and finally his study, though it belatedly occurred to him that he ought to have made some effort to tidy before inviting her inside. There were books and papers everywhere, as if the place had been ransacked. His desk was almost hidden beneath a giant map of the estate.

'Is this your study?' She looked vaguely impressed by the scale of the mess.

'It used to be called that, though I believe Mrs Gargrave now refers to it as a disgrace.' He lifted an eyebrow as her lips twitched. 'Is something funny?'

'I believe that's her favourite word. *I* was a disgrace yesterday.'

'You were? I find that hard to believe.'

'Both of us were, I think. Although in this case I'm afraid I agree. It's not very tidy.'

'I won't let her tidy it. If I she did, then I'd never find anything ever again. I've never been very organised.'

'So I see. What's this?'

She leaned over the desk to examine the map and he moved to stand at her shoulder, closer than was strictly necessary. After so many months it felt strange being so close to a woman. After what had happened the last time he would have thought he might be repelled, but instead he felt quite the opposite. The fresh smell of her hair, the light sound of her breathing, even the faint heat from her body were all provoking a physical reaction he'd almost forgotten. Odd, when those of his female acquaintances who'd called upon him since his return had failed to stir even the faintest interest.

'It shows the whole of the estate.' He reached past her to trace a line around the edge of the map. 'I've just opened a mine in this valley over here.'

'*You* have?'

'A couple of months ago, yes. I'd like to open a few more, too. There's an ironworks in Grosmont already, but there's plenty of potential for more.'

She twisted her face towards him, though she seemed not to notice his close proximity. Whatever effect he was feeling appeared to be entirely one-sided.

'But I thought you were a recluse?'

He laughed aloud. 'Is that what they're saying in Whitby about me, that I'm sitting in a dark room wallowing in my own misery? Well, I've done my fair share of that, too, as you observed last night, but I like to do a bit more with my time. I want to improve the estate, not just for me, but for everyone who lives here. The mine is just the first step.'

'So that's why you want my inheritance?'

'Yes.' He bent his head closer, lowering his

voice to a sardonic undertone. 'Or did you think I intended to spend it all on brandy?'

'Not all of it.' Her expression didn't falter. 'I expected some to go on whisky as well.'

He straightened up again, smiling appreciatively. 'Was that a joke, Miss Harper? You wound me, though I suppose I deserve it.'

'You do.' She turned around and leaned back against the desk, gazing up at the bookshelves that covered two of the walls. 'It's a beautiful room—what I can see of it anyway.'

'No expense spared.' He leaned against the table beside her, taking the weight off his legs for a moment. 'My father didn't care what my mother did to the place as long as she paid for it.'

'You sound as if you didn't like him.'

'Sometimes I didn't, though I loved him all the same. But he didn't make her happy. He only married her for her money and, yes, I do appreciate the irony.'

'Did she know that was why he married her?'

'I don't know. She was an intelligent woman so maybe she knew what she was doing. I hope so. I hope that she wasn't deceived.' He glanced sideways at her. 'For what it's worth, I never intended to be a fortune hunter myself.'

'Our fathers were the fortune hunters. At least you're honest.'

'To a fault. It's what gets me in trouble.'

'I doubt that's the only reason.' She gave him a pointed look. 'But I do appreciate the truth.'

'Then I promise always to give it.'

'Thank you.' She pushed herself upright again. 'Can we see the ballroom now?'

His rising spirits plummeted. 'If you wish.'

He led her back to the hall and along a corridor towards a pair of vast double doors. The ballroom occupied the whole east wing of the house, though he'd hoped to avoid this part of the tour. Somehow he'd assumed that she'd want to as well, though perhaps she was braver than he was.

'Here we are.' He pushed the doors open reluctantly.

She appeared to take a deep breath as she stepped inside, her expression pensive. 'It's bigger than I remember.'

'It was full of people that night.'

'I suppose so. It all felt so overwhelming at the time.' She walked slowly into the middle of the floor, then gestured towards the far corner of the room. 'That's where it happened.'

He felt a tightening sensation in his chest. There was no need to ask what *it* referred to. She meant the spot where they'd argued, where he'd last seen his father and brother. *It* was the reason he never came in here—why, even now, he refused to go any further than the doorway. The whole room was full of ghosts. If he went any further he was afraid he might be overwhelmed by them. She really *was* braver than him.

'Did you ever reconcile with your father?' She glanced back over her shoulder.

'No.' His voice sounded rougher somehow. 'We were far too alike. While my mother was alive she was a kind of buffer between us, but after she died, we did nothing but argue. We were both far too pig-headed to back down. That evening was the last time we ever spoke. Neither of us wrote. When I got shot, I thought perhaps it might be a means to reconcile, but then they told me about his collapse. You know, it all happened in the same week.'

'You mean you and your brother and father... all in the same week?'

'Last August wasn't the best month for us Ambertons. I'm the only one who survived. The wrong one, as it turns out.'

'You shouldn't say that.'

'Why not? Ask anyone and they'll tell you. Arthur was the only decent one among us. You would have been far better off marrying him.'

'Except that he didn't want me.'

She dropped her chin as she murmured the words, staring at her feet for a few seconds before crouching down suddenly.

'There a pattern here.'

'It's a Yorkshire rose.' He watched the graceful sweep of her fingers across the floorboards. She was so small, so delicate, and yet there was something entrancing about her. 'There's one on the ceiling as well.'

'Oh!' She tipped her head back so that her hair fell in a heavy coil to the floor. 'It's beautiful.'

'I'm glad you like it. They're all round the house if you care to look for them.'

'How many?'

'Fifty, perhaps. I don't really notice them any more. Except for the maze, of course.'

'There's a maze?' Her eyes seemed to catch light suddenly. 'Can I see it?'

'I'm afraid it's covered with snow.' He smiled at her obvious excitement. 'Although we can probably see the outline from upstairs.'

He closed up the ballroom with relief and led her back to the main staircase, gripping the banister for support as he dragged his injured leg up behind him. This ought to teach him to drink to excess, he thought bitterly. His leg always hurt more afterwards, making the stairs feel like a mountain this morning. Miss Harper, however, stepped lightly alongside, neither looking away nor directly at him, yet matching his pace as if it were natural for her to move so slowly. He appreciated the gesture even if he didn't deserve it.

'This way.' He turned right at the top.

'What are these rooms?'

She gestured at the long row of doors, though he kept his gaze fixed straight ahead.

'They're the family rooms.'

'Is one of them yours?'

'Not any more.' He jerked his head. 'That one used to be.'

'But why—?' She stopped abruptly, halting mid-step and mid-sentence to stare at the door before them. 'That's the room you locked me in yesterday!'

'That's where we're going. It has the best view of the maze.' He turned to confront her accusing expression. 'I won't do it again, I promise.'

'What about the window in this room?' She gestured towards another door. 'Can't we see it from there?'

'Yes, but that was Arthur's room.' His throat turned dry at the words. 'I told you, I don't use these rooms.'

'Can't we even go inside?'

'*No!*' He adjusted his tone quickly. 'I don't go in. I hadn't been in the tower for ten years until yesterday, only…'

He scowled as he tried and failed to find a way to finish the sentence. *Only what?* Only it had seemed to suit her? He could hardly say *that*. He limped on to the end of the corridor instead, unlocking the door and then holding the key out towards her. 'Here, I'll go in first. You can take your revenge if you want.'

'It's tempting.'

'Which is why I'm relying on your better nature.'

He opened the door and limped across the room. The tower had eight walls, four of which had windows, one of them with an almost perfect bird's-eye view of the maze. If she chose to follow him, that was.

'You can see it from here.' He beckoned to her and she edged forward warily, looking ready to turn and run at the slightest provocation.

'See those hedges in the shape of a flower?' He stood to one side of the window and pointed.

'Yes.' She stood at the opposite edge. 'It's an unusual design.'

'It was specially commissioned.'

'What's in the centre?'

'Can't you guess?'

'Another rose?'

'Something a bit more Arthurian.'

'A stone?' She clapped her hands when he nodded, her face shining with a look of pure delight. 'With a sword in it?'

He smiled, admiring the glow. 'I think you would have got along with my mother, Miss Harper.'

'Violet.'

'Violet,' he repeated, but she was already looking away from him, staring out of the window as if her life depended on it. There were two spots of colour high up on her cheekbones, he noticed, as well as a small tick at the base of her throat, a nerve fluttering lightly beneath the skin, as if she weren't quite as immune to his proximity as the rest of her behaviour suggested.

He felt a sudden impulse to reach out and stroke his fingers down the smooth line of her neck. What would an ice maiden feel like? he wondered. Would her skin feel warm? Would she melt in his arms? The idea made both his chest and groin tighten uncomfortably. Strange how intensely aware he was of her small body standing across from him. He could hardly have been any more aware if they'd actually been touching.

'Violet.' He said her name again, hearing the trace of huskiness in his own voice. 'I can't alter the terms of your father's will, but I can make them more bearable.'

She seemed to sway slightly towards him. 'What do you mean?'

'I mean that if you marry me, then I'll give you your freedom. I want your father's money, that's true, but not at any cost. I understand your objections to me, but I'd rather not see you destitute because of them. Our fathers have left us in this bizarre situation for better or worse, so to speak, but it seems to me that we can help each other. We can abide by their agreement on our own terms. You can live however you want and go wherever you want. I'll do everything I can to make you happy. We'll share the money equally.'

'You'd give me half?'

'Why not? He was your father and I presume there are other old walls you'd like to visit. I believe Chester has some.'

'So I'd be able to travel?'

'Of course, if that's what you want.'

She half turned her head, though she still didn't look at him. 'How do I know if I can trust you?'

'You have my word as a gentleman, for what it's worth.'

'I'll need to think about it.'

'Take as much time as you need.' He grimaced. 'As long as it's no more than a week. I'm afraid that's when the terms of your father's will expire.'

'And then we'd both lose the money.' She sounded thoughtful. 'What if the snow doesn't clear before then? We might not be able to get back to Whitby to be married.'

'Then we'll marry in the village. Your father didn't specify a venue.'

'And if I still don't want to?'

'Then I'll take you home personally with no

hard feelings. We can still salvage your reputation.'

This time she looked straight at him. 'I thought it was already too late for that?'

'You're fortunate enough to be under the same roof as Mrs Gargrave. She's a staunch defender of the family reputation, not to mention her own. The poor woman has her hands full with the task, but she'll vouch for you if I suffer one of her interminable lectures first. Think of her as your chaperon.'

To his surprise, she actually smiled at the suggestion. 'All right. Then I'll stay for the week and think about it.'

'Thank you.' He felt as if a heavy weight were being lifted. 'In that case, I hope you've forgiven me for last night?'

She pursed her lips, looking around the tower with a speculative expression. 'What is this room?'

'This was my mother's private sitting room. Our old playroom, too, when we were little. She liked to keep us close to her.'

'I like it better in daylight.'

She caught at one of the dust covers, tugging it away to reveal a blue-velvet chair, and he felt a sharp pang in his chest, struck with the memory of his mother sitting there, reading to him and Arthur. For some bizarre reason he hadn't thought that the tower would affect him as much as the family bedrooms, but now he felt as though his heart were being gripped in a vice, so tight he could hardly breathe. Maybe it served him right for having imprisoned Violet yesterday.

'Captain Amberton?' She sounded concerned. 'Are you all right?'

'Lance,' he corrected her, struggling to get his features back under control. 'Yes. It's just my leg. It hurts sometimes.'

'Perhaps you should sit?'

'No,' he answered too vehemently. 'I'm all right.'

'Are you sure?'

'It'll pass. It always does.'

'If you say so.' She looked faintly dubious. 'In that case, I'll forgive you on two conditions.'

'Name them.'

'One, if I stay, I'd like to have this room as my own. It seems a waste not to use it.'

'Very well.' He supposed he deserved that, too…

'And two, whilst I'm thinking about it, you have to let me do whatever I want. No telling me where to go or watching me or even asking where I'm going. If you're offering me freedom, then you have to prove that you mean it.'

'As you wish.'

'Good.' Her eyes sparkled with a look that was borderline mischievous. 'Because apart from yesterday I've never been outside in the snow before and I'd like to know what it feels like. I want to explore. If that's acceptable to you—*Lance*?'

Chapter Seven

❧

Violet kept up a dignified manner as she crossed the courtyard, waiting until she was out of sight of the front door before charging headlong through the snow towards the maze. It was harder to run than she'd expected. Her feet stuck in deep trenches every few steps, making a crunching sound that seemed especially loud in the otherwise eerie silence. The snow seemed to be muffling the real world—all the sights, sounds and smells of nature—and yet she relished the feel of it. The hem of her dress was heavy and wet, the cold air stung her face and she was panting heavily, but she didn't care. It felt good not to be cosseted, to be outside on her own, to prove that she wasn't so small and delicate after all.

The memory of Lance's expression when she'd told him she wanted to go outside made her smile, too. He hadn't been happy about it, that had been obvious, but considering what they'd just been talking about, he hadn't been able to refuse. He'd arranged a luncheon for her first, however, still claiming not to be hungry himself, and then offered to accompany her, but she'd declined. Even if it hadn't been for his leg, she'd needed for him to prove that he meant what he'd promised. Freedom.

She stopped at the entrance to the maze and looked back at the hall, wondering if he was watching from one of the windows, but there was no sign of anyone, not so much as a twitch of a curtain. From a distance, the building looked unreal and slightly forbidding, though that was only fitting, she supposed. Not much that had happened over the past few days seemed to make a great deal of sense, as if she'd actually slipped into a fairy tale.

The very hall seemed to belong to some imaginary realm, looking like someone's fantasy of a medieval castle, which in fact it was. All it needed was a moat and portcullis to complete the effect. It was Lance's mother's fantasy made real, though Violet wondered how much the rest of her life had lived up to it.

According to Lance, it hadn't. He'd said that his father had only married her for her money, as if there had never been any other bond between them. No romance, no comfort, no love, just money. And now he was offering her the same. Could she bear to accept such an arrangement? *Could* she live with it? More importantly, could she risk giving any man that much control over her life again?

She heaved a sigh. Perhaps his parents' relationship explained the faint air of sadness that hung about the place, as if the history of the family who'd lived there had seeped into its very walls. Its current owner certainly seemed tainted with it, too. When she'd woken that morning she couldn't have imagined feeling any emotion but anger towards him, yet when he'd mentioned his mother she'd found herself wanting to offer sympathy. Not that he'd asked for it. He'd been almost matter-of-fact about the details of his parents' marriage, but the emotion behind the words had been palpable.

Perhaps he wasn't quite the heartless beast she'd taken him for after all. His reputation was appalling, justifiably so by his own admission, but perhaps she'd misjudged him, too. She certainly hadn't seen him at his best the previous night and now he *seemed* to want to make amends for it...

After crying herself to sleep, devastated by his accusations, she'd come down to breakfast ready to demand that someone take her back to Whitby, snowdrifts or not, but he'd actually come to find her to apologise. More than that, he'd told her that what had happened to Arthur wasn't her fault. If there was any blame on her shoulders, he'd forgiven her and, in so doing, given her licence to forgive herself. Amazingly, she'd actually felt grateful to him.

So she'd stayed.

She turned her back on the hall finally and headed into the maze, selecting the path to her left. The snow was shallower between the hedges, the paths being better sheltered from the wind, though there was still enough that she could follow her own footprints back. Which might be a good thing, she decided, since her mind was spinning with so many emotions that she was finding it difficult to concentrate.

That was the other reason she'd wanted to come outside, to get some space to think—something that seemed impossible to do in the company of her erstwhile suitor. As much as she hated to admit it, there was something about him that seemed to disrupt her thoughts even more, not to mention her body. When he'd stood beside her that morning, first at the desk and then at the window, she'd felt as though she'd been standing too close to a fireplace. All of her nerves had seemed to tingle and vibrate at once, making her whole body pulse alarmingly. She'd avoided looking at him so he wouldn't be able to tell.

She shivered at the memory, though not with cold. How was it possible for her to be so strongly affected by a man she didn't even like? Because she didn't like him…did she? No! She had to remind herself of that fact. Not so much had changed between them since that morning. And yet she *had*, a small voice at the back of her mind whispered. Once upon a time she *had* liked him, far more so than his brother, and not just because Arthur had been so completely uninterested in her. Lance Amberton had been like no one she'd ever met before, charming, irrepressible and ridiculously handsome, with a streak of rebelliousness and aura of potent masculinity that had been both shocking and dangerously attractive at the same time. Alarmingly, it still was.

Attraction. Was that what she'd felt five years ago? She hadn't wanted to admit it to herself, but now the feeling was back, stronger than ever, and she could no longer even pretend to deny it. She was attracted to him—and he'd been 'quite taken' with her, or so he'd said.

Had he really meant it, or had he simply been trying to persuade her to marry him? She didn't think he would lie, given how brutally honest he'd been in every other regard, and he *had* seemed to like her five years ago. If she hadn't known better, she might have suspected that he'd been flirting with her at the ball, but she *had* known better. Her father had warned her about rakes and fortune hunters beforehand, reminding her of how small and insipid she was, of how unscrupulous men would try to take advantage of her wealth, and yet...

She sighed. She'd spent so many years believing the worst about herself that the possibility of somebody actually admiring or liking her for *herself* had never even occurred to her back then, but if Lance was telling the truth, then maybe she hadn't been so unappealing after all. Had he really found her attractive? Was it possible?

The peculiar throbbing sensation in her stomach was back, as if she were longing for something, even if she didn't know what. Of course, if he had actually been 'taken with her' at the time, his feelings were clearly very different now. He'd told her last night that she was the last woman in the world he would ever have chosen to marry, that his only motive was her fortune. Whatever interest he might once have had was obviously long gone. All he wanted now was her money, just as her father had always said would be the case. Lance was only more honest about it than most fortune hunters.

Not that she wanted him to want anything else, she reminded herself, no more than she wanted any kind of romantic attachment. Attractive as he was, she wasn't fool enough to offer her heart to such a notorious ladies' man, even if she were tempted to do so, which she wasn't. There were other things she wanted—places to visit, sights to see, a whole world to experience away from Whitby, none of which involved Captain Lancelot Amberton.

In which case, why shouldn't she marry him on the terms that he'd offered, freedom in exchange for her fortune, not to mention an equal share in the money? His proposal was a surprisingly fair one. He wasn't trying to deceive her, or intending to squander the money as she'd first suspected. He must surely have been joking, albeit in poor taste, when he'd said that he intended to drink himself into oblivion. And she *did* owe him a debt. Despite his apology that morning, she still felt partly to blame for his banishment. If she married him, it would go some way towards repaying it…

She rounded a corner and then stopped. She'd been so lost in thought that she'd come upon the heart of the maze unawares, but there it was, just as he'd said, a large stone with a metal sword protruding from the top. She ran forward and tugged on the hilt, but the metal was welded fast to the rock. Probably there was no other half to the sword to extract, but the effect was still enchanting.

There was a sweet-looking arbour in one

sheltered corner of the clearing, too, though even a quick glance showed that the wood was rotting and the rose bushes on either side, which must once have trailed elegantly over the trellis, were hopelessly overgrown. It was a pity to see a place once so obviously loved now so neglected. If she stayed, then she'd have to do something about restoring its former loveliness...

If.

She leaned back against the boulder and clutched the edges of her shawl tightly beneath her chin. She'd never expected to marry, but she'd always assumed that if she did, then it would be for love. Ianthe and Robert seemed to have such a marriage, but how often did that happen? Could someone as small and strange as she was ever be so lucky? In which case, perhaps she ought to consider Lance's offer after all...

But this was exactly the situation she'd been afraid of, that she'd let herself be persuaded into following her father's orders, into letting him govern her life even after his death. If she agreed to his final demand, then it would be as good as admitting that she'd never break free of him, never be free to make her own choices...

On the other hand, Lancelot Amberton hadn't been, would never have been, her father's choice. If she married him, then she'd only be submitting to the wording, not the actual intention of his will. If Lance was genuinely offering her freedom, then it wouldn't be a real marriage anyway, would it? He'd said they could live on their own terms, in whatever way they chose. In one way, it would be the perfect form of revenge...

She pushed herself away from the rock and started back through the maze, ashamed at the thought. She oughtn't to think of revenge. Whatever her father had done, he'd done to protect her, to ensure that she was looked after. All his controlling behaviour had only ever been for her own good. That was what he'd said—what she'd had to believe. Why else would he have treated her so badly, keeping her bound by his side for twenty-three years, demanding that she live her life in the shadows, unable to make acquaintances, let alone friends? Why else would he have kept her a prisoner?

She staggered as the numb, hard feeling in her chest, the ice that seemed to have settled there when Mr Rowlinson read out the will, splintered apart suddenly, letting loose a wave of pent-up emotion. How could her father have done it, not just the will, but all of it?

She'd been asking herself that question for weeks, but now it was more than a question. It was a burst of anger, fierce and hot and all-encompassing. And she didn't really need to ask why because she already knew the answer, had always known it deep down, only some vestige of loyalty had stopped her from acknowledging the whole truth. He'd done it because he could, because he'd wanted to control every aspect of her life, because he'd wanted a nursemaid who would never leave him, but most of all because he'd blamed her for her mother's death.

That was the truth that no one had ever spoken out loud, though there had been hundreds of clues over the years. So he'd made her feel worthless, telling her that she was small and insipid and unattractive, and he'd made *her* believe it, too. He'd been punishing her for something he'd never even told her about and now she was simply furious. Why *shouldn't* she want revenge? What she really wanted was to scream and to shout and to rail at him, but since she couldn't do that, why not marry Lance, a man he'd despised, instead? When she'd run away from Whitby, she'd thought that she'd been running away from the pair of them, but the truth was that they weren't on the same side at all.

She charged out of the maze as if there were hounds on her tail, though strangely enough her mind felt clear. No matter how painful the truth, just acknowledging it made her feel better. She still didn't know if she could marry Lance, but there was one thing she definitely wanted to do, one way to show that she wasn't going to be controlled any more.

She ran back across the lawn and through the front door, discarding her damp shoes by the fireplace and hurtling upstairs to her room. Then she sat in front of her dresser, staring into the mirror as she tried to summon up the nerve to continue.

Oddly enough she already looked different. The last time she'd looked at her reflection had been the evening before she'd run away, when she'd stood in front of her long glass, pale and nervous, looking to all intents and purposes like the child her father had always told her she was. Yesterday, she hadn't looked at herself at all, too ashamed by the failure of her plans to do so. But today…

Today there were subtle but noticeable differences, as if all her features had come into sharper focus overnight. Today she looked like someone with her own mind, who'd taken the first step, however faltering, towards securing her freedom and becoming her own woman.

There was only one problem, one she intended to remedy straight away. She twisted her shoulders, looking at the long lengths of her silvery-blonde hair with dislike. It fell, as it always had, in an inflexible straight line to her waist. Her father had never let her wear it up, insisting that she keep it down like a girl even when it had become ridiculous to do so. She reached up and twisted the lengths around her hands, coiling it up into a bun. The effect was…also ridiculous. With her tiny size, she looked as if she were wearing a cat on top of her head. Which meant there was only one thing *to* do.

She rang the bell for Eliza and asked for a pair of scissors, waiting patiently for her return before setting to, hacking away at the long lengths until her hair fell to a point midway between her shoulders and ears. It wasn't much of a rebellion, she conceded, but it felt like a start, as if she were cutting away the ties of her old life and starting anew.

Then she looked at her reflection again and wondered if she'd just made a terrible mistake. Piles of white-gold lay on the floor around her feet like another snowdrift, but what remained on her head looked as if it had just been mauled by the same animal it had just resembled.

'What do you think?' She looked up at Eliza hopefully, though one glance at the maid's expression was enough to confirm the worst. 'Is it so very bad?'

'It's not good,' the girl answered awkwardly. 'Perhaps you'd let me try, miss? I cut my brother and sisters' hair and I don't do too badly. Yours is a bit straighter than theirs, but if we neaten it up at the sides…' She tapped her chin thoughtfully. 'Maybe if we tuck it back behind your ears? That would frame your face nicely.'

'Would it?'

She relinquished the scissors at once. Anything was worth a try, she supposed, since there was no way to make any more of a mess than she already had. Then she squeezed her eyelids shut, listening in silence to the click of the scissors until she felt a brief tap on her shoulder. Nervously, she opened one eye, then both in amazement. Only a few minutes had passed, but she could scarcely believe the transformation. Eliza had trimmed what was left of her hair into a neat line around her chin. It looked and felt wonderful.

'I feel so much lighter.' She twisted her head, looking at it sideways in the mirror and marvelling at the cool feeling of air on her neck. 'Thank you.'

'It suits you, miss.' Eliza smiled shyly. 'Not that it wasn't nice before, but there was a lot of it. This shows up your cheekbones, too.'

Violet leaned forward, struggling to recognise herself in the mirror. Eliza was right, she *did* have cheekbones. They were high and sharp, though she'd never noticed them before. Briefly, she wondered what Lance would think of her new style before admonishing herself. What he thought didn't matter. He wasn't marrying her for what she looked like and she didn't care for his opinion anyway. What mattered was what she thought of it—and she loved it.

'Dinner will be ready soon.' Eliza brushed a few errant strands from Violet's shoulders. 'Begging your pardon, miss, but I noticed that you didn't bring many dresses. Perhaps you'd like to wear one of the new ones?'

'What new ones?' She spun around on her stool in surprise.

'The ones the master ordered from Newcastle. He had them specially made as a wedding present.'

'For me?'

'He's not marrying anyone else, miss.' Eliza giggled. 'Mrs Gargrave says she thought she'd never see the day.'

'Oh.' Violet glanced towards the wardrobe. On the one hand, if the gowns were a wedding gift, then she could hardly wear them without implying something about her intentions. On the other hand, she had so few pretty dresses...

'He must have had them made very quickly.'

'I suppose so, miss, though I thought there must have been some mistake when they were delivered on account of their size... Oh!' Eliza put her hand to her mouth quickly. 'I'm sorry, miss. I didn't mean anything by it.'

'That's all right.' Violet smiled reassuringly. The maid looked so mortified that it was impossible to be angry. Besides, she'd come to another realisation out in the maze. She was small. That was a fact. There was no point in being offended by the truth so she might as well try to embrace it. And if the dresses had been specially made, then it wasn't as if they were going to fit anyone else. She might as well take a look at them. Surely there couldn't be any harm in that?

She opened the wardrobe with a building sense of anticipation. Inside were two new dresses beside her own drab ones, one day gown and one evening gown. The day gown was a sombre dark grey, perfectly suitable for a woman in mourning, but the evening gown...

She let out a gasp. It was a bright azure blue, silken and shoulderless, gathered at the back in the latest fashion, with a trim of delicate, white lace around the sleeves and hem. Her father had never allowed her to wear anything remotely fashionable or luxuriant, let alone silk, and the temptation to try it on was overwhelming.

'I think the captain must have ordered that for when you came out of mourning, miss.' Eliza sounded vaguely apologetic. 'Though it seems a shame for it to just sit there.'

Violet gave a murmur of assent, too busy stroking her hands over the fabric to answer. If she followed the rules of etiquette, then it would be another eleven months before she was out of mourning and allowed to wear it, but today she didn't want to follow rules or be respectful either. Her father had made her feel colourless for long enough. Eliza was right. It *was* a waste to hide away something so beautiful. No matter what her wearing it might suggest, Lance could hardly criticise her for wearing something that *he'd* bought! He could hardly criticise anyone for being rebellious either.

'I'll wear it tonight.' She pulled it out of the wardrobe decisively.

'But…' Eliza took one look at her face and bit her tongue. 'Yes, miss. Would you like a bath before dinner, Mrs Gargrave wanted to know?'

'Yes, please. And Eliza?' She called out as the maid headed for the door. 'I'd be grateful if you didn't mention my haircut downstairs. I'd like it to be a surprise.'

Chapter Eight

Violet made her way purposefully down the staircase, moving quickly so that she wouldn't change her mind. Her new gown rustled as she walked, but it fitted perfectly, surprisingly so given that most dressmakers seemed unable to accept the accuracy of her measurements and generally made her dresses a couple of inches too long. Somehow Captain Amberton had managed to order one of exactly the right length. How? Surely he couldn't have remembered her height from five years ago. She would have assumed that he'd asked someone her size, but who?

'Good evening.' She passed Mrs Gargrave in the hallway. 'Is Captain Amberton in the drawing room?'

'He's in the dining room, miss,' a footman answered as the housekeeper gaped at her speechlessly. 'Dinner's ready to be served.'

'Thank you.'

She gave a polite nod and swept on, hearing a muffled exclamation of outrage in her wake, though she didn't have time to dwell on it. The door to the dining room was open and she could already see Lance standing inside. He was leaning against the chimney breast, dressed in a pair of form-fitting black trousers, matching leather boots, a crisp white shirt and perfectly tailored jacket. If she hadn't known better, she would have thought him the very model of genteel respectability. He wasn't even holding a drink.

She paused in the doorway, lifting her chin and pulling her shoulders back before announcing herself. 'Good evening, Lance.'

'Violet.' He glanced up and then did an abrupt double take, his gaze flickering first over her hair and then down to her gown. 'You look... different.'

'Oh.' She couldn't help feeling disappointed. It wasn't quite the compliment she'd been hoping for. 'I wanted a change.'

'Evidently.' His gaze travelled back to hers and held, though his expression was unreadable. 'That colour suits you. I thought that it might.'

'Eliza said you ordered the gown from Newcastle. Thank you.'

He inclined his head. 'I thought I ought to get you something as a wedding present.'

'I'm afraid I've shocked Mrs Gargrave.'

'It doesn't take much.'

She still couldn't read his expression. 'Are you shocked, too?'

'A little.' He smiled finally, though his gaze never left hers. 'Though that's not necessarily a bad thing. I quite like to be shocked sometimes.'

'What about my hair?' She felt nervous asking. 'Do you like that?'

He raised a hand to his chin and rubbed it thoughtfully. 'Do you know, the first time I saw you I thought you looked like a kitten. I wanted to pat you on the head. Now I do even more.'

A kitten? She felt a wave of dismay. How many more ways were there of calling her helpless?

'You are *not* patting me on the head.'

'Then I promise I won't, no matter how tempted I am, but for the record, I approve. Wholeheartedly, in fact.'

'Because I look like a kitten?' She couldn't conceal the resentment in her voice, and he arched an eyebrow.

'I meant it as a compliment. Kittens are generally considered quite sweet.'

'They're small and timid.'

'Ah.' His eyes flashed with a look of understanding. 'You're right. But kittens grow into cats. Beautiful, sleek ones with claws, and we've already established that you have those.'

She made a harrumphing sound, only partially mollified, and he laughed. 'Not good enough? All right then, Violet, you look quite scandalously beautiful tonight. That hairstyle suits you.'

'Thank you.' Her cheeks flushed at the compliment. No one in her whole life had ever called her beautiful before, nor looked at her with such obvious appreciation—no one except him five years before when she'd thought he'd been mocking her. Was he mocking her now? She peered up at him from under her lashes. No, amazingly enough, he didn't look as though he was.

'More importantly,' he continued, 'do *you* like it?'

'Yes. I never realised how heavy my hair was before. I always felt like it was dragging me down, but I never realised how much. It's as though I can finally move.'

'Then I approve even more. Did you do it yourself?'

'Yes, but it looked awful. Eliza fixed it.'

'Remind me to raise her wages. She might make an excellent ladies' maid. If you decide to stay, that is.' He held out a chair for her to sit down. 'Now I hope that you're hungry. Cook has provided a feast.'

'Have they finally forgiven us in the kitchens, then?'

'It appears so. We'll just have to eat everything or they might never cook for us again.' He picked up a bottle from the centre of the table. 'I didn't know what you'd care to drink. I thought maybe lemonade?'

'I'll have some wine, thank you.' She smiled at his look of surprise.

'I thought that you didn't approve?'

'My father didn't approve. I've never tried. I'd like to have a taste before I make up my mind.'

'Very well.' He put the lemonade down and picked up a different bottle, pouring a splash into her glass.

'I thought you didn't like half measures?' She gave him a pointed look.

'*Touché.*' His lips quirked as he poured again. 'I admire your good taste. This is a particularly fine claret. Is that sufficient?'

'Yes, thank you.'

She reached for the glass and took a tentative sip. The wine had a far mellower taste than Mr Rowlinson's brandy and made her stomach feel pleasantly fuzzy. She took a few more mouthfuls.

'Strictly speaking it's meant to be savoured, not gulped.' There was a smile in his voice. 'Trust me, when it comes to alcohol I'm an expert.'

'Oh.' She took another mouthful and let the wine sit on her tongue for a few seconds before swallowing. Instantly the flavour seemed richer and more intense.

'You know your hair really does suit you.' He sat down opposite. 'I like it more and more.'

She peered across the table suspiciously. 'You don't have to say that.'

'I know.'

'I've already said that I'll consider your offer.'

'I know that, too.' He reached for his own glass. 'Do you think that I'm trying to charm you?'

'Aren't you?'

'I was simply offering a compliment based on fact. That's allowed, isn't it?'

'Just as long as it's honest.'

'I've told you before, Violet, I'm many things, but not a liar.'

'I'm sorry.' She watched as he filled his own glass to the brim. 'I just tend to assume...' She bit her lip. She didn't want to say what she tended to assume. She didn't want to think that way any more, but old habits were hard to break.

'That I'm lying because I'm a fortune hunter and wouldn't dream of giving you a compliment otherwise?'

She winced at his bluntness. 'I suppose so.'

'You have so little confidence in yourself,

then?' He put the bottle down with a thud. 'You know, sometimes I wish I'd hit your father when I had the chance.'

'So do I.'

Both of his eyebrows shot up, though whatever response he was about to make faded as two maids entered the room carrying bowls of steaming Julienne soup.

'This looks delicious.' Violet licked her lips with anticipation. 'I feel famished. It's funny, but ever since I got here I've felt as though I could eat a horse.'

'You could do to eat a couple.'

'Father never let me eat much. He said it wasn't ladylike.' She swallowed a spoonful and sighed with pleasure. The soup was so delicious that she was half tempted to pick the bowl up and drink. 'I feel as though I've been hungry my whole life. Now I want to make up for lost time.'

'Then I'll stop pestering you with conversation and let you enjoy. I do believe Cook will be very pleased.'

They ate in companionable silence, finishing off a first course of baked salmon before the arrival of braised beef, roast potatoes, parsnips, carrots and peas. Violet ate it all up with relish. She wanted to make up for lost time in so many ways. Food was just the beginning. If she could only have her freedom…

She studied Lance surreptitiously across the table. He'd said he was prepared to give her just that if she married him and the idea was becoming more and more tempting. He wasn't the beast she'd thought he was, the house was captivating and she'd already made a friend in Eliza.

There was just one important question that needed answering, one that had been playing on her mind all afternoon, the very last one she wanted to ask aloud, but one that needed asking none the less. He'd said that their marriage would be one of convenience, a way of helping each other out, but how much freedom would he allow her really? How much of a marriage would it be? Given his reputation, how much of a real marriage did he want? And how could she possibly ask?

'You know, you really are full of surprises.' Lance leaned back in his chair, watching her through hooded eyes as she scooped up her last spoonful of citrus ice. 'I misjudged you the first time we met. I thought you were timid and unassuming, albeit with an occasional flash of those claws. I never imagined you were the kind of woman who'd run off over the moors on her own. It was brave of you.'

'I thought you said it was childish?'

She gave him a pointed look and he made a face.

'I was angry when I said that. I'm afraid my temper isn't my most endearing quality.'

'What is?'

'I've no idea.' He smiled sheepishly. 'I never expected you to cut off all your hair and drink wine either.'

'Sometimes appearances can be deceptive.'

'Yes, they can. By the by, how did you enjoy your walk in the snow?'

'Very much. I found the sword in the stone.'

'Any success?'

'Unfortunately not.' She gave an exaggerated sigh. 'It seems I'm not destined to be a queen.'

'I'm glad to hear it. If you were, then I'd have to wait for you to propose.'

'But then I wouldn't need to marry you. I'd already have my freedom.'

'Then I'm doubly glad. I won't call you Guinevere after all.'

'Good. I always felt sorry for her.'

'For Guinevere?'

'Yes. In the stories, her husband—' she avoided saying the name Arthur '—was always putting her on trial and then leaving it to Lancelot to save her. It was no wonder she preferred him.'

'I never thought of it that way.' He looked faintly amused. 'So you think she loved him because he rescued her?'

'Not necessarily. Maybe she never wanted to

marry Ar—that is, her husband in the first place. But I always thought it was a tragic love story. Lancelot had to do the honourable thing in the end and leave her.'

'You wanted a different ending?'

'I don't know. I just thought she deserved a better husband.'

'A lot of women do.' He grinned wolfishly. 'Do you like reading?'

'Yes, but…' Her voice trailed away and he arched an eyebrow.

'Let me guess. Your father didn't approve?'

She gave a self-deprecating shrug. 'He chose what I read, although I had a few of my mother's old books for a while. I found them in a chest in one of the guest chambers and read them all in a month. There was Malory and Marvell and Thackeray and Richardson, too, I remember, but when Father found out he took them away. I don't know why, or what he did with them.'

'Well, feel free to read whatever books you want while you're here.' He looked at her broodingly. 'Speaking of your being here, have you given any more thought to my proposal?'

'I have.' She toyed with the stem of her wine-glass. 'I just have a few questions.'

'Such as?'

This time she picked up the glass and took a fortifying mouthful, starting to understand why he liked alcohol so much. It made certain subjects easier. 'I was wondering about…bedrooms.'

'Bedrooms.' He repeated the word quizzically. 'What about them?'

'If I stay, will I keep the room I'm in now?'

'If you wish.'

'So I—*we*—wouldn't move back into the old family quarters?'

A shadow crossed his face. 'I hadn't thought that far ahead, but you can choose whichever bedroom you like.'

'Oh…' She faltered. Didn't he know what she was trying to ask? He was supposed to be a libertine! Surely she didn't have to come straight out and say it? But apparently she did… She cleared her throat with embarrassment.

'Would we share it?'

'Share what?'

'The bedroom?'

A pair of dark eyebrows rose upwards in unison. 'Would you want to?'

'No!' She felt her cheeks flare a vivid shade of crimson. She was trying to understand what *he* wanted, not saying what she did!

'Forgive me…' he sat up a little straighter '…but given your upbringing…'

'You didn't expect me to think of it?' She willed her face to cool down, although it seemed determined to do the opposite. 'I probably never would have, but my friend Ianthe and her husband are very…affectionate. She's told me a few details as well.'

'Indeed?'

'And I wanted to know…' Somehow she forced herself to keep talking. Now that she'd started, she had to at least finish her question, no matter how mortifying. 'That is… I wanted to know what exactly our marriage would involve?'

'Ah, and your friend has told you it involves sharing a bedroom?'

'Yes. She and Robert do, but she says that sometimes, for some couples, it's only occasionally.' She picked up her glass again and took several long draughts.

'I wouldn't gulp it like that when you're not used to it.' His voice sounded strangely gravelly. 'It might make you feel ill later.'

She stopped drinking although she didn't put the glass down, tapping a finger against the side while she waited for him to respond. Judging by the silence, he didn't know quite what to say.

'What else has she told you?' he asked finally.

'About marriage?'

'Yes.'

'That they share a bed, too.'

'Anything else?'

She cleared her throat awkwardly. Ianthe had

told her a little more than that, but she certainly wasn't going to repeat it.

'I see.' His voice softened slightly. 'Violet, I would never ask you to do anything that you objected to. I certainly wouldn't force you to share a room or a bed with me. My initial plans are simply to save the estate. The rest can follow afterwards.'

'The rest?' Her voice seemed to have jumped up an octave.

'I'm afraid that providing an heir is another one of those duties my father would have expected me to fulfil. It would make sharing a bedroom—a bed—necessary on occasion, though only with your consent, of course.'

She took another mouthful of wine, mind whirling. She wasn't sure how she felt about the word duty. Somehow it implied a distinct lack of freedom. It wasn't particularly flattering either, as if that was the only reason he'd want to share a bed with her, and as for children... A month ago she'd never envisaged being married, let alone anything else. It was becoming hard to keep up with all the changes in her life, yet the thought wasn't unpleasant. She *would* like to have children some day.

'As I said, there's no rush.' Lance's gaze was searching, as if he were worried about her reaction. 'Especially since I can't legally inherit my brother's title for seven years.'

'Oh.' She blinked. 'I'd forgotten about that.'

'In which case, why don't we agree to think about children in seven years? That's seven years of freedom for you, seven years of trying to put this place right for me. After that we can settle down to a life of quiet domesticity. You might even have learned to like me by then.'

'What about your plan to drink yourself into oblivion?' She frowned at the memory of what he'd said the previous evening. 'You might not last seven years.'

'I appreciate the confidence.' He looked down at the glass in his hand. 'All right. You drive a hard bargain, Miss Harper, but what if I refrain from drinking during daylight hours?'

'Only in daylight?'

'There's only so much a man can do.'

She scrunched her mouth up thoughtfully. 'So we'd live together as brother and sister for seven years?'

'If that's what you want. No one else need ever know. Even lawyers can't stick their noses into private bedrooms. We can both sleep where we choose.'

She nodded, struck with an unexpected combination of relief and disappointment. She ought to be pleased, but it was hard not to be offended by such a genteel offer from such a notorious ladies' man. She could hardly have asked for a clearer indication of his interest in her. Apparently he didn't find her remotely attractive. Which led to another problem... Considering his reputation, if he didn't want to share a bed with her, then whose would he?

'What about in the meantime?' She tried to ask the question nonchalantly. 'Would there be other women?'

'Would I take a mistress, do you mean?' His teeth flashed in a grin.

'It's not a joke!'

'Apologies. You caught me by surprise, but in answer to your question, no, I would not. I haven't always had the highest regard for marital vows—other peoples', that is—but I've learnt my lesson in that regard. If it's my reputation you're worried about, then I promise you, those days are over. I haven't so much as looked at a woman in the past seven months. Ask Mrs Gargrave if you don't believe me. All the maids have their virtues intact, though, of course, I can't vouch for their behaviour with the footmen.'

'I'll ask no such thing!'

'Not that I've lost any physical functions beyond my leg.' He glanced pointedly downwards. 'My injury wasn't quite as interesting as I'm sure some of the gossips would have you believe.'

'Lance!'

He raised his hands in a gesture of apology. 'I'm only trying to reassure you that when it comes to producing an heir, the rest of my body's still in full functioning order. I've only lost interest in the process, so to speak. I'm more than willing to fulfil my husbandly duties from a purely procreational perspective, but in all other respects you'd find me one of the most loyal husbands in England.'

'Oh.' She picked up her spoon and scooped up the remains of the melted ice from her bowl, hoping it might do something to cool her flaming cheeks. Well, she'd asked the question and he'd given her an answer. A pretty definitive one, too.

Lost interest in the process...

Somehow those words were the most disappointing of all.

Chapter Nine

Lance watched as Violet ate the last of her dessert, vaguely amazed at how much she'd eaten. For a small woman, she clearly had a voracious appetite, clearing away every last morsel of food that was set in front of her. Now she was licking what remained of the ice on her spoon in a way that made him feel hungry in a different way altogether. The feeling was even more powerful now than it had been that morning.

She seemed to be full of surprises this evening. Her appearance for starters. Not just the fact that she was out of mourning and had shed almost two feet of hair, but that she looked quite jaw-droppingly gorgeous as well. He'd ordered the blue gown on a whim, partly because he hadn't been able to think of anything else as a wedding present and a grey mourning gown on its own had seemed somewhat dismal, partly because he'd never forgotten how vibrantly blue her eyes were. It seemed to fit her perfectly, too, despite his having to guess the measurements based solely on the memory of one dance. A memory that struck him now as uncannily accurate.

Her questions about their marital sleeping arrangements had taken him by surprise, too, though in all honesty they'd also come as something of a relief. He'd been wondering how to broach the subject himself, afraid of scaring her off, but it turned out that she already knew more about marriage than he'd assumed—although still not enough, apparently, to give it a try. She'd looked mortified the whole way through their conversation.

Of course, that might simply have been shyness, but the readiness at which she'd agreed to a seven-year delay suggested otherwise. What the hell had he been thinking, coming up with such a ridiculous idea? He'd just suggested seven years of celibacy! *That* was another surprise. A week, even a day, ago he wouldn't particularly have cared, but watching her lick up the remains of her dessert, he suddenly, very definitely did. Just when he'd claimed to have lost interest in the process, too!

'Shall we move next door?' He cleared his throat huskily.

She nodded, draining the last of her wine before following him through the hall to the drawing room. A fire was roaring in the grate and she rushed forward to sit on a footstool in front of it.

'Are you cold?' He looked down at her with concern.

'No. I've just always wanted to sit right in front.'

He guessed the implication. Yet another thing she hadn't been allowed to do…

'Was your father worried about you getting too close?'

'Maybe, although in that case I could have sat beside him, but my chair was always set behind his.'

'Then how could he see you?'

She shrugged. 'I don't think he wanted to see me. Sometimes I think he didn't like looking at me at all.'

Lance levered himself down into his armchair, swallowing a varied assortment of swear words. 'Why on earth wouldn't he like looking at you?'

She didn't answer, leaping to her feet suddenly instead. 'I'm sorry. This footstool's for your leg, isn't it?'

'My leg be damned.' He gestured for her to sit down again. 'I said you could go wherever you wanted. That includes footstools.'

'Here.' She perched on one edge, leaving room for his foot. 'We can share.'

'You look uncomfortable.'

'Well, I'm not.' She reached down, wrapping her hands around his boot and lifting it up beside her. 'How about that?'

He stiffened at her touch, his whole body tightening as a thrill of desire coursed through it. The view was even more stimulating. She was sitting lower down than he was, so that he had a perfect view of the tops of her breasts, moving gently up and down as she breathed. They were an exquisite size, too, he noticed, perfect handfuls...

'Better.' He dragged his gaze away quickly.

'What happened to your leg?' She looked at it curiously, as if she might somehow guess the injury by staring at his trousers.

'I was shot.'

'In battle?'

'Nothing so grand.'

'In a skirmish?'

'In a duel.'

Her eyes darted back to his. 'I thought they were illegal?'

'They are, but my opponent had a legitimate grievance.'

'Which was?'

He sighed. 'I doubt you'd like me very much if I told you.'

'You promised to always tell me the truth.'

'So I did, but there's a difference between telling the truth and telling everything. Suffice to say that the answer doesn't reflect very well on me. I deserved everything I got and more. Besides, you haven't answered my question yet. Why didn't your father like looking at you?'

She seemed to exhale slowly. 'I think it was to do with what you said earlier, about me looking like my mother. I was a reminder of her when he didn't want any.'

'Didn't he care for her?'

'The opposite.' She gave a sad-looking smile. 'It's hard to imagine my father in love, I know, but he did love her. No one's ever told me so directly, of course, but I've heard things and pieced them together. There were never any pictures or mementoes of her in the house because he didn't allow them. No one was even allowed to mention her name in his hearing. He wasn't always the way he became, but when she died he was heartbroken, and…' she paused briefly '… he blamed me.'

'For what?'

'For killing her, I suppose. You see, I was sick first. I don't even know what kind of illness it was. All I know is that she nursed me and then she fell sick, too. Only I got better and she didn't. I think he blamed me for that.'

'You were only a child.'

'I know. He knew it, too. I suppose that's why he never accused me directly, but there were times when I caught him looking at me as if he resented me for it. As if he hated me even.'

Lance frowned. He'd thought of Harper as a miserable, cranky old curmudgeon, but he'd never realised just how much of a monster he'd truly been.

'You said he controlled you.'

'Yes.' She stared into the fireplace. 'Although he always said that he was trying to protect me. I wanted to believe it, but I think it was a form of punishment, too, as if he were trying to stop me from living my own life because I'd ruined his somehow. But I went along with it, always trying to please him, to make him happy. I never asked for anything. I never argued back. I thought that maybe one day...'

'One day?' He prompted her as her voice trailed away.

'I don't know.' She shook her head. 'Maybe I hoped that he'd tell me he loved me and let me go, but he never did. He spent his life warning me about fortune hunters and men who might pretend to care for me, but he never cared either.

It was as though he refused to care for anyone ever again after my mother died.'

Lance felt a dull ache in his chest. Hadn't he experienced something similar after his own mother's funeral, when he'd told himself that he never wanted to feel hurt or pain like that again? Like her father, he'd closed his heart a long time ago, too—or thought that he had. Was that why he'd been so self-centred and reckless with everyone else's feelings, because he'd thought himself immune to caring for anyone else deeply?

The past seven months had given the lie to that. Here he was, right back to where he'd started, grieving a brother and father he hadn't realised he loved so much until it was too late. Maybe he'd been just as much a monster in his own way as her father had, taking his grief out on everyone around him. The thought made him distinctly uncomfortable. If that were the case, then he truly was the last man on earth she ought to marry.

'I never really admitted to myself how angry I was with him until today.' Her face wore a guilty expression. 'I know it sounds wicked, but after the funeral, a part of me was relieved.'

'That doesn't sound wicked. It sounds perfectly natural.'

'I thought that maybe I could finally make

some choices of my own, but then Mr Rowlinson told me about the will.'

'And you discovered that your father had shackled you into marriage instead?'

'Yes, but then I thought that it might be a good form of revenge, marrying you. He would have hated the idea.'

'There you go, then.'

She gave him a remonstrative look. 'I don't want to marry you for revenge.'

'So call it rebellion.'

'I was never very good at that. I did almost everything I was told.'

'You're doing it pretty well tonight.' He smiled approvingly. 'I must be a worse influence than I thought. Besides, you just said *almost* everything. What *didn't* you do?'

She twisted her hands in her lap as if she felt genuinely guilty. 'He told me to stop seeing Ianthe. He didn't approve of her.'

'Really? Then I definitely want to meet her.'

'She's the only real friend I ever had.'

'One real friend is better than a lot of false ones. A man can have lots of friends, but there's usually only one who'll help you bury the body, so to speak.'

'Is Martin yours?'

'Martin? No, he just won't leave me no matter how many times I tell him to.' He laughed and then sobered again almost instantly. 'I suppose Arthur was always my best friend.'

'I'm sorry.'

He caught his breath, fighting back a sudden fierce onslaught of emotion. Arthur *had* been his best friend. Why hadn't he known that until now?

'Speaking of Martin—' he forced himself to keep speaking normally '—he thinks he might be able to make it to Whitby tomorrow.'

'Are the roads clear?'

'No, but it hasn't snowed any more and the man likes a challenge. So you can write to your friend Ianthe and tell her you've been imprisoned by a madman.'

'I never said you were mad.'

'You might as well make it exciting.'

'Then I will.' She gave what looked like a genuine smile. 'Thank you.'

'Thank Martin.' He leaned back in his chair. 'Now tell me how else you defied your father. I like this rebellious side of you.'

She got to her feet instead. 'Can I have another drink first?'

'Help yourself.' He gestured to the sideboard. 'There should be some more wine somewhere.'

'Would you like some?'

'No, thank you, I'm trying to accustom myself to sobriety.'

She rummaged in the sideboard for a few moments and then sat down again with a full glass. 'The night of the ball, my father told me not to talk to you, let alone dance.'

'Really?' Another surprise. That *was* interesting...

'But then we were introduced and you were friendlier than your brother. Not that I didn't like him, but...'

'But he was a little less than charming.'

'Yes, although at least now I know why. You were much friendlier.' She took a sip of wine and licked her lips. 'You didn't tell me how small I was either.'

'Didn't I?' He was so distracted watching her tongue brush along her top lip that he honestly couldn't remember. At that moment, he was having a hard enough time following the conversation at all.

'No. Usually it's the first thing people say to me.' She peeked up at him. 'Doesn't it bother you?'

'Your height? Not at all, but then it occurs to me that you're the perfect size for a walking stick. I can lean on your shoulder.'

She gave him a look that was part amused, part admonishing. 'Are you never serious?'

'I told you, I'm trying to learn.'

'Sometimes I wondered if my size was the

reason my father behaved the way he did.' She sounded thoughtful. 'Maybe he genuinely thought I was too small to look after myself. Maybe if I'd looked more like a woman…'

'You do look like a woman…' he dropped his gaze appreciatively '…especially tonight.'

'But it would explain why he treated me like a child.'

'He treated you like a child because he was a miserable, self-centred old man and took it out on everyone else, you especially.'

She looked at him strangely. 'Is that why you were so angry at him at the ball? I didn't understand at the time.'

'I suppose so. I thought what he'd told you about fortune hunters was cruel, too. He implied that you weren't worth marrying without a fortune. Believe me, Violet, there are plenty of other reasons.'

'You agreed with him.'

'What?' He felt genuinely shocked. 'When?'

'When he asked if you'd marry me without a fortune and you said no. Not that I expected you to say yes,' she added quickly.

His brow furrowed. 'That wasn't because of you. I would have said the same about anyone. I told you, I never wanted to marry.'

'Until now.'

'I'm willing to give it a try.'

'For the money.' She gave a small sigh. 'Just as he said.'

Lance felt a fresh stab of guilt. Damn it all, the last thing he wanted to do was to prove her father right about anything, but he'd promised her honesty.

'Surely that doesn't mean we can't be friends?'

'No, I suppose not. It's really quite ironic when you think about it. Neither of us ever expected to marry and yet here we are.' She paused and then nodded emphatically. 'All right, Captain Amberton, I accept.'

'You accept?' He wondered if he'd misunderstood.

'Friendship. Marriage. The money. I'll marry you.'

Chapter Ten

'What would you like to do with the house?'

Lance shifted forward on the bench, trying to catch a glimpse of Violet's averted face as they sat side by side in the rolling carriage. The tops of the moors were still covered in snow, but the valleys had cleared sufficiently for them to make the journey to Whitby without too much difficulty. The weather had improved markedly over the past week, so that it felt like spring today instead of winter. Now they were on the outskirts of town, two scant hours before their wedding, although there was somewhere else they needed to go first.

'Sell it.' She didn't hesitate. 'Unless you want to keep it?'

'Not if you don't want to.'

He shook his head, not that there was much point in doing so when she wouldn't look at him, but at least she was speaking now, which was more than she'd done since breakfast. She seemed to be lost in her own thoughts, her small hands gripped rather than folded together in her lap, her jaw a tightly drawn line. If he wasn't mistaken she was clenching her teeth. If she didn't relax soon, then she'd break a tooth for certain.

He only hoped that it was pre-wedding nerves and not that she'd changed her mind and felt honour-bound to go ahead, although he was reluctant to ask the question out loud. It had been a week since she'd accepted his proposal and he'd thought that they'd been getting along well enough.

Admittedly, he'd been busy at the mine during the days, but they'd spent their evenings together in the drawing room, either talking or reading or playing cards. She'd seemed reasonably calm until that morning—happy, even. Strangely enough, it had felt good to make her happy, as if he were doing something positive for once in his life. To his surprise, *he'd* felt reasonably happy, too. He'd even been sleeping better. He'd never imagined spending his life with any woman for a prolonged period of time, even so much as a week, but he'd actually enjoyed being with her.

Today, however, was the real test. It was now or never. He'd given her as long as possible to be certain, but in another day, the terms of her father's will would expire. They could either be rich together or poor separately, although, somewhat alarmingly, that seemed to be a more difficult decision for her than he'd thought. Dressed in a plain grey morning gown, her small face pale and drawn, she looked more like a woman on her way to the gallows than a bride on the happiest day of her life.

'Very well, then.' He did his best to sound cheerful. 'I'll ask Mr Rowlinson to look out for a buyer. I just wondered if you'd like to keep your own establishment in Whitby.'

'No.' She pressed the flat of her hand against her stomach. 'After today, I never want to go back.'

He lifted an eyebrow at the uncharacteristic edge in her voice. Going to the house that morning had been his suggestion. He'd thought that collecting some of her own belongings might make her feel more at home in Amberton Castle, but apparently the idea had only made her feel nauseated. Now that he thought of it, she'd seemed to turn a little paler when he'd mentioned it, though she hadn't objected. She hadn't said much at all. Was that why she seemed so withdrawn then, or was he grasping at straws, trying to persuade himself that her behaviour wasn't about their impending nuptials?

'Violet?' He reached across and folded one of his hands gently around hers. 'We don't have to visit the house if you don't want to.'

She gave her head a small, determined shake. 'It's all right. I'm being silly, but I just never expected to go back there again. I know it's only been a week, but it feels like an age since I ran away. So much has happened.'

'Not all of it bad, I hope?'

'No.' Her lips parted, although she didn't smile as he'd hoped. Her tone wasn't particularly reassuring either. 'Not all of it.'

Her fingers tensed beneath his as the carriage rolled to a halt. He looked past her, out of the window and up at the red-brick facade of her father's mansion. Even in the bright morning sunshine, it looked gloomy and forbidding. And he'd thought that his mother's architectural designs had been Gothic This looked more like the stuff of nightmares.

He tightened his grip reassuringly. 'If you don't want to go inside, then let me. I'll collect your things if you tell me what you want.'

'No.' Her voice sounded forceful, as if she were trying to spur herself on. 'I'm not running away again.'

'Then let me come with you?'

'Yes.' Her tone softened again. 'Thank you.'

He smiled, relinquishing her hand as Martin

opened the carriage door. She climbed down and he followed behind, berating himself inwardly as she mounted the front steps of the house. Damn it all, this was his fault again! Considering what she'd told him about her father, he ought to have considered how coming back here might affect her, but he'd been insensitive again and on their wedding day, too! It wasn't exactly a promising start...

Oddly enough, there seemed to be no one around to open the front door, so he did it for her, leading the way into a vast, marble-floored hallway that echoed loudly with the sound of their footsteps. He looked around, repressing a shudder. It was the gloomiest, most spartan-looking room he'd ever been in, as if the owner had been determined to have as much space as possible and yet not to fill it.

'Have the servants started packing up the house already?'

'No. It's always been like this.' Her voice sounded strained. 'I'll go upstairs and fetch my things. It won't take long.'

He nodded and wandered into the drawing room. Surely here the servants must have started putting ornaments and furniture into storage? But, no, there was no sign of trunks or boxes anywhere, nor any marks on the floor to suggest that anything had recently been moved. Unbelievably, the room must have been intended to be just as it looked, almost empty and cheerless, its windows draped with heavy velvet curtains to shut out all trace of the outside world.

His eyes alighted on two chairs by the fireplace, one large leather armchair and one small, uncomfortable-looking wooden one behind it. The other side of the hearth was empty. The sight made him unaccountably furious.

He swung on his good heel and strode determinedly out of the room. An ancient-looking butler had appeared from somewhere, though he seemed unperturbed by the sight of a stranger in the hallway. He simply stood at the bottom of the stairs, looking to all intents and purposes as if he'd turned to stone.

'Which one is Miss Harper's bedroom?' Lance asked as he mounted the stairs.

The ancient face barely moved as it answered, 'At the end of the corridor on the left, sir.'

Lance started up the stairs and then stopped. 'How many people are employed here?'

'Myself and Cook, two maids and a boy, sir.'

'Send the boy up.'

He made his way as quickly as he could up the staircase and along another barren corridor to her bedroom. Considering the size of the house, it was surprisingly small, though there was no sign of her in it. He might have thought he had the wrong room if it hadn't felt so much like her. It shouldn't have, given that it looked as empty as the rest of the house, but somehow it felt lighter and less oppressive.

Absently, he ran his hand down the frame of her four-poster bed before stooping to press his face into the pillow. That was her scent, too. Not perfumed, but clean and fresh, like soap and… Violet. He frowned at the thought. Wedding-day nerves must be getting to him, too. He wasn't usually sentimental.

He lifted his head, straightening up again at the sound of several loud thuds coming from the opposite end of the corridor.

'Violet?' He called her name out as he followed the noise back down the corridor, drawing to an abrupt halt in the doorway of another, much larger room, taken aback by the sight of an enormous heap of clothes and papers piled high in the centre. Every cupboard in the room appeared to have been opened and emptied, every drawer pulled out and upturned over the floor. It looked as though a storm had just blown through the room and there in the midst of it, looking slightly dazed, stood Violet, as if she had no idea what had just happened either.

'Are you all right?' He took a tentative step towards her.

'Yes.' She was panting heavily. 'I was just looking for something.'

'Then let me help you.' He edged forward again, moving slowly as if she were a wild horse to be steadied. She looked almost skittish. 'Two of us are better than one. What are we looking for?'

For a moment, he thought she wasn't going to tell him, before her face crumpled into a look of heartfelt appeal.

'Something to do with my mother. I wanted to find *something*—a letter, a diary, anything. I thought there might at least be a picture of her, but there isn't.' Her eyes glittered with unshed tears. 'I think perhaps I got carried away.'

'Sir?' A boy of around twelve years old skidded up behind him suddenly, staring wide-eyed at the mess on the floor. 'Mr Jenkins said you wanted me, sir? Oh, begging your pardon, Miss Harper.' He attempted a bow when he noticed her. 'I didn't see you there.'

Lance looked the boy over appraisingly. He could hardly have presented a greater contrast to the butler if he'd tried, with a mop of tousled red hair, a cheerful-looking face and a generous sprinkling of freckles. 'What's your name?'

'Daniel, sir.'

'All right, Daniel. Do you know where the family portraits are kept?'

'Mr Harper didn't like pictures, sir.'

'What about family heirlooms, that sort of thing? Where did he keep them?'

Daniel scrunched up his small face thoughtfully. 'I don't know about anything like that, sir.'

Lance reached into his pocket and drew out a shilling. 'Do you like a challenge, Daniel?'

'Yes, sir!'

'Good. Then take this. If you want to earn another, see what you can find. Tell the other staff, too. We're looking for a picture or keepsake, anything to do with the late Mrs Harper, understand?'

'Yes, sir.' The boy's face lit up enthusiastically.

'And, Daniel?' He winked. 'You have Miss Harper's permission to break as many ornaments and tear down as many walls as it takes to find them. Enjoy yourself.'

'I will, sir!'

The boy ran off and Lance held an arm out towards Violet. She still looked vaguely stunned and for the hundredth time he wished he'd never so much as mentioned her father's house. The visit certainly hadn't gone the way that he'd hoped. The idea that he'd caused her anguish made his chest ache almost painfully. All he wanted now was to get her out of there as quickly as possible.

'Shall we go?'

'Yes.' She gripped his arm tight, holding on to it like a lifeline. 'Let's go.'

Violet stepped back out into the street, heart hammering violently against her ribcage. What had just happened? It all felt unreal, like a dream, or a nightmare. She'd gone up to her old bedroom with every intention of simply collecting a few belongings, but once she'd reached the top of the stairs she'd found herself walking towards her father's old chamber instead. She didn't care about her own belongings, she'd realised. She cared about something else, something that had been bothering her ever since Lance had told her she looked like her mother and she hadn't known if it was true.

But she ought to have known! Surely any daughter ought to know what her mother looked like. And so she'd gone to her father's room looking for clues, starting off calmly enough by opening a few drawers and simply peering inside, then somehow become possessed by the idea, rummaging through every cupboard and hurling all his belongings to the floor—still finding nothing.

'I'm sorry.' She glanced awkwardly towards Lance as he stood on the pavement beside her. 'I don't know what came over me.'

'There's no need to apologise. I've ransacked enough rooms in my time. You did quite a good job for a beginner.'

She tried to smile, but her face fell instead. 'I just wanted to find something of hers.'

'I know.'

'Thank you for what you did.'

'You mean Daniel?' He brought his spare hand up to cover hers on his arm. 'Hopefully he's sufficiently motivated.'

'It was a good idea. I just wish…' She dashed a hand across her cheeks, the words dissolving into a sob.

'Shall we walk for a while? Get some sea air?' He spoke softly, almost kindly, and she felt an even bigger lump swell in her throat. She hadn't expected kindness from him.

'Yes. I'd like that.'

He led her in silence along the clifftop streets, across to the promenade that ran along the edge of the north bay, into the fresh sea air until she started to feel her mind calm again.

'It's so beautiful here.'

She stopped finally, her arm still hooked inside his as they looked out over the rippling expanse of the North Sea. It shone like an emerald carpet rolling out endlessly into the distance, calm today even though its moods could, and frequently did, change quickly enough.

'It's funny. Our house was so close to the sea, yet I only saw it once a week when we drove by. We never went down to the shore. I always wanted to walk on the sand.'

'You never have?'

'I have now. My father slept a lot when he was sick. I nursed him most days, but there were times when I had to get out or I thought I'd go mad. Ianthe was setting up a school for some of the shipyard children and I helped her sometimes. One day we all went for a walk on the beach in our bare feet.'

'How did it feel?'

She brushed aside a lock of hair that had blown across her face. 'Wonderful.'

'Freedom does feel wonderful.' He reached out and caught the hair before it blew back again, tucking it gently inside her bonnet. 'Especially your first taste of it. You can walk barefoot on the beach as much as you want from now on.'

She held her breath as his fingers skimmed across her cheek. Brown eyes smiled down into hers, softer and gentler than she'd ever imagined they could be, reminding her of how little she knew about him, this man she was going to spend the rest of her life with. *Was* she doing the right thing in agreeing to marry him?

'Violet?' He put a finger beneath her chin, tipping it upwards. 'What is it?'

'Everything's just happening so fast.'

'Our wedding, yes. As for our marriage, we have another seven years to get to know each other. Think of it as a long engagement.'

She pressed her lips together. He was trying to make her feel better. Surely his words *ought* to make her feel better, but they didn't. She was going to be married and yet not married. To a man who wasn't the marrying kind, who'd told her that she was the last woman he would ever have chosen. If she married him, then she'd be making the same bargain his mother had done, a marriage based on money, not love. Could she be content in a loveless marriage, too? Would it be enough? In all honesty, she didn't know, but she was running out of time to decide.

'How long do we have?'

'Until the fateful hour?' He pulled out a fob watch. 'Half an hour. Time enough to collect your maid of honour.'

'Yes.' That thought at least made her smile. 'It'll be good to see Ianthe again.'

'I have to admit I'm rather intrigued by the sound of her. What was it about her that your father disapproved of? You said he forbade you to see her.'

'You didn't hear the rumours?'

'I might have. Mrs Gargrave feels it her duty to regale me with the comings and goings of

Whitby society, though I try not to listen. Being the subject of so many rumours myself, I have a certain amount of sympathy for the victims.'

'Well, Ianthe *is* the victim. She was pursued and blackmailed by Sir Charles Lester.'

'Lester…' He drew his brows together. 'Wait, I do remember something about that. He fell off the cliff, didn't he?'

'Yes, but it wasn't just a fall. He was trying to shoot Robert and lost his footing. I saw the whole thing from their house. It was an accident, but there were still rumours. People said that Ianthe must have done something to encourage his attentions and that Robert attacked him in a jealous rage.'

'Neither of which was true, I suppose?'

'No. Lester was obsessed with Ianthe, and Robert only fought back in self-defence, but my father hated any hint of scandal. He was going to sell Robert his shipyard until that happened, but afterwards he refused to have anything to do with either of them. He sold it a few months later for half the price.' She looked at him askance. 'I don't suppose Mr Rowlinson mentioned that when he told you about the will.'

'No, but I'm not greedy. You're still pretty good value.'

'How amusing.'

He chuckled softly. 'Then I'm even more

intrigued by your friend. Though under the circumstances I suspect she might not be so delighted to see me.'

'No, maybe not.' She had to admit she felt mildly apprehensive about that herself. Considering how determined she'd been in planning her escape, she wasn't sure what Ianthe would think of her sudden decision to marry. She'd tried to explain in the letter Martin had delivered to Whitby, but she had a feeling her friend might not be completely convinced.

'I just need a few moments…' she unthreaded her arm from his gently '…on my own, if you don't mind?'

'Of course not. I'll take a walk along the front. Slowly, of course.'

'Are you afraid that I'll bolt at the last minute?' She smiled ironically, but he only looked sombre.

'I've put all my cards on the table, Violet. I know what I want, but you must do whatever you wish. When you're ready, *if* you're ready, we'll go to the Felstones' house together.'

She watched him limp away, feeling a rush of gratitude. There was still time to change her mind, he was saying, if she wanted to—but she didn't *want* to, she realised. Whatever else, life with him wouldn't be dull. He might never be entirely respectable, but he wasn't the man she'd feared he was either. Reprobate or not, he had more depth than she'd previously suspected. More pain, too, however much he tried to conceal it. He seemed to understand how she felt about her father as well and he *did* seem to have changed. He was prepared to change even more to marry her. She hadn't seen him touch a drop of alcohol since the night she'd agreed to marry him.

Most importantly, he wanted to use her father's money to build something, not just for himself, but for the good of others. He had a plan, a purpose, and he was prepared to let her live her own life, too. Most of all, he'd been honest with her about the nature of their relationship, hadn't deceived her by pretending that his heart was involved. As long as she protected hers, too, they ought to be content.

'Lance?' she called out before he'd gone barely ten paces, pointing towards the Royal Crescent on the other side of the promenade. 'That's their house over there.'

He turned around slowly, meeting her gaze with a look of such searing intensity that she felt as if all the breath had left her body suddenly. He'd removed his hat and the combination of sun and sea breeze made his hair seem to glow with golden tints, making him look more ruggedly dishevelled than ever. He even looked younger, too, though his expression was stern, as if he'd been bracing himself for her to refuse him at the last moment.

She forced herself to start breathing again. He was, without any doubt, the handsomest man she'd ever laid eyes on—a realisation that seemed to be having a disturbing effect on her body, making her breasts and stomach tighten, so that she wondered if she were making a terrible mistake after all. She didn't want to feel any kind of effect. *That* wasn't part of their arrangement, not for seven years anyway. How mortifying would it be to want a man who didn't want her back? Especially when that man was a renowned libertine!

Then he smiled and she forgot everything else.

'Come along, then, Miss Harper.'

He started towards her and she found herself drifting forward to meet him, her feet seeming to move of their own accord.

'You won't regret it, Violet, I promise.'

He took hold of her hands as they met on the pavement, lifting them slowly to his lips and kissing each in turn. She felt a thrill of pleasure, unexpectedly touched by the gesture. He really did want her to be happy, it seemed. Maybe that in itself would be enough. Whatever other unsettling physical effects he might have on her, she could control them. There was certainly no need for *him* ever to know about any of it.

They walked arm in arm along the crescent to the Felstones' house, though they'd barely entered the hall before Ianthe came hurtling out of the drawing room, enveloping her in a none-too-gentle embrace.

'Violet! I've been so worried!'

'I'm sorry. I got word to you as soon as I could, but the snow...' She hugged her back just as tightly. 'I didn't mean to upset you.'

'It wasn't your fault.' Ianthe took a step back and glared daggers at Lance. 'You didn't intend for any of this to happen.'

'No, but...' She looked between the two of them, wondering how to ease the atmosphere of tension. Ianthe looked as if she wanted to throw Lance out on to the street. Nine out of ten men would have quailed and fled from such a virulent glare, but he only bent his head courteously.

'Mrs Felstone, I presume?'

'You presume correctly.'

'Then I'm honoured to meet such a good friend of Violet's.'

'Indeed?' Ianthe's voice was clipped with anger. 'Then I'm sorry to inform you that the feeling's *not* mutual.'

'Captain Amberton?'

Ianthe's husband, Robert, emerged from the

drawing room at that moment, and Violet felt a surge of relief. At least *he* sounded civil. Not that she could blame her friend for being protective, but there was so much to explain…

'Mr Felstone.' Lance took the other man's proffered hand with a smile. 'I'm glad to meet you again under better circumstances.'

'So am I.' Robert turned to face Violet with a serious expression. 'I hope you can forgive me for what I did. It wasn't my wish to betray you.'

'I know.' She smiled reassuringly, too grateful at that moment to do otherwise. 'You were trying to help.'

'I was. And believe me, I've been reprimanded enough.'

'Oh!' She threw a quick glance towards her friend. 'I hope I haven't caused any trouble.'

'No more than he deserved.' Ianthe seized hold of her arm, throwing one last venomous look towards Lance before dragging her off to one side.

'It's all right.' Violet threw an apologetic look over her shoulder. 'He's not as bad as I feared.'

'So you said in your letter, but are you certain?' Ianthe spoke in a fierce whisper. 'You don't have to go through with this. Robert and I have been talking and you're welcome to—'

'No! I know what you're going to say and, no.

I don't want to live on your charity, although I do appreciate the offer.'

'But marriage is such a big step.'

'It is, but I know what I'm doing. This is my decision, not my father's, and I was wrong about Lance. He wasn't mocking me that first time we met at the ball and he isn't a reprobate, at least not any more. In any case, we've come to our own agreement.'

'What do you mean?'

'Just that we're adapting our fathers' plans to suit us. Half of my inheritance will go towards the new ironworks. The other half is for me to keep and do whatever I want with.'

Ianthe looked dubious. 'Do you trust him?'

'Yes.' Violet surprised herself with the readiness of her answer. 'He's been a perfect gentleman most of the time.'

'*Most* of the time?'

She gave an evasive shrug. She had the distinct feeling that mentioning her imprisonment in a freezing cold tower wouldn't help Lance's cause.

'People aren't always who we think they are.'

'True.' Ianthe threw a quick glance in Robert's direction. 'All right, if you're certain, then I'll support you.'

'Thank you.' Violet hugged her again. 'Besides, if it doesn't work out, then I can always run away again.'

'Don't joke. You'll be trapped up there on the Moors with him.'

'I was trapped here before with my father, but this marriage won't be a prison, you'll see.'

'It won't be.' Lance approached her solemnly. 'But now I believe that it's time, Violet.'

She looked around at the three faces surrounding her. It was hard to tell which of them looked the most anxious, though oddly enough, the sight was reassuring. The fact that they cared enough to be anxious made her feel warm inside, despite the fluttering of nerves in her abdomen. It still wasn't too late to change her mind, but she liked him, she trusted him—and she was going to marry him.

'Yes.' She took his arm, all her fears dissipating in the sudden warmth of his smile. 'It is.'

Chapter Eleven

'Welcome to your new home, Mrs Amberton.' Lance caught Violet's waist as she stepped down from the carriage and twirled her around in mid-air. 'I hope this is a better welcome than I gave you the first or second times. Shall we say third time lucky?'

'I hope so.' She felt breathless as he set her back on her feet. 'It's been a strange day.'

'It has, but it went well, I think.'

'Yes.'

It *really* had, she thought with some residual amazement. With just Robert, Ianthe, Mr Rowlinson and Martin in attendance, their wedding had felt intimate, personal and unexpectedly moving. Lance had been uncharacteristically serious, too, reciting his vows with a depth of feeling that had taken her by surprise. When he'd dipped his head to kiss her at the end of the ceremony she'd almost imagined that it was all real and not simply a marriage of convenience. For one fleeting moment, it had *felt* real.

He captured her hand in his as they entered the hall. To her dismay, she felt even more nervous now walking beside him, just as she'd felt uncomfortably aware of his close proximity in the carriage on the journey back. Not that she ought to feel any more uncomfortable, she reminded herself. Nothing between them had changed, not really. They'd agreed that nothing about their relationship would be any different, not for seven years anyway, and yet despite that, something was. They were married. Somehow that made a big difference.

What had she done?

'Captain Amberton. Mrs Amberton.' Mrs Gargrave greeted them with a look that bordered on approval. 'I'll have some tea brought to the drawing room.'

'That won't be—'

'Thank you, Mrs Gargrave.' Violet cut short Lance's refusal. 'Tea would be perfect.'

'It would?' He held open the drawing-room door, murmuring in her ear as she brushed past.

'Yes.' She accelerated quickly, alarmed by the tingling sensation that raced through her body as his breath tickled her neck. 'We had enough champagne with Ianthe and Robert.'

'True, though I'm afraid it didn't make any difference. Your best friend still hates me.'

'She doesn't hate you.'

'She doesn't like me.'

'No-oo.' She felt compelled to be honest. 'But she doesn't know you, not yet. She only knows stories about the old you. You seemed to get on well enough with Robert though.'

He made a non-committal sound and she stopped in the middle of the room, spinning around in surprise. 'What's wrong with Robert?'

'Nothing, annoyingly. I'd like to detest the man, but I can't.'

'Why would you want to do that?'

'For all the wrong reasons.' Lance dropped into his armchair with a thud. 'Because he's intelligent and successful and has a wife who gazes at him adoringly.'

She blinked in surprise. 'Do you want *me* to gaze at you adoringly?'

'I could hardly expect that.' He slouched further down in his chair and stared broodingly into the fire. 'Only you don't have to look at him in the same way, too.'

'I do not! He's Ianthe's husband!'

'Yes, and a paragon of male virtue. The man has no right to set such high standards.'

Violet took a seat on the sofa opposite, amused

by his petulant tone. He sounded almost jealous, though surely he couldn't be…could he?

'I never thought of it before, but I suppose he does set a high standard…' she feigned a wistful-sounding sigh '…and he's very handsome.'

'I hadn't noticed.'

'A talented businessman, too.'

'As I said.'

'Quite perfect really.'

'In your opinion.' Lance's tone was distinctly annoyed.

'Not really.' She relented at last. 'He's perfect in a lot of ways and definitely for Ianthe, but I've never thought of him like that.' She tilted her head thoughtfully. 'I wonder why not.'

'Never?'

'No. Not even when he used to visit my father to discuss buying the shipyard.'

'Visit?' His gaze seemed to sharpen. 'You never told me about that. Was it often?'

'I suppose so. Once a week maybe.'

'Was he kind to you?'

'Very. More than he needed to be.'

'I suppose you never thought he was mocking you?'

'Never, but then he never chased me across the moors or locked me in a tower either. It makes him seem quite boring now.'

'Really?'

Lance looked faintly pleased and she couldn't resist smiling back.

'I suppose I like adventure more than I thought. Oh, thank you, Mrs Gargrave.' She looked up as the housekeeper reappeared with a tea tray. 'I can manage from here.'

'Of course, Mrs Amberton, but just so you know, your new rooms are both ready.'

'Our *what*?'

Lance's tone hardened abruptly and the housekeeper's spine stiffened like a ramrod. 'I presumed that you'd want to move back into the family quarters now that you're married. I've prepared both your parents' old rooms.' She pursed her lips primly. 'I wasn't sure which you'd be using tonight.'

'Neither! And you presumed wrongly.'

'That was very thoughtful of you.' Violet interjected again. 'We appreciate your efforts, Mrs Gargrave.'

'Very good, Mrs Amberton. I've already moved your belongings.'

'Then you can damned well m—'

'*Thank you*, Mrs Gargrave. That will be all for now.'

'Damned woman!' Lance burst out of his chair as the housekeeper closed the door behind her.

'She was only trying to help.'

'Help?' He snatched up a glass from the sideboard and then remembered himself, putting it down again without filling it. 'She's been trying to make me move rooms ever since I got back. Typical of her to use today as an excuse!'

'Ye-es.' Violet chose her words with care. Uncomfortable as she was with the subject of their sleeping arrangements, the strength of his reaction surprised her. 'But I suppose it might look suspicious for us to be sleeping at opposite ends of the house.'

His eyes flashed accusingly. 'Are you on her side now?'

'No, but those are the family rooms. Maybe we ought to be using them.'

'We should be allowed to sleep wherever we want. It's our house!'

Despite his temper, she felt a warm glow at the words. *Our* house. Somehow she'd always thought of herself as a guest even in her father's house, somebody who was tolerated under sufferance, and yet Lance seemed more than willing to share his home. All except for the family quarters.

'Why don't you want to use those rooms?' She remembered his tense reaction that first day when she'd suggested looking at the maze from Arthur's window. It had seemed strange at the time.

'They're family rooms. I'm not part of a family any more.' His voice sounded strained.

'You mean it's too upsetting?'

He gave a small nod and then sighed. 'I mean I don't have the courage to face it.'

'Then maybe it's time.' She made the suggestion as gently as she could. 'We'll go together, if you like. You came with me to my father's house today.'

She reached out a hand before she could think to stop herself, but to her surprise, he took it.

'As I recall, it only ruined your morning.'

'Not completely.' She swallowed, trying to keep her mind on the subject. She'd never touched his hand without gloves before and his fingers felt warm and strong, sending a vivid tingling sensation up her arm and all through her body before it pooled in her stomach. 'I won't deny that it was difficult at the time, but it helped me, too. I'd like to repay the favour.'

'Very well. Since I made you do it…' He tightened his grip slightly, his eyes darkening as he stared across at her. 'You *do* realise that Mrs Gargrave expects us to share a bed tonight?'

'Yes.' She dropped her gaze, struck with the uncomfortable impression that he could see straight into her mind. Their hands were still joined, his fingers interlaced with hers, making her skin feel red-hot suddenly.

'Then again, I don't suppose she'll be peering in at the keyhole. Now there's an unpleasant thought.' He gave an exaggerated shudder. 'All right, I'll let her win this time. Back to the family rooms it is, but don't get used to it. You won't have time.'

'What do you mean?' Violet looked up again in alarm, but he was smiling.

'It means that I thought you might enjoy a honeymoon.'

'We're going on honeymoon?'

'No. *You* are. I'm afraid I have work to do, and besides, I thought you might enjoy it more with your friend Mrs Felstone. I spoke to her perfect husband about it after the wedding.'

'Is that what the two of you had your heads pressed together about? It all looked very secretive.'

'It was. I thought I'd have more success speaking with him than his wife. Somehow I doubted she'd appreciate the offer coming from me. I suggested Scotland for six weeks, but he refused to be parted from her for so long. We compromised on a month, providing she agrees, of course. The weather's positively summery now.'

'Scotland? But that's wonderful!' Violet tore her fingers away from his to clasp her hands together. It *was* wonderful, even if she felt torn between excitement and disappointment that he wasn't the one going with her. 'When do we leave?'

'Tomorrow morning.'

'So soon?' Her stomach plummeted. Less than a day after their marriage... She couldn't help but feel a little hurt. Clearly he had no feelings for her at all if he was happy to send her away so soon.

He leaned forward suddenly, capturing both of her hands this time, just as he'd done on the promenade earlier. 'I know you're eager for a taste of freedom, Violet. I know what that feels like, too. I would have sent you off today except that it might have raised some questions over the legitimacy of our marriage.'

'Oh.' She felt her cheeks redden at the insinuation. 'Yes, of course.'

'But after I've had my wicked way with you tonight, theoretically of course, you're free to run away wherever and whenever you choose. I believe that those were the terms we agreed on. My only condition is that Martin accompanies you.'

'Martin?' She narrowed her eyes suspiciously. 'To keep an eye on me?'

'To make sure you don't run away with any Highlanders, naturally, but for your own safety as well. He's a useful man to have around.'

'All right, if he wishes to come.'

'Good.' He gave her a smile that appeared to

be completely genuine. 'Then I hope you enjoy your freedom, Mrs Amberton. You deserve it.'

Half an hour later, Lance stood in the doorway of his father's old chamber, without even the faintest hint of a smile on his face, wondering if time had reversed itself and it was actually five years before. Nothing about the room seemed to have changed at all.

'Are you all right?' Violet's voice was soft at his side.

'Yes.' He forced himself to take a step over the threshold. 'It's just strange.'

'If it's too upsetting…'

'No. As much as I hate to admit it when Mrs Gargrave's right, it's about time I moved in. It's what my father would have wanted.'

'But if it reminds you of him too much?'

'It does, but that's not what bothers me most.' He ran a hand through his hair with a sigh. 'It's Arthur. This was supposed to be his room, the heir's room. It was never meant to be mine. It feels wrong to be here.'

'You didn't take his place on purpose.'

'No, but he was just so much better than me. In every way. He should have been the one who…'

'Don't!' She put a hand on his arm. 'Don't say

that. We've both ended up in places we didn't expect, but we have to make the most of it.'

He frowned at the understatement. Did she feel as confused as he did, then? Did the place she'd found herself feel wrong? He didn't like that idea. Then again, it had been an emotional day for both of them. The ceremony had been more of a sombre experience than he'd expected, but then he'd taken it seriously. He'd never intended to marry, let alone to marry for money like his father. The least he could do to compensate for that fact was to behave properly.

And he *would* make her happy. He'd made that resolve on the promenade after their visit to her father's house. He'd do whatever he could do to make up for the unhappiness of her upbringing, to compensate for his own earlier behaviour towards her, too. Somehow that purpose seemed almost as important to him now as saving the estate.

The honeymoon he'd arranged was a start. It would give her the freedom she craved—although she hadn't seemed as happy with his gift as he'd hoped she would be. Ironic when he'd been trying his best to be happy *for* her. The idea of her leaving so soon made him feel strangely bereft, but it was what she wanted.

'Speaking of your place…' He led her across to a door in the far corner. 'Your bedchamber's through here. It's known as the blue room for obvious reasons...' he frowned as he turned the handle '...though it's not so easy to tell in the dark.'

He tensed as she leaned past him, holding her candle up to peer into the unlit chamber. Judging by the lack of a fire, or indeed any lighting at all, it seemed that Mrs Gargrave had her own definite ideas about where his new bride ought to spend her first night as a married woman. So much for both their rooms being ready. The next time his housekeeper offered him tea, he'd tell her exactly what she could do with it.

He turned back into his own room and looked around apprehensively, noticing the little touches he'd missed at first glance. There was a bottle of champagne and two glasses set out on a table—even a faint scent of perfume in the air if he wasn't mistaken. That definitely hadn't been there in his father's day. There was even a nightdress laid out on the bed, damn it! He supposed he ought to be grateful that there weren't rose petals sprinkled over the floor as well.

He cleared his throat, trying to sound matter-of-fact. 'It appears that we'll be sharing a bed tonight after all. For the sake of appearances,' he added quickly.

'Yes.' She turned around slowly to face him, though her expression didn't waver. Instead she looked very much as if she were trying not to have any expression at all. 'For appearances.'

'It won't happen again. I'll speak to Mrs Gargrave in the morning.'

'It's all right. It was a reasonable assumption for her to make.'

'Violet, you know I had nothing to do with this?' He felt a powerful urge to defend himself. After promising her that they'd sleep in separate rooms, he was uncomfortably aware that he appeared to be breaking his word on the very first night.

'I know that.' Her expression flickered with a look that he couldn't interpret. Suspicion? Fear? No, incongruously enough, it looked more like hurt, though surely it couldn't be that.

'If I could just have a few moments to get ready for bed?' She lifted her chin up slightly.

'Of course.' He found himself clearing his throat again. 'Should I call for Eliza?'

'No, I can manage.'

'Very well. In that case, I'll wait outside.'

He stepped out into the corridor, feeling relieved and slightly ridiculous at the same time. The whole situation was ludicrous. He'd never been so formal with a woman in his life and this was his wedding night. He sounded as priggish as his father, for pity's sake! Maybe the room was affecting him even more than he'd thought.

The thought of sharing a bed with her made him as nervous as a youth with his first encounter and he wasn't even intending to sleep with her!

She opened the door again after a few minutes, dressed in what appeared to be a small tent. It managed to conceal everything, from the point of her chin down to the tips of her toes, yet the effect was oddly enticing. Such a concerted attempt to conceal her body only made him ten times more curious about it. Oh, hell…

'I'm ready.' She seemed to be avoiding his eyes. 'Shall I wait outside while you undress, too?'

'No.' He shook his head. She looked and sounded so sincere that he had to clench his jaw to stop himself from laughing. 'Get into bed if you like. You must be tired.'

He watched as she fled across the room, uncertain about how to proceed. Usually he slept naked, but considering her somewhat excessive apparel, he supposed he ought to modify his habits tonight. Slowly, he untied his cravat and pulled off his shirt, undershirt and trousers, leaving only his drawers, before moving cautiously across to the bed, extinguishing all the candles so that the only remaining light came from the fireside.

'May I?' He felt even more ridiculous asking permission to get in, but she had the covers pulled up to her chin, as if she were afraid her voluminous nightgown wasn't armour enough, and he didn't want to alarm her. She gave a tiny nod and he climbed in, resisting the urge to spread out, as usual, in the centre.

'Comfortable?' He felt the need to say something, anything, to ease the tension he could feel emanating from her side.

'Yes. It's just…strange.'

'Would you prefer me to sleep in the chair?'

'No.' She shook her head quickly. 'It wouldn't be good for your leg. And we *are* married.'

'Yes.' He hoisted the covers up over his chest. 'So we are.'

They were silent for a few moments, both staring at the canopy as if there were something of intense interest above them.

'I haven't shared a bed with anyone for years.' She broke the silence finally. 'Not since my mother died. She used to sleep with me when I was frightened.'

'My mother used to let Arthur and me sleep in her bed when we had bad dreams, too.' He smiled at the memory. He hadn't thought about that for years…

'It was nice, having someone to curl up with.' She stiffened suddenly. 'Not that I mean…'

'I know what you mean.' Although he was inclined to agree in either case. The warmth radiating from her small body was already tempting him across the centre of the bed. It would be more than nice to curl up with her. It would be nice to do other things, too. More than nice, in fact... Damn it. Even the thought made his body react in a way that was definitely *not* in keeping with their agreement. He shifted on to his side and flicked at the covers, trying to hide the evidence.

'Didn't you have a nurse to sleep with?' He tried to distract himself with the question.

'Yes, for a while.' She twisted her head towards him with a perplexed expression. 'Are you too hot?'

'No.'

'We can take the covers off if you like?'

'What? Oh, no, I was just rearranging. You said you had a nurse?'

'Yes, but she never slept with me. She never touched me if she could help it. My father told her not to. He thought it was bad for me.'

'To be touched?'

'Or embraced. Or kissed. He said it was all sentimental nonsense.'

He propped himself up on one elbow to look down at her. Did she sound wistful or was he just imagining it?

'Didn't you have other relatives? Aunts? Uncles? Grandparents?'

'My father didn't have any family as far as I know, although some of my mother's family came to her funeral. They said they'd visit me, but they never did.'

'They never wrote to you? Never invited you to stay?'

'If they did, my father never told me.' Her eyes looked very bright in the firelight suddenly, as if there were tears glistening inside them. 'But perhaps I'm blaming him unfairly. Perhaps they didn't want me.'

He felt an ache in his chest, a combination of sympathy for her and anger towards her father. How lonely must she have been, growing up in that vast, empty prison of a house without any love or affection, just a miserly old man hoarding her all to himself for company? He had the sudden strong conviction that if he could wind the clock back five years, then not only would he call Jeremy Harper a few more choice words than liar, but he would rescue her, too. He would have refused to leave the ballroom without her. Then he would have gathered her into his arms the way he wanted to now.

That would *definitely* give the wrong impression.

'I'm sure your mother's family wanted you, Violet. They would have been mad not to. Do you know where they live?'

'No.'

He drew his brows together thoughtfully. 'Did your father have a study?'

'Yes, but he always kept it locked. I think Mr Rowlinson has the key.'

'Then it belongs to you now. We ought to take a look. There might be some clue as to where they live.'

'No.' She shook her head vehemently. 'I know it sounds wicked, but I don't want to go back there ever again.'

'Then let me.'

She looked surprised. 'You wouldn't mind?'

'Not at all, and if that doesn't work then there are plenty of other ways we can find them.'

She pursed her lips together as if she were trying to control some emotion. 'I'd like that.'

'Good. Then I'll look into it while you're away.'

Impulsively, he reached out and brushed his knuckles across her cheek, surprised by a feeling of tenderness. Even now, she looked radiant, albeit swathed in enough material to make a pair of curtains. How was it possible for such a warm, vibrant woman to have emerged out of such a cold, lonely childhood? One in which she'd never been hugged, held or kissed…

His gaze dropped to her lips. No wonder she'd been so sensitive about the subject of suitors when they'd first met. She'd never been touched or caressed by any man. Even *he* hadn't kissed her at their wedding, no more than a chaste peck anyway. Considering their agreement, it hadn't seemed appropriate to do more at the time, but now he wished that he had. It seemed wrong now *not* to have kissed her, even if it was too late to do anything about it. If he tried to kiss her now, even chastely, then she might think he wanted more—which, given the strain in the lower part of his body, he did.

What the hell had he been thinking, suggesting seven years?

'You ought to get some sleep.' He dragged his hand away and rolled on to his other side, wishing he'd ordered a cold bath for the evening. 'You have a big day ahead of you.'

'Yes.' He thought he heard a faint sigh before she spoke, her voice sounding oddly subdued. 'Goodnight, Lance.'

Chapter Twelve

'You're early, Amberton.'

Lance twisted his head to find Robert Felstone standing on the railway platform beside him. He'd been staring at the track so fixedly, looking for any hint of steam in the distance, that he hadn't seen him approach.

'Yes, I must have got the wrong time.'

He frowned as he said it, wondering why he was bothering to lie. He knew exactly what time the train was due, having checked the schedule repeatedly over the past few days and at least five times that morning, but for some reason he didn't want the other man to know that.

'Ah.' Robert gave a wry smile. 'I'm early, too, as it happens, though you know there's nothing wrong with being eager to see your wife, Amberton.'

'I hardly know my wife.' Lance had to consciously restrain himself from looking back down the track. 'How could I miss her?'

He pulled at the rim of his top hat, asking the question as if it were simply rhetorical, though in truth he was somewhat curious to know the answer himself. The past three weeks had felt at least double that length.

'I knew Ianthe for less than ten minutes before I asked her to marry me—' Robert was still smiling '—though it took her another two days to say yes. Then I had to wait three months before seeing her again. They were the longest three months of my life.'

'Lucky for me it's only been three weeks, then.'

'True, although I wouldn't have agreed to any longer than a month. I really ought to be angry with you for sending my wife off on your honeymoon, but then they say absence makes the heart grow fonder.'

'They do, but as I said, I must have got the time wrong.' Lance cleared his throat awkwardly. 'Any idea why they're coming back a week early? Violet's letter was somewhat vague.'

'So was Ianthe's, though I suppose we'll find out soon enough. Do you care for some company while we wait?'

'By all means, as long as you don't mind being stared at.' Lance nodded his head towards a group of men clustered together on the far platform. The frequent glances in his direction made their topic of conversation quite obvious. 'I seem to be attracting a lot of attention this morning.'

'Which makes a refreshing change for me.' Robert arched an eyebrow. 'Usually I'm the one being gossiped about, but your reputation seems to be even more jaded than mine. The two of us together ought to be the talk of Whitby.'

'I thought you were an esteemed man of business?'

'Man of business, yes. Esteemed, no. I was on my way towards becoming a gentleman once, but I'm afraid circumstances put paid to that.'

'Because of Charles Lester? I heard the rumours.'

'I didn't push him.'

'I never thought that you did. Besides, I think Violet would have refused to marry me if I had.' He felt a tug of jealousy at his own words. 'She's one of your greatest defenders.'

Robert laughed. 'I put that entirely down to Ianthe. Old Harper made his disapproval of me quite obvious.'

'Then we've something in common. He called me a reprobate—quite rightly, of course.'

'And now you're married to his daughter.'

'I doubt he would have been pleased.'

Robert glanced at him speculatively. 'I understand that you're setting up in business yourself? Iron, isn't it?'

'Yes. I've opened a new mine close to Rosedale.' Lance hesitated briefly. 'As it happens, I wouldn't mind your opinion on a few matters. I heard you invested in the works at Grosmont.'

'I did, though I'm no expert on mining, I'm afraid.'

'Neither am I. I'm learning as I go along, but I wouldn't mind another opinion.'

'Then I'd be glad to discuss anything you want.'

'Good. I'm there almost every day. Come and visit when you—'

He stopped at the sound of a whistle blowing, his heart seeming to do some kind of violent somersault in his chest as he turned to see the locomotive already rolling into the station, chuffing slowly to a halt in a billowing cloud of steam. The whistle blew again and it stopped, the compartment doors all bursting open, seemingly at once, as passengers started to get off.

Lance peered over the top of the crowd, resenting the height of the other travellers that made it impossible to spot his wife, about to make his way forward when a flurry of green silk flew past him and threw itself headlong into Robert's waiting arms. He watched in amusement. *That* would give the crowd of onlookers something else to talk about. It seemed Ianthe Felstone was just as excited by the prospect of a reunion as her husband. He felt a brief pang of jealousy, quickly followed by a whole different pang as he turned again and caught sight of his wife.

'Lance.'

She was standing just a few feet away, dressed all in blue, his new favourite colour, smiling up at him, though for a few moments he seemed oddly incapable of answering. She looked positively transformed, her whole face seeming to glow with health and happiness. She looked slightly bigger than before, too, as if her body had rounded out in the time since she'd left. Even her hair looked fuller and softer, with feathery tendrils stroking the sides of her newly rounded face.

Whatever that first pang had been, it stabbed him anew, a bittersweet combination of pleasure at seeing her again and resentment that such a dazzling transformation had happened in his absence. She seemed to have blossomed during their separation, while he'd spent his time counting the days.

'Violet.' He smiled stiffly and extended an arm, acutely aware of how formal his behaviour must seem next to the enthusiastically informal couple beside them. Frankly, if the Felstones started to behave any more informally, then he might have to suggest they adjourn to one of the nearby waiting rooms. 'It's good to see you again. I trust that you've had an enjoyable trip.'

'Very enjoyable, thank you.' She threaded her arm through his. 'Goodbye, Ianthe.'

Lance lifted a hand to the rim of his hat, though by the look of things, saying goodbye was the very last thing on either of the Felstones' minds.

Violet giggled. 'I don't think she heard me.'

'No, I think not.' He led the way out of the station, pressing her arm tightly against his side so that she couldn't pull it away again. Now that he had her back, he didn't want to let go, even for a second. 'She almost knocked me over to reach him.'

'I noticed. I hope you weren't waiting long.'

'Not at all,' he lied. 'It was perfect timing.'

'And the weather's so fine today.' She gave a sigh of pleasure as they walked out of the station on to the harbourside. 'I don't think I've ever seen Whitby looking more beautiful.'

'Me neither.' He glanced down at her radiant expression, still oppressed by that same bittersweet duality of emotions. In truth, he hadn't paid any attention to the weather that day, but beautiful seemed the most appropriate word for his view now.

He let go of her arm reluctantly, handing her up into his waiting carriage before turning to greet his batman. 'Did you enjoy yourself, too, Martin?'

'Very much, sir.'

Lance lifted an eyebrow. If he wasn't mistaken, his retainer's usually taciturn features were arranged in something resembling a smirk.

'Something the matter?' He narrowed his gaze suspiciously.

'No, sir. It's just good to see you looking so happy, sir.'

'I don't recall saying anything of the kind. *Am* I happy, Martin?'

'You must just look that way, sir.'

'We've had a wonderful time.' Violet twisted around enthusiastically as he threw his batman a last pointed look and climbed in beside her. 'Edinburgh was wonderful. The castle, the museums, Princes Street Gardens. It was the most thoughtful wedding present you could ever have given me.'

'A honeymoon without the groom?' The words sounded more bitter than he'd intended.

'That's not what I meant.' Her expression sobered instantly. 'And it was more than just a holiday, you know that. It was freedom. You gave me that, Lance. I'm grateful.'

'Then I'm truly glad that you enjoyed it, although I'm sorry you never made it to the Highlands. What made you curtail the trip?'

'Ianthe wasn't feeling well.'

'Oh.' He felt a fleeting sense of disappointment, but then what other reason had he expected? That she'd missed him as much as he had her? He pushed the thought away as the carriage started moving. 'Is she unwell?'

'Not exactly.' She beamed suddenly. 'She started to feel sick in the mornings and when she consulted a doctor, he told her she was going to have a baby. She said she'd be happy to keep travelling, but I knew she'd want to tell Robert as soon as possible.'

'Ah.' Nothing at all to do with him, then. 'In that case, I'm happy for them, but still sorry it cut your holiday short.'

'I'm not.' She rested her head against the seat cushion with a tired smile. 'It feels good to be back. I think I appreciate it more for having been away. Does that make sense?'

'Perfectly.' He leaned back beside her, warmed by the words. 'Five years ago I was desperate to escape and see new places. I never wanted to come back. When I was shot and they said I had to leave the army and come home, I was half tempted to shoot myself again, but now that I've seen a bit more of the world, I appreciate my own small corner of it a bit more. Now I can see it in the same way I did as a boy. Arthur and I loved the moors. We spent all our free time roaming up there.'

'Just the two of you?'

'We thought so, but there always seemed to be somebody around when we got into trouble. I think my mother set people to watch us. The terrain can be dangerous if you're not careful. There are cliffs and bogs, and the weather can change completely in ten minutes.'

'I never realised how unique the landscape is here.'

'This is a wilder landscape than most.'

She leaned towards him so that her head brushed lightly against his shoulder. 'I must like things to be wild, then.'

'In that case, we'll definitely have to make sure you reach the Highlands next time. You must have a wild soul.'

She burst into a peal of laughter. 'No one's ever suggested that before.'

He smiled, starting to share in her happiness. After all, she was right, he *had* played some small part in her transformation. It felt good to have made her happy and he liked her laugh. He'd missed it, he realised with a jolt, as if missing *her* hadn't been bad enough.

'Maybe no one else knows you the way I do.'

He stretched an arm out, resting it along the top of the carriage seat behind her.

'*Do* you know me?' She craned her neck towards him with a look of surprise.

'I think I'm starting to. You look different, Violet, in a very good way, I might add. As if you're the person you were always meant to be, independent and adventurous and carefree.'

'Now I know you're talking about someone else.'

'That's because you still think of yourself as Violet Harper, downtrodden daughter. You're Violet Amberton now, my rebellious, runaway bride. She's a whole different woman.'

'In that case, I think I like being Violet Amberton.' She leaned a little closer towards him and he brought his arm down, wrapping it around her shoulders. She seemed to fit there perfectly.

'Good. I like you being her, too.'

'Will you really come with me to the Highlands?'

'Me?' He felt a twinge of surprise. He hadn't said anything about going himself, though he felt ridiculously pleased at the invitation to join her. He gave a small tug on his arm, pulling her closer. 'All right. Just as soon as things are more settled at the mine.'

'How is it going?'

'I can show you if you like. We're travelling back that way.'

'Yes, please.' She nodded eagerly. 'I'd like to see the reason we got married.'

He winced inwardly, although it was a fair comment, he supposed. He *had* married her for the mine, for the money to expand it at least, even if that didn't feel quite like the reason any more.

Twenty minutes later, he helped her down from the carriage, gesturing towards a ramshackle collection of wooden, shed-like structures on a rock-strewn plateau halfway up a hillside.

'It's not as chaotic as it looks, I promise you.'

'I didn't expect a palace.' She looked around with interest. 'Is your office in one of those?'

'Not so much an office as a desk, but in that small shack at the end, yes. The rest are where we store the equipment.'

'Are those all entrances to the mine?' She pointed towards a few holes in the hillside.

'Yes, there's four altogether. It's safer to have several escape routes.'

'I see.' She peered inside one of the sheds, looking around as if she were genuinely interested. 'How many people work here?'

'At the moment, about thirty. Only men

though. I don't allow women or children. They spend three hours in the mine, then I insist on an hour outside. I pay good wages and I make sure it's as safe as it can be.'

She nodded thoughtfully. 'You said you wanted to expand. What is it that you want to do? More tunnels?'

'Not yet.' He gestured down into the valley. 'But if we build our own blast furnace, then we won't have to take the ore to Grosmont for smelting. We can do our own smelting and puddling and then sell it as wrought iron instead of pig. We're not far from Rosedale and we can use their supply line to transport it directly to the ports. I've already struck a bargain with the owner.'

'Is it expensive to build a furnace?'

'Extremely, in the short term, but in the long run, we can reinvest in the estate. If we build it in the valley away from the villages, then it won't ruin the countryside or the air either. It'll be a good thing for everyone, I hope.' He turned to face her again, unable to stop a feeling of happiness from bursting out of him suddenly. 'I'm glad that you're home, Violet.'

To his surprise and delight, she didn't hesitate to answer. 'So am I.'

Chapter Thirteen

Violet awoke to the sight of a turquoise-blue canopy. Smiling, she let herself sink deeper into the comfort of a generously proportioned, lavishly cushioned four-poster bed. She was in the blue room, her mother-in-law's old chamber, reclining on a feather-filled mattress that surely had to be the most comfortable place in the world.

According to the clock on the mantel it was well past eight o'clock in the morning, but she had no desire to move, let alone to get up. Given the chance, she'd be more than happy to spend the rest of the day lying there. Even if something seemed to be missing…

'Mrs Amberton?' There was a small knock on the door, followed by the sound of Eliza's voice.

'Come in.'

'Morning, ma'am.' The maid poked her head

around the door with a bright smile. 'The master thought you might like breakfast in bed today.'

'Oh.' She wriggled up to a sitting position, thoughts of slumber forgotten after all. She'd never had breakfast in bed before, but the idea had always been wickedly tempting. 'Yes, I would.'

'Here you go.' Eliza placed a large tray over her lap, piled high with ham and eggs, toast and jam.

'You said this was Captain Amberton's idea?'

'Yes, ma'am, though he said to wait awhile because you were fast asleep.'

'I was? I mean…he did?' She blinked in surprise. How had he known if she was asleep or not when they'd slept in separate bedrooms? 'Is he having breakfast in his chamber, too?'

'No, ma'am, he left for the mine two hours ago.'

'Oh.' Violet picked up a cup of hot chocolate and sipped at it thoughtfully. They'd had a pleasant dinner together the previous evening, catching up on each other's news, before Lance had escorted her up to her new chamber and then left her at the door. But if he'd known that she was still asleep that morning, then surely that meant he'd been in her room at some point—to say goodbye, perhaps?

'He said I should ask if there's anything else you might fancy?' Eliza nodded at the tray.

'Something *else*?' Violet echoed the word incredulously. Considering the massive amount of food piled up in front of her, it was hard to imagine what else she *could* want. 'No, this is plenty, thank you. Would you like some? Here…' she patted the bedcover '…why don't you sit down?'

Eliza stole a fleeting look at the door, hesitating for a moment before perching on the edge of the bed.

'Can I have some toast?'

'Of course. Jam and butter?'

'Yes, please. Cook watches how much we have.'

Violet smeared a generous amount on to two pieces of toast, offering one to Eliza and biting into the other herself.

'The master seems very keen to make you happy.' Eliza gave her a conspiratorial look. 'He's been like a different man this past month, Mrs Gargrave says.'

'Mrs Gargrave says that?' Violet swallowed a mouthful of toast in amazement. It was hard to imagine the housekeeper approving of her husband in any way at all. 'As a compliment?'

'I think so, as much as she ever gives one anyway.'

'How has he changed?'

'Well, for starters, he gets up early in the mornings now and goes to bed at what she calls a reasonable hour. And she hasn't filled the decanters in a whole month.'

Violet took another bite to stifle a smile. She hadn't necessarily expected Lance to stick to that part of their bargain while she was away, but apparently he had.

'*And* he was eager to get to the station in good time yesterday. Left a whole hour early, Mrs Gargrave says.'

'Really?'

She felt her cheeks flush with a mixture of embarrassment and pleasure. She was starting to think that Mrs Gargrave said a little *too* much, not that she wasn't pleased by the thought of Lance himself being eager to see her. She'd had mixed feelings about seeing him again, but when she'd seen him waiting on the platform, she hadn't been able to stop her heart doing some kind of jig in her chest. She'd told him that she was glad to be back and it was true. Despite her eagerness to travel and her resolve *not* to think about him in Scotland, she'd felt more homesick than she'd expected, not for Whitby, but for here…for him.

And yet, something about their relationship seemed to have shifted in her absence as well, as if he really *had* missed her. The way his eyes had seemed to light up when he'd seen her again had made her want to run into his arms the way Ianthe had into Robert's. When she'd accidentally brushed her head against his shoulder in the carriage, he'd put his arm around her as if he wanted her close too, even if he *had* chosen to sleep in a separate bedroom last night. Was *he* what felt missing from her bed?

Having taken the opportunity of travelling with Ianthe to ask some more pointed questions about that particular aspect of marriage, she was half excited, half alarmed by the idea of sharing a bed with him again. Not that it was going to happen for another seven years. Not unless they changed their minds about their arrangement anyway...

'Your new sitting room is ready, too,' Eliza continued. 'Freshly painted and everything.'

'My what?'

'Your sitting room. Captain Amberton said you wanted to use the tower.'

'Oh!' She swallowed the last of her hot chocolate and wrenched back the bedcovers, wriggling into a dressing gown. Apparently he really did want her to be happy. The very thought of her new sitting room achieved that. She couldn't wait another moment to see it!

She ran down the corridor and stopped in the doorway of the tower, rendered speechless. Her former prison had been transformed into the prettiest, cosiest room she could ever have imagined, with cream-coloured walls complemented by an assortment of pink-and-white-striped furniture and a dark, dusky rose carpet. Pictures of seascapes adorned the walls and there were bunches of bluebells arranged in vases on every spare surface, as if someone were trying to make the room as homey as possible.

'What's that?'

Her eyes fell on a battered and ancient-looking wooden chest beneath one of the windows. It seemed incongruous, out of place with the rest of the furniture and yet familiar somehow. It certainly hadn't been there the last time she'd been in the room. She would have remembered it.

'I don't know, ma'am, but Captain Amberton said not to open it without you. Would you like me to help you unpack it now?'

'No.' She felt a sudden urge to be alone. 'That's enough for now, thank you, Eliza. I'll manage.'

'Very good, ma'am.'

She crouched down by the chest, waiting until the sound of Eliza's footsteps had receded before unfastening the metal clasp, a feeling of anticipation making her feel slightly dizzy. Nervously, she opened the lid, pressing a hand to her mouth as she did so. Sure enough, there they were, all her mother's old books, just as she remembered them, like a group of long-lost friends. She reached in and picked up the uppermost tome, a copy of Malory's Arthurian legends, hugging it to her breast and laughing aloud with happiness.

A few hours later, she looked up from her newfound favourite position, comfortably ensconced in an armchair by the fireplace. Her sitting room was finished. Her mother's books were arranged in pride of place on her bookshelf, while the chest remained under the window, ornamented with cushions to provide an additional seat. She'd been so engrossed in her books that she'd declined lunch, although Mrs Gargrave had appeared on several occasions bearing a tea tray, tutting loudly each time to find the mistress of the house still clad in her dressing gown.

She didn't care. She was wearing a pair of spectacles, too, the ones she needed for reading, though she was starting to wish that she'd purchased a new pair on her travels. The tiny metal frames had an irritating habit of sliding down her nose at inopportune moments, making the words in front of her go suddenly blurry, though it was a minor irritation at best. Nothing could spoil her mood today. Everything else was perfect. She'd come to the pleasing conclusion that her husband could lock her up every day if he wanted to.

'Happy?'

The sound of his voice made her leap out of her chair in surprise, as if her very thoughts had conjured him.

'Lance!' She put a hand to her chest. 'You startled me!'

'Apologies.' He grinned from the doorway, the whiteness of his teeth contrasting vividly with the black flecks all over his skin and clothes. He looked even more dishevelled than usual, his hair tousled and windblown, as if he'd just arrived home and come straight to find her. Somehow that idea made him even more attractive.

'You were smiling.' He seemed to be studying her intently. 'I hope that means you're happy.'

'Very. I love my new sitting room.'

'Good.' His grin spread even further. 'Do I need permission to enter this private domain?'

She pursed her lips thoughtfully and then relented. 'I'll let you off for today, seeing that you found my mother's books.' She gestured towards the new window seat. 'Where was it?'

'In the attic, as it turned out, though I'm afraid I can't take the credit. My leg isn't much use around ladders, but our young friend Daniel was very helpful.'

'I hope you gave him more than a shilling.'

'I did and a job, too. He's down in the kitchens right now.' He advanced a few steps towards her. 'You look very studious.'

'Oh!' She raised a hand to her head self-consciously. She'd forgotten that she was wearing her spectacles, the ones her father had said made her look even more unattractive. He'd always hated them. No doubt Lance would, too.

'Don't take them off.' He put a hand out to stop her before she could pull them away. 'They suit you.'

'They do?'

'Very much.' He advanced a few steps into the room. 'Do you know, I've never kissed a woman in glasses before.'

'Oh.' It seemed a woefully inadequate answer, but she didn't know how else to respond.

'May I?'

'May you…what?' Her mouth felt very dry all of a sudden.

'May I kiss the bride? I didn't do it properly on our wedding day and you know what they say—the longer you wait to do something, the harder it becomes.'

'Do they say that?'

'They might.' He shrugged. 'I thought it sounded persuasive.'

Her heart sank. *Persuasive.* That was all his words were then, empty words intended to charm and convince her. He'd probably used them a hundred times before. It was just a casual kiss for him, nothing more. After all, he wasn't attracted to her. He was happy to wait seven years…

'And…' he seemed to read the scepticism in her face '…because you look quite enchantingly pretty.'

'In spectacles?'

'You can take them off if you want.' He moved yet another step closer. 'Though I'd prefer it if you didn't.'

She swallowed, trying to keep her head. *Enchantingly pretty.* She ought not to be charmed, but he didn't look as if he were either mocking or toying with her. He looked serious. He looked as if he were really about to kiss her and she, apparently, was going to let him. Her legs were showing no signs of bearing her away. On the contrary, she was afraid that if she tried to move, then they might simply give way beneath her.

'May I, Violet?'

He said her name softly, like a caress, and she nodded. Slowly, he raised both hands to her face, cradling it between his fingers as his thumb trailed a light path over her skin, leaving a trail of heat that seemed to penetrate deep into her body. She closed her eyes as he leaned in towards her, then his lips were on hers, pressing gently, as if he were taking deliberate care not to disturb her spectacles. His mouth felt tender and yet hard at the same time, barely touching her at first and then starting to move, nudging hers to respond.

For a few seconds she didn't know what to do. Then the heat seemed to build in intensity until she couldn't *not* move any longer. Instead she responded instinctively, moving her lips against his in a way that made all her insides turn to liquid at once. Her mind seemed to go silent as her body took over. The tip of his tongue slid inside her mouth, stroking the edge of her lips and she reached her own tongue out to meet it, sucking and tasting and exploring as her hands found their way up around his neck.

She felt his own hands move away from her face and slide down over her throat, down the sides of her breasts and around her waist, scooping her up off the floor until she was standing on tiptoe, pressing against him so closely that she could feel the taut, muscular lines of his chest and something else, even harder and more muscular, pushing between her legs.

He released her abruptly and she was able to start thinking again—if it could be called anything as coherent as thinking, that was. Her mind seemed to be in turmoil, only slightly less than her body, which seemed to have received some kind of violent physical shock. Her limbs were all quivering with the after-effects.

'There you are, Mrs Amberton.' His voice sounded distinctly husky. 'Consider yourself kissed.'

She opened her eyes. Why had he stopped? She'd had the impression that they were just getting started... Except that maybe he wanted to stop, she thought in mortification. Maybe he'd had enough. He was smiling as if it had been easy for him to stop when her whole body was still trembling with desire.

'Our young friend also found something else you might like.'

'Really?' She forced her scattered thoughts to focus. 'That sounds mysterious.'

'Wait here.' He walked to the door and reached for something just outside. Judging by the shape and size it was clearly a painting, though with the back of the canvas towards her, she couldn't see what the subject was.

'This was in the attic, too.' He turned the frame around slowly, his gaze fixed on her face the whole time. 'Judging by the resemblance, I believe it must be your mother.'

She pressed a hand to her mouth, stifling a gasp. It was undoubtedly her mother. The similarity was more striking than she could ever have imagined, as though she were looking into a mirror, at a serious-looking young woman with white-blonde hair, luminous blue eyes and large, wide-set features that perfectly matched her own. She felt a stinging sensation behind her eyelids, as if there were tears pressing against them.

'Violet?' Lance sounded concerned. 'I'm sorry. I didn't mean to upset you.'

'You haven't.' She shook her head, hardly able to express what she was feeling. She seemed unable to drag her gaze away even as he placed it to one side, leaning it against a chair before coming to stand just in front of her. 'It's just a shock.'

'Then you're pleased?'

'Yes. I just never knew...never imagined...'

'That you were so much like her?' He looked down at her intently. 'You are. You're just as beautiful, too, Violet. Would you like to hang it in here?'

'Yes.' She rubbed a hand across her face as a lone tear escaped and trickled downwards. 'How about over there, instead of the seascape?'

'Wherever you like.' He lifted down the old painting and hung the portrait in its place. 'There. What do you think?'

'Perfect. I think she looks perfect. I could look at her all day.'

'Then what if we eat dinner in here tonight?

You've made it so cosy, it seems almost a shame to go downstairs.'

'That would be lovely.' She gave a small start. 'What time is it?'

'Almost six o'clock.'

'In the *evening*?' She looked down at her dressing gown in dismay. 'But I never even got dressed!'

'I did wonder about that.' He grinned. 'Not that I mind informality, of course.'

'No wonder Mrs Gargrave looked so disapproving.'

'Wait until she finds out that we plan to have dinner in here.'

'I'll tell her that you're a bad influence.'

'And she'll believe you.' He put a hand to his heart as if he were wounded. 'She'll be scandalised, of course, though I do believe it'll be one of my lesser crimes.'

'Shall I tell her?'

'No, let me. I need to have a bath and a shave first anyway. I'm still covered in dust.'

'Then I'll get dressed finally.'

'Pity. I rather like you in your nightclothes.' His gaze flickered downwards, lingering over her hips, and she felt her blood start to heat again. What did it mean when he looked at her like that? What did their kiss mean? Surely it had to mean something! *What was he thinking?*

'You know, you really are just like your mother, Violet.' He gave her the answer as their eyes met again, his own dark and intense, as he made for the door. 'You look perfect, too.'

Chapter Fourteen

Lance pulled his shirt over his head and flung it aside in exasperation. Had he really just told his wife she looked perfect? The words had taken him by surprise—even more so the fact that he'd genuinely meant them. He hadn't simply been flirting with her, though in truth he'd been starting to feel almost like his old self again—with one significant difference.

In the past, flirtation had always been a game, one played with willing partners, but a game none the less, the women largely interchangeable with each other. This time he was only interested in one woman, a tiny fairy-tale creature in a rumpled dressing gown and pair of wire-rimmed spectacles, with tousled blonde hair and a look of pure joy when she'd been gazing at her books. She'd looked…perfect. That was truly the only word for it. And altogether more gorgeous than he was quite comfortable admitting, as if she'd somehow grown into her body while she'd been away.

So he'd kissed her. He shouldn't have, but he hadn't been able to help himself. She'd looked so serious and studious at her reading that he'd found his mouth pressed against hers almost before he knew what he was doing.

Not that she'd stopped him or pulled away either. On the contrary, her lips had parted and her tongue had sought his with an ardour that had seemed equal to his own, though perhaps he'd imagined that. She'd felt soft and warm and deliciously tempting, but he'd known he *had* to resist. If it hadn't been for their agreement, he would have been seriously tempted to take her to bed right then and there, but instead he'd forced himself to step away.

That hadn't been easy. He let out a low moan at the memory. Never mind seven years, he hadn't been able to keep his hands off her for one day! He had no idea how he was going to get through tonight. But he'd made her a promise. Freedom was what she deserved, not to mention a better man for a husband, but since she was stuck with him, he could at least do the decent thing and leave her alone. He wouldn't sully her by dragging her down to his level. She was a hundred times better than that.

He tore off the rest of his clothes and lowered himself into a steaming hot bathtub. The heat eased the pain in his leg, soothing the damaged muscles and making it feel almost restored again. Almost. Not that it could ever be truly restored.

He ducked his head under the water so that he was completely submerged. His body would never be completely the same, the camp surgeon had been clear about that, but he felt no resentment about the fact. His leg was simply the punishment he had to accept for his past misdemeanours, but what about the rest of him? Could his *self* be restored?

He emerged out of the water and rested his head against the back of the tub. He'd come home from Canada with only two intentions. To save the estate and then drink himself into an early grave. Violet had helped him with one and prevented the other, although to his surprise he didn't resent that either. He'd been afraid that if he stopped drinking then he might be overwhelmed by his memories, but instead he'd found himself slowly coming to terms with them.

While she'd been away, he'd forced himself to keep sleeping in his father's old chamber, to the point where it now finally felt like his. For the first time in six months, he was starting to feel that he might be able to accept the past and move on. The only problem was that he didn't want to do it alone. He wanted to do it with his wife—a real wife, one he could share both his heart and his body with. He wanted to do it with Violet, the woman he'd promised to set free.

He had to force himself to wait another hour before returning to the sitting room, refreshed but no less frustrated, to find all the armchairs pushed back and a small dining table set in the centre.

'What do you think?'

Violet gestured at the arrangement proudly. She was wearing her azure-blue evening gown again, the one she'd worn for their first dinner, though her new fuller figure made the neckline somewhat more close-fitting. The mounds of her breasts were bulging in a way that affected him in a much lower area, too, intensifying his sense of frustration.

'Very snug.' He tore his gaze away from her cleavage. 'Perhaps we should do this more often.'

'I don't think we could get away with it too often. Mrs Gargrave already came to ask if you'd gone mad.'

'And you said?'

'I said you seemed the same as ever to me.'

'I'm not sure that's a compliment. I don't suppose anyone's ever called your Mr Felstone mad.'

She gave him a reproachful look. 'He's not

my Mr Felstone and they've called him lots of other things.'

He snorted derisively. 'Anyone can get a bad reputation. It takes a lot more commitment to be called mad as well.'

She laughed as a pair of kitchen maids appeared carrying plates of winter salad and a basket of fresh bread.

'May I?' Lance pulled out a chair for her.

'Thank you.' She sat down and spread a napkin over her lap. 'I was so engrossed in my books that I missed lunch. I didn't realise how hungry I was.'

'I see you've been eating well.'

'What do you mean?' Her hand wavered in mid-air as she reached for a piece of bread.

'Just that you look well.'

'Because I'm bigger?'

'I didn't mean…' He took the chair opposite, wincing at his own tactlessness. 'I meant that you look better.'

She held his gaze suspiciously for a moment and then smiled. 'It's funny, Ianthe's the one who's having a baby and I'm the one who looks like I am. I won't fit into any of my dresses soon.'

'Good. You were far too thin before. I've never understood why some women compete to wear the tightest corsets. Whoever invented the garment clearly didn't like your sex very much.'

She looked mildly shocked. 'Are you allowed to mention corsets in polite conversation?'

'Probably not, but then, you *are* my wife. Surely we can keep etiquette for other, less agreeable occasions?'

'All right.' Her lips curved upwards. 'Then I have to admit I agree with you. They can be very uncomfortable.'

'Hence the dressing gown?' He winked. 'Then perhaps you shouldn't wear them at all when you're at home. As part of your pursuit of freedom, I mean.'

Her expression became incredulous. 'You don't think I should wear underclothes?'

'As far as I'm concerned, you can wear as much or as little as you want. A modest wrap should be enough to spare Mrs Gargrave's blushes.'

She stared at him open-mouthed for a few seconds before bursting into a peal of laughter and he found himself grinning back. He'd promised himself that he'd behave, but somehow he couldn't resist flirting with her. The sound of her laughter was almost intoxicating. And he was only joking after all—half joking, anyway.

'I might have to abandon corsets altogether if I keep on eating like this.' She popped a potato into her mouth as if to demonstrate her intention of doing so. 'Or I might burst out of mine one day.'

'I'd like to see that.' He grinned broadly. 'I'd be there to catch you, of course. Trust me, Violet, you have curves in all the right places.'

She dropped her gaze to her plate as her cheeks darkened. 'It's funny, but I love food. I never realised it before, but I do. Isn't that strange?'

'That you never realised it? I suppose so.'

'My father said it was unladylike to eat large portions so I thought I was always just hungry, but it's more than that. I *love* food. Now I can decide what to eat and how much, I relish every mouthful.' She made a face. 'I'm not sure I'm explaining myself very well.'

'I think you are. You mean you're learning new things about yourself.'

'Yes! Who I am, what I like, who I want to be... My father used to make every decision for me. Now that I have my own choices to make, I feel like I'm finally discovering who I am.' She gave a self-deprecating smile. 'Better late than never.'

'Some of us get too many choices too early.' He put down his knife and fork, losing his appetite suddenly. 'I had all the choices I ever wanted. Second sons are lucky that way. The oldest son gets the money and the title, but the second gets to take more risks—in my case especially.'

'Why especially?'

He frowned. Why had he started this? They'd been talking about corsets and food. Why was he spoiling the evening by bringing the past up again, telling her things he'd never told anyone, even Arthur?

'After my mother died, my father let me do whatever I wanted. He put all the pressure on Arthur and left me alone.'

'Didn't it make you happy to do whatever you wanted?'

'For a while—or maybe not even that. I thought it did, but…there was always something missing.'

'Maybe you wanted some of your father's attention, too?'

He rubbed a hand over his face. 'Maybe, though I would never have admitted as much back then, not to myself or him. I resented him too much. I blamed him for her death, you see. I was only eleven, but even at that age I knew there had been something strained between my parents. She was so full of love and he… In any case, I knew he hadn't made her happy. I thought that if he'd loved her then maybe she wouldn't have left us, that maybe she would have wanted to stay. I know it sounds ridiculous, but there's a difference between knowing something in your head and in your heart.'

'Did he know that you blamed him?'

He grimaced. 'Subtlety was never my strong suit. Not that we saw each other very often. He just shut himself up in his study and we never spoke of it. We rarely spoke at all, and when we did, we argued. It's strange, but in some ways, I suppose I behaved just like your father.'

Her face froze. 'What do you mean?'

'He blamed you for your mother's death. I blamed my father.'

'You were just a boy.'

'I still took my grief out on someone who didn't deserve it.'

'True, but you loved him. You said so when you gave me my first tour of the house.'

'So I did.' Though the fact that she remembered took him by surprise.

'Then maybe love and hate aren't so far apart after all.' Her brow creased thoughtfully. 'If you could love him despite blaming him, then maybe my father loved me, too. I've always assumed that he didn't, that love and resentment couldn't go hand in hand, but maybe I was wrong. In which case, maybe he really did think he was protecting me from the world.'

'Maybe he was frightened of losing you as well as your mother.'

'So many maybes…' She smiled sadly. 'I never spoke to him about any of them either. Maybe I ought to have tried arguing back once in a while.'

'Maybe I should have tried doing what I was told.'

'*Maybe* again.' She sat up straighter. 'I know that my father resented me, but now I'd prefer to believe that he loved me as well. It would make it all seem less of a waste.'

'Can you forgive him for blaming you?'

'Yes.' She didn't hesitate. 'I think that his heart was genuinely broken by my mother's death. I don't agree with what he did, but I can understand why he did it. Can you forgive your father?'

'What is there to forgive? He didn't love my mother, but he didn't kill her.'

'He could have reached out to you.'

'I don't think he was capable of that. I was the one who caused the rift between us.'

'Is that why you were so wild, to get back at him?'

'That would be the easy answer, though I suppose it was a kind of revenge. The family name meant a lot to my father so I set out to sully it. It was selfish and adolescent of me, but I wanted to embarrass him. I was always the wildest of my friends, the risk-taker. Poor Arthur was left to be the good one, the dutiful son, the one who bore all the pressure while I simply enjoyed myself. It was no wonder he snapped eventually. It took me a long time to understand that my behaviour was hurting more people than just my father. I was hurting everyone around me, but by the time I realised, it was too late. I acted like an immature boy for too long. I only really grew up eight months ago, just when it was too late to put anything right. I failed Arthur when he needed me. Everything that went wrong in my family was my fault.' He met her gaze across the table. 'You're still finding out who you are, Violet, but I already know who I am—a worthless reprobate, just like my father said.'

'No.' Her voice sounded surprisingly firm. 'What happened to your father and brother was tragic, but they were responsible for their own lives. You can't blame yourself for everything that happened.'

He arched an eyebrow. If only it were so easy... If only there were some way to redeem himself... If only that was *all* there was to forgive...

'You have to move on, Lance.'

He smiled at her optimism. 'And how do you propose I do that?'

'I have an idea.' She tucked into the last of her salad. 'Although you might not like it.'

'I'm all ears.'

'We'll throw a ball.'

'A ball?' He felt as shocked as if he'd just been shot again.

'Yes. I've only been to one and it didn't go so well, if you recall?'

'How could I forget?'

'Then let's go back to the start, as if we were meeting all over again.'

Back to the start… A fresh start… The idea was certainly tempting. The thought of the ballroom and all its memories appalled him, but perhaps she was right and it *was* time for them both to move on. *Could* he put the past behind him? He wanted to, and she seemed to want to do it with him, almost as if she wanted a real marriage, too. Having her at his side made it seem easier and at least this meant she wouldn't be leaving again straight away…

'So you're not in a rush to go travelling again?'

'No. I have a few other things I want to do first, like prove to the world I'm not a timid mouse any more.'

He lifted an eyebrow. 'You're not timid at all. In fact, I'm starting to think you might be more than I can handle. Very well, Mrs Amberton, if you want a ball, let's throw a ball.'

Chapter Fifteen

❦

'Is that everyone, do you think?'

Violet peered around the edge of the front door hopefully. She'd been standing in the hallway greeting guests for so long that her feet were aching. So many new faces had paraded past her in the last hour that they'd all started to blur. Some had been vaguely familiar, though Ianthe, Robert and Mr Rowlinson's were the only ones she'd recognised with any certainty. There was no way she was going to remember more than a dozen names.

'I certainly hope so.' Lance leaned against the doorjamb beside her. 'If it's not, then I think we should start refusing entry. Whitby must be deserted this evening. Did *anyone* refuse the invitation?'

'No, though I'm starting to wish a few had.'

'Then I'd say your ball is an unqualified success. Everyone's come to catch a glimpse of the mysterious Violet Amberton, née Harper.'

'I'd say that just as many have come to see the reclusive Captain Amberton.'

'To see if he's mended his wicked ways, do you mean? No, I refuse to believe that I have quite the same appeal. They were all looking at you, not that I can blame them. You look quite exquisite, by the way.'

'I thought I looked enchanting.' She gave him a teasing look. 'That's what you said earlier.'

'Exquisite and enchanting and anything else beginning with *e*. Effervescent?'

'I think I'll stick with enchanting.'

He grinned and she felt the corners of her mouth tug upwards. Over the past month she'd come to realise that there was a vast difference between spiteful mocking and affectionate teasing. Lance was an expert at the latter. He was irrepressible really. She'd laughed more in the past few weeks than she had in the whole of her life before, had lost count of the number of times she'd ended up doubled over at something he'd said, or simply just at the way he'd said it. It was almost impossible to believe that he was the same stern, brooding man that she'd married.

Even if he *hadn't* kissed her again.

That fact was the only thing spoiling her contentment. As much as she tried to convince herself that she didn't care, she couldn't repress a vague feeling of disappointment. She'd come to the conclusion that she must have read more into that first real kiss than was actually there, although she'd caught him looking at her on a number of occasions as if he wanted to do it again. As if he wanted to do more, in fact, though he'd never laid as much as a finger on her.

On the other hand, he definitely liked her appearance that evening. As vain as it sounded, he'd looked almost thunderstruck, though she'd put the effect down to her dress. She'd had it specially made for the occasion, selecting a silvery-blue satin fabric with a pattern of tiny white butterflies embroidered over the skirts. It had felt decadent buying something so gorgeous for herself, but she'd wanted to make a good impression at her second ball.

She'd wanted to match up to her husband, too, though surely that was impossible. He was looking quite breathtakingly handsome in his black formal evening suit, his chestnut hair swept back off his face, with his moustache neatly trimmed for once. She almost wished that he was dishevelled again so that he wouldn't look quite so intimidating. She already felt a strong impulse to run her hands through his hair and ruffle him up.

'I noticed quite a few disappointed bachelors

among our guests, too.' He gave her a faintly accusing look.

'You did not!'

'I assure you, I did. All those potential suitors you always denied having. Some of them were staring quite blatantly.'

'They were probably thinking about how small I was.'

'No.' His tone shifted subtly. 'They were thinking about how beautiful you are, Violet, and how I'm the luckiest man in the whole of Yorkshire, possibly all of England. You're the only one still thinking about your size.'

She blushed at the compliment. Maybe he was right. Maybe she *was* the only one still preoccupied with her tiny size. She *had* detected a few looks of admiration, incredible as that still seemed.

'I suppose I really can't blame them for staring.' His tone became teasing again. 'I'm finding it hard to keep my eyes off you myself.'

'Stop it!' She laughed. 'And don't think I didn't notice how some of the ladies were making eyes at you.'

'Were they? If they were, then I certainly didn't reciprocate.'

She gave a private smile. That was true. Engrossed as she'd been in greeting her guests, she'd still detected a few flirtatious advances towards her husband, all of which had been politely but firmly rebuffed.

'I suppose we ought to go in?' She glanced in the direction of the ballroom nervously.

'Yes, but there's no need to look so terrified. This is *our* ball in *our* house to celebrate *our* wedding. I'm on my best behaviour, you look elegant and enticing and...' he waved a hand in the air '...ethereal. Why don't we just go and enjoy ourselves?'

'You're right.' She took a steadying breath. 'It's just... I want everything to be perfect.'

'Which is why you've spent the last month making it so. You've spent so much time with Mrs Gargrave that I've become quite jealous. Though, of course, she adores you now, just like the rest of my staff.' He heaved an exaggerated sigh. 'I'm really quite aggrieved to have been replaced in her affections.'

She grasped hold of his arm and tugged him unceremoniously in the direction of the ballroom. 'You're incorrigible, but if you're trying to make me relax then it's working. Thank you.'

'Good. Just remember that everyone's come to have a good time. To appease their curiosity about us, too, but mostly to enjoy themselves. Now...' he stopped in the doorway and made an exaggerated bow '...shall we give them something memorable to look at?'

'What do you mean?' She felt a moment of panic. Everyone in the room was turning to look at them, bringing all her anxieties back with a vengeance.

'Will you start the dancing with me, Violet?'

'But…dancing?' She glanced down at his leg. 'Can you?'

'I can shuffle. It might not be the most edifying spectacle, but I should be able to manage a couple of turns around the room at least.'

'Are you sure?'

'I am. I've even been practising, mortifying as it was when Mrs Gargrave walked in on me.'

She had to stifle a laugh. 'You should have asked her to partner you.'

'I thought of it, but the poor woman looked horrified enough.'

'Then you should have asked me.'

'Ah, but I wanted to surprise you. Now, will you do me the honour?'

She nodded and let him lead her into the centre of the floor, vividly aware of the muscles of his arm bunching beneath her fingers as they walked. He must be nervous, too, she realised, although she guessed it was less due to the prospect of dancing than the room itself. She'd found him there that afternoon, sitting on the piano bench, looking around with such a sombre, almost mournful expression that she'd been half tempted to cancel the ball on the spot, but then he'd looked towards her and smiled, and the impulse had passed. This evening was as significant an event for him as it was for her, she'd realised, perhaps even more so since this was his family home, but it was also a necessary one. They were confronting their pasts together— and if her injured husband was brave enough to dance, then she could overcome her self-consciousness, too.

He made a gesture to the orchestra and then swung round to face her, placing one hand on the small of her back as the other clasped her gloved fingers. For a moment, her nerve failed her, as though she were back in this very ballroom five years before, dancing her first and only dance with this same man, feeling small and incredibly foolish. She was briefly tempted to run, but then her eyes met his and her spirits rallied again. He wasn't the same man she'd danced with back then. He'd never been that man. She hadn't known him at all five years ago, but she did now. Over the past month they'd spent living together, she'd come to know the real him—and she loved him.

She *what*?

She'd barely had a chance to acknowledge the thought before the music started and his grip on her hand tightened.

'I requested a waltz…' he leaned forward to whisper in her ear, so close that she could feel the warmth of his breath on her cheek '…but I'll try not to lean on you too much. I've always said you make a handy walking stick.'

'It's all right.' She forced her voice to remain calm despite the trembling sensation in her knees. 'You can lean on me as much as you need.'

'You might regret saying that.'

He grinned and then they were moving, swaying and swirling around the floor, somewhat stiffly perhaps, but still dancing. If he felt any discomfort in his leg, he gave no sign of it, gazing into her face with a smile that held no hint of mockery. She felt suddenly, unexpectedly, acutely happy. She loved him. Of course she did. And she wanted to dance—to truly enjoy a dance for the first time in her life. She was hardly aware of the crowd watching them any more. There was only him, sweeping her around the ballroom in his arms with a hundred candles blazing around them, as if they were the only two people in the world.

'Do you know, ethereal might be the perfect word.' His gaze clung to hers. 'Did I mention how beautiful you look tonight?'

'Once or twice.'

'Well, it bears repeating a third time, possibly a fourth and fifth before the evening's out. Alas, anyone would think I'm hoping for a compliment in return.'

'Oh!' She bit her lip guiltily. She hadn't thought to offer *him* any compliments, but why on earth would a man as handsome as he was need to be told? 'Do you want one?'

'It would be nice to know what my wife thinks of my appearance. Martin's made quite an effort with me.'

She laughed. 'Then tell Martin you look very handsome. You always do. It's quite unfair.'

'Unfair?' He looked puzzled. 'What do you mean?'

'I mean, how can I ever hope to match up?'

His eyes lost their look of merriment. 'You exceed me, Violet, in every possible way. You're beautiful inside and out, didn't anyone ever tell you that?'

She gazed at him speechlessly as the waltz ended and other couples made their way on to the floor. No, no one had ever told her anything so poignant before. Any compliments she'd received had always been perfunctory at best. No one else had ever sounded as if they truly meant them, whereas he—he sounded as if he truly did. He made her *feel* it, his amber eyes glowing with an intensity that made her heart leap into her throat.

'I suppose we ought to see to our guests.' He pressed a kiss to the inside of her wrist and then winced.

'What's the matter? Is it your leg?'

'Just a twinge.' He made an apologetic face. 'I'm afraid I might have been a tad overambitious with a waltz. Forgive me, Violet, but I think I've done enough dancing for tonight.'

'Of course. You should sit down and rest.'

'No, I ought to reintroduce myself to Whitby society. I've put it off long enough.' He escorted her back to the edge of the floor. 'You go and enjoy yourself. It's about time you had some fun, only not too much without me. I'll be watching.'

Violet stared after him as he limped stiffly away. *I'll be watching*…as if he wanted to watch her. Was it possible that he might care for her after all, then? That he might not want to wait seven years? Everything about his behaviour seemed to suggest it…

'Mrs Amberton?'

Her father's old lawyer appeared in front of her and she inclined her head politely.

'Mr Rowlinson, good evening. Are you enjoying the ball?'

'Very much. It's good to see Amberton Castle all lit up again. These balls have been sorely missed over the past few years.'

'We thought it would be a good way to celebrate our wedding since the event itself was so small.'

'Indeed.' The lawyer lowered his voice confidentially. 'And I'm glad to hear that your marriage *is* a cause for celebration. You must know I was most uncomfortable carrying out the terms of your father's will.'

'I do know it, but it's all right. They were my father's wishes, not yours.'

'No, but as events have transpired…' He faltered, as if unsure whether or not to go on.

'What do you mean?' She looked at him enquiringly. 'Is something wrong?'

'Not wrong exactly, only there's something I ought perhaps to tell you.' He threw a swift look over his shoulder, as if to make sure no one could hear them. 'It relates to your father's will.'

'Yes?'

'Well, the fact is that besides your own inheritance, there were a number of other small clauses in the document. Minor ones, mostly relating to the party who was to inherit the estate should your marriage to Captain Amberton not go ahead. Considering the somewhat unusual circumstances, I felt obliged to travel to Cumberland to explain matters to that gentleman in person.'

'And?' She felt a vague prickle of unease.

'He disavowed the will.'

'He what?'

Mr Rowlinson cleared his throat awkwardly. 'It seems that, despite being a second cousin of your father's, the pair of them were never close. In fact, the gentleman said a few choice phrases, quite unsuitable for a lady's ears, that makes that quite an understatement.'

'He didn't want the money?'

'No. He said he was well enough off, had no children of his own and wanted nothing to do with any of it. He also added that the will itself was just what he would have expected from your father. He was, if you'll forgive my saying so, a great deal like him.'

'I see.' She blinked a few times, mind racing. 'But how does this affect me?'

'It doesn't, at least not now. Two months ago, however...'

'It would have made a difference?'

'Yes. I'm afraid it probably means that your marriage was unnecessary after all. Your father had no other close relatives and, without any other claimants to challenge the will, I believe that the money would have reverted to you anyway.'

'So you're saying there was no need for me to marry Lance?'

'I think not.' Mr Rowlinson looked distinctly

uncomfortable. 'Which is why I'm delighted to see you both looking so happy tonight.'

'Yes.' She looked across the room at her husband, the lawyer's words ringing in her ears. Lance was standing in a group of elderly gentlemen, wearing his most courteous, charming expression. There was no need for her to have married him…and yet she was married to him—and she loved him. Mr Rowlinson's news didn't change anything, yet it struck her suddenly that there *was* a way out of the marriage if she still wanted it. Lack of consummation would be grounds for an annulment.

'Theoretically then, if there were a way to dissolve our marriage, would I keep my inheritance?'

Mr Rowlinson looked positively alarmed. 'Yes, I believe so, although a divorce would be very costly. It would cause quite a scandal, too.'

She was seized by the desire to burst out laughing. Clearly the idea of a non-consummation hadn't occurred to him, although given Lance's reputation with women that was easy to understand. She would probably have a hard time convincing a court of her innocence in that regard, too. Funny how different they were now, the man and his reputation. A giggle escaped past her lips.

'Mrs Amberton?'

'Forgive me. It's just, my poor father… His plans could hardly have gone any further awry.'

The lawyer inclined his head. 'No, I do believe that you're right.'

'He would have been appalled. The funny thing is that I'm genuinely happy. Despite all his plans, I'm actually grateful to him for making that will. Isn't it odd?'

'I suppose so.'

He was looking at her as if she'd had too much to drink and she swallowed another giggle. 'Have you told my husband any of this yet?'

'No, I didn't think it was necessary. Unless you think so?'

'Not tonight. I'll tell him later. As you say, it doesn't make any difference now.'

Mr Rowlinson looked relieved. 'There was just one other matter, Mrs Amberton. A few weeks ago, your husband asked me to look into your mother's side of the family. It took me a while to go through your father's papers, but I eventually found an old birth certificate and was able to trace them from there. I'm afraid that your grandparents are already deceased, but your mother also had a sister who's still living. In York, as it happens.'

Violet caught her breath. 'So close?'

'Yes, your mother was from the city originally. I took the liberty of bringing your aunt's address with me tonight.' He reached into his pocket and fished out a piece of card.

'So I have some family…' She gazed at the card with something like wonder, then caught sight of Robert approaching. 'Oh, Mr Felstone, you know Mr Rowlinson, of course?'

'I do.' He made a formal bow to both of them. 'But I've come to request the honour of a dance. My wife tells me that she's in no condition to polka.'

'Then I'd be delighted.' She slipped the card into her reticule and then reached up impulsively to press a kiss to the lawyer's cheek. 'Good evening, Mr Rowlinson, and thank you. You're completely forgiven for everything.'

Lance looked across the ballroom and frowned. His wife was dancing with Robert Felstone. He ought not to be jealous. It was ridiculous to be jealous and not just because Robert was clearly besotted with his own wife, Violet's best friend. Not because Violet was looking so happy in his company either. Not even because, damn it all, he actually liked the man. He was jealous simply because someone else was dancing with his wife while he stood on the sidelines watching. She looked vibrant and glowing and, as he seemed unable to stop repeating, beautiful, like a long-dormant rosebud blossoming in the sunshine. She'd faced up to her fears and triumphed. Beautiful was the only word for her.

He flexed his leg muscles tentatively and grimaced. Damn this injury. If it weren't for his bullet wound, he would happily have danced with Violet all night, never mind the gossip. Damn his injury, damn the man who'd shot him and double damn the woman who'd caused it.

He gave a start of surprise. He'd never allowed himself to feel anger about the events or people connected with his injury before, only guilt and an intense sense of self-loathing. The feeling was strangely liberating, as if he'd taken some kind of step forward. Maybe Violet was right and he *had* finally punished himself enough to move on, to seize a second chance at happiness. Even if he didn't deserve her, could he allow himself to be happy? Could they be happy together?

He wasn't sure when exactly he'd fallen in love, though he suspected it was the moment he'd seen her standing on the station platform a month ago and the feeling had only got stronger every day since. Had it really only been a month? That meant only another six years and ten months before he could actually touch her, before he could…

He stopped the thought before he could finish it. No matter what he wanted, or how badly he wanted it, it wasn't his place to suggest any change to their domestic arrangements. They'd made a bargain—at *his* suggestion. He couldn't renege on it now, not unless she wanted to. Did she? He'd had the distinct impression on a couple of occasions over the past month that she might, but what if he was wrong?

If he was, then that kind of mistake could ruin everything between them. He'd likely scare her away for ever. Never mind the fact that if they were going to have a real marriage then he'd have to tell her the whole truth about himself and his injury—he owed her that much—and there was no way he wanted to do that. Better to be celibate for ever than have her despise him.

'You know, my husband's a good judge of character.'

Ianthe Felstone appeared at his shoulder and he twisted around in surprise. It was the first time she'd spoken to him since the wedding.

'Is that so?'

'Yes, and he likes you. It's not easy to admit when we've been in the wrong, Captain Amberton, but in this case I'm pleased to do so. You make Violet happy.'

He felt a lurch in his chest. 'I hope so.'

'I know so. I was afraid that if she married you, she'd be just as trapped and unhappy as she was before. I expected the worst, but you've brought out the best in her.'

'That wasn't me. I just gave her the freedom to find out who she was.'

'But you set her free. A lot of men wouldn't have. I should have known better than to believe all the gossip about you. I'm sorry.'

She held out a hand and he bowed over it. 'Don't be sorry. You were protecting your friend. She deserves to be happy.'

'And loved.' She gave him a searching look. 'It's funny, but when I came over here you looked very much like a man in love with his wife. I'm lucky enough to know what that looks like. I want Violet to know it, too, but I'm afraid she might not recognise the emotion when she sees it. She hasn't had a great deal of affection in her life. It's entirely possible she might need you to tell her how you feel.'

He opened his mouth to deny it and then reconsidered. 'It's not so easy. We made an agreement.'

'Ah.' Ianthe took a small sip of lemonade. 'You know, my marriage to Robert was complicated, too, at the start. I should have told him how I felt about him a long time before I did, but I had a secret and I didn't want him to find out and regret marrying me. I was afraid.' She gave him a smile that held more than a hint of challenge. 'Of course, that's where you're fortunate, Captain Amberton. The one thing I never took you for was a coward.'

Chapter Sixteen

'That was wonderful.'

Violet spread her arms wide and twirled along the upstairs corridor, humming softly to herself as they made their way slowly to bed.

'I'm glad you enjoyed it.' Lance followed behind, watching in amusement.

'Didn't *you*?'

'Yes, surprisingly enough. It was a triumph, thanks to you.'

'And you.' She tipped her head back and gave him an upside-down smile. 'Both of us.'

'Because I managed not to lose my temper with anyone and spoil the evening like five years ago?'

She clucked her tongue reprovingly. 'You were the perfect gentleman. Never mind all my disappointed suitors, I believe a fair number of ladies were quite devastated to find you off the marriage market as well.'

'I could have been standing in a sea full of women this evening and still noticed only one.'

'Mrs Gargrave?'

'Is it so obvious?'

He chuckled and bent down suddenly, ignoring the pain in his leg as he scooped her up off her feet and into his arms.

'Lance!' She squealed in surprise as he spun her round in a circle. 'Your leg!'

'Has it fallen off?' He adopted a look of mock horror. 'We're in a tricky situation if it has. I may be forced to drop you.'

'Don't be silly.'

'Then let me worry about my leg.'

'All right.' She smiled and rested her head against his shoulder, snuggling into the space beneath his chin. 'Will you tell me what happened to it—your leg, I mean?'

He froze mid-step. 'I told you, I was injured in a duel.'

'You never said what the duel was about.'

'No.' He lowered her gently to her feet again, though he kept his hands clasped tight around her waist. 'Although I *did* say you wouldn't like me very much if I did.'

'It's a risk I'm willing to take.' She looked up at him pleadingly. 'Won't you tell me now, Lance, please?'

He sighed and rested his chin on the top of

her head, gathering her closer towards him. 'I think I'd prefer it if my leg really had fallen off.'

'It might make you feel better to tell someone.'

'I doubt it.'

She pressed her face into his chest, though her muffled voice sounded distinctly guilty. 'I asked Martin when we were in Scotland.'

'And?' He found himself holding his breath.

'He wouldn't tell me.'

'Good.'

'He *did* tell me that you were a good commander, though. He said that your men would have followed you into battle without question.'

'Lucky we were in Canada then. There weren't many battles.'

'*And* that you saved his life. He said he fell down a rock face and you carried him ten miles to safety rather than abandon him in the wilderness.'

'It was easy terrain.'

'He said it was a forest full of wolves and bears.'

'You know he's always exaggerating.'

'Stop joking.' She gave him a small shake. 'You still saved his life. And whatever your duel was about, Martin didn't abandon you afterwards. He must not think what you did was so bad.'

'Only because he thinks he owes me a debt.

He doesn't. He was my batman. It was my duty to get him back to safety.'

'That's not what he says. He says there were half a dozen of you in the scouting party and the rest told you to leave him behind.'

'All that proves is that I'm stubborn. It doesn't make me a hero, Violet.'

She curled her arms around his neck, pulling herself up towards him. 'Then tell me why you're a villain. I won't let go until you do.'

He gritted his teeth. Her face was just a few inches from his. He was half tempted to kiss her just to stop her from talking, except that he had a feeling she wouldn't let the matter drop even then. But perhaps he owed her the whole truth after all.

'All right, but not here. Come inside.'

He drew her arms from around his neck and opened his bedroom door, standing back to let her precede him inside. He couldn't touch her any longer, not until after he'd told her—though he doubted she'd want him to hold her then...

'This isn't easy to do without a drink.' He closed the door behind them with an ominous thud. 'You might need one, too.'

'No, thank you.' She took a seat on the edge of the bed, looking up at him expectantly.

'All right.' He strode across to the fireplace, feeling chilled all of a sudden. 'You might recall that I have—I *had*—a certain reputation. With women, that is.'

'Yes.' He could almost feel her eyes boring into the back of his head.

'It was a fair one. In all honesty, it might have been a lot worse. I've no excuse for my behaviour. It was reprehensible. I'd like to say that being in the army changed me, made me more of a gentleman, but it didn't. I was a good officer, my men liked me, but I still behaved badly.'

He threw a quick look over his shoulder, but her expression was unreadable. 'The major of our unit was about twenty years older than me. He was a good man, someone I liked and respected, but he had a younger wife... Pamela. He adored her, but suffice to say she wasn't quite so enamoured. She was pretty and bored and easily distracted. You can probably guess the rest.'

'I don't want to guess.'

'Very well.' He gripped the edge of the mantel. 'We had an affair. It was only a handful of times, but one evening he found us together in bed. I suppose I ought to be glad he didn't shoot me there and then, but unlike me, he was a man of honour. He challenged me to a duel instead.' He ground his teeth at the memory. 'I slept with his wife and he gave *me* a chance to shoot him.'

He sensed rather than heard her come to stand behind him. 'Only a chance? Didn't you take it?'

'I stood and faced him with a loaded pistol, if that's what you mean, but when I saw the look of pain on his face I realised that it didn't make any difference who shot whom. No matter what happened, I'd already destroyed something inside of him that couldn't be repaired. I'd broken his heart over a woman I didn't even care about. It was the first time in my life I knew what guilt felt like. The first time I realised my actions had real consequences. So I shot into the air and waited. I thought it was the least I could do under the circumstances.'

'Then he shot you?'

'Only in the leg. At ten paces on a perfectly still day with a clear target. He was too good a man to punish me the way I deserved.'

'Did you *want* him to kill you?'

'No. I didn't want to die, even though I thought I probably deserved it. When I woke up in the infirmary, I didn't mind the pain either because I knew I deserved that, too. But after that, everything seemed to unravel. I got the news about Arthur and Father, I was discharged from the army, I had to face everything I'd done, all those mistakes…' He bent his head over his hands. 'So now you know. I'm not a war hero, Violet, not even close.'

'No…' Her voice sounded flat, without any inflection at all. 'You're not.'

They lapsed into silence for a few moments, with only the sound of the fire crackling between them. He couldn't even hear her breathing, but he could still sense her there at his shoulder, as if all his nerve endings were straining towards her.

'So what now?' At last he couldn't bear the tension any longer.

'What do you mean?' Her voice was the same flat monotone as before.

'I mean, how soon will you be leaving now that I've told you the truth?' He gave a bitter smile and then grimaced. 'Forgive me, Violet. I shouldn't have said it like that. You've every right to leave if you want to. I'll even take you to the station if you wish.'

'I don't wish it. I don't want to go anywhere. I'm tired.'

'Tired?' He felt a stab of disappointment. Was that it? Wasn't she going to say anything about what he'd just told her? He'd expected condemnation, disgust, tears even, but not *tired*-ness. He'd have rather she railed at him than said nothing at all, though maybe silence was a more fitting punishment. Maybe there *was* nothing to say. He limped stiffly towards the interconnecting door that led to her bedroom and held it open, but she didn't follow.

'Violet?'

'Will you help me undress?' Slowly she peeled

her gloves off and then turned around, gesturing at the clasps that ran down the back of her gown. 'I told Eliza not to wait up.'

He made a noise intended to be agreement, though it sounded more like a growl as he moved back towards her again, lifting his fingers to the nape of her neck and slowly unfastening each clasp. To his surprise, his hands were shaking slightly.

'There's a bow, too, at my waist.' She half twisted her head. 'Could you untie it?'

He didn't even try to answer this time, half wondering if he'd somehow fallen asleep and was dreaming. Surely only that could explain her asking him to undress her? If it *was* a dream, however, he didn't want to wake up.

He did as she asked, untying the bow and easing the silken fabric away from her skin. Her skirts came loose with a swooshing sound, falling to the floor like a silvery pool around her feet.

'Thank you for telling me the truth.' She turned to face him at last, dressed in only her corset and undergarments. 'I'm glad that you did.'

He kept his eyes fixed on her face, not daring to look any lower. 'You deserve the truth, Violet. No matter what I've done in the past, I intend to act honourably from now on. That means towards you, too. I won't break my promise.'

'You mean seven years…' She put a hand on his chest, spreading her palm flat over his heart. 'What if *I* don't want to wait that long?'

His mind seemed to go blank for a moment. 'What?'

'What if I don't want to go away again either?' Her fingers flexed against his chest as her gaze flickered up to his. 'Unless *you* want me to go?'

'I never wanted you to go the first time.' His voice sounded hoarse, hardly like his own any more. 'But I promised you your freedom.'

'Can't I have freedom and you, too?'

'Violet.' Somehow he managed to keep his hands at his sides. 'Weren't you listening to what I just told you?'

She looked straight into his eyes, her own bigger and bluer and more mesmerising than any he'd ever seen before. 'Yes. You wanted to be punished. That shows you were sorry.'

'That's not the point.' He shook his head obstinately. 'I *still* deserve to be punished, Violet. Not just for that, but for Arthur and my father, too. I'm not worthy of someone like you. I don't deserve to be happy.'

Her eyes flashed with anger before she raised her other hand to his chest and shoved hard. 'Well, I do! And don't you dare call yourself unworthy! You're worth something to me. You gave me back a piece of me that was missing.

You gave me my mother. Even if it doesn't mean much to you, it does to me!'

She started to whirl away, but he reached up and clutched her wrists.

'Wait!'

'No!' She glared at him. 'I won't live with someone who says he can't be happy. I can't bear it again! If you won't let go of the past, then you really *are* like my father!'

'Violet!' He caught at her waist this time, hauling her back towards him so that her chest heaved against his. 'Forgive me.'

'Not if you won't forgive yourself. You're not that man any more! You don't have to let who you were in the past define you now. You don't have to let it destroy our marriage either!'

He leaned forward, lowering his forehead to hers. 'I don't want to destroy our marriage. I want it—I want *you*—more than I've ever wanted anything before.'

'Then you have to let go of the past. Be my husband—my *real* husband.'

She lifted her hands and placed one on either side of his head, slowly drawing his mouth down to hers. He didn't resist, hardly dared to move as her lips touched his with a sweetness that took his breath away. She tasted like lemonade, he thought inconsequentially, before he stopped thinking altogether and let feeling take over. Her hands slid up into his hair and he gathered her into his arms, claiming her mouth again with a need that caught him by surprise. She felt warm and yielding and irresistible. He wanted her. And she wanted him. Despite everything that she knew about him now, she *still* wanted him.

'Violet?' He moaned her name against her lips. 'Are you certain?'

'Yes.' She murmured the word and he didn't hold back any longer, his lips never leaving hers as he half lifted, half staggered with her across the room. She tugged at the arms of his jacket while he pulled at the lacings of her corset, tearing it away before they reached the bed and tumbled down on to it together.

Gently, he slid his hands beneath the rounded curve of her bottom, revelling in the softness of her skin as he pulled the full length of her body against him, tearing at the rest of her undergarments. It would make more sense, a small part of his mind argued, to move away and undress her, but he didn't want to move away. He couldn't bear to be parted from her, not for a moment. He wanted there to be as little space between them as possible. Somehow he freed himself from the remainder of his clothes, too, and then they were naked, side by side, arms and legs entangled as they explored each other's bodies with a hunger that made his whole being ache with need.

He rolled on top of her and she tipped her head back, arching her back beneath him as he drew a hand across her thighs and then between her legs, caressing her gently until she moaned aloud. Then he nudged her legs apart, pushing himself against the apex of her thighs. She felt wet already and he had to stop himself from rushing, from taking her before she was ready. He wanted her to be ready. He wanted her to enjoy the experience, even if waiting felt like an unbearable torture.

Slowly, he trailed his lips over her throat, kissing and sucking and tasting her skin all the way down to her breasts, before gently suckling each nipple. *Almost.* He moaned as she ran her hands over his back, raking her nails over his skin as she squirmed and panted beneath him. *Almost.* She lifted her head to meet his, sliding her tongue inside his mouth, and he couldn't wait any longer. He came inside her with one hard powerful thrust, holding her hips steady as he met some inner resistance and then pushed deeper.

'Violet?' He stilled as she cried out and stiffened beneath him. He'd heard that it was painful the first time, although he'd never slept with a virgin before. And she was so small, so delicate... Had he hurt her? He hardly dared ask.

'Are you all right?'

'Yes.' She sounded breathless.

'Should I stop?'

'No.' She shook her head determinedly and he almost panted with relief. Even now, lying vulnerable and exposed beneath him, there was something indefatigable about her. Something that made him want to push even deeper, to possess every part of her. So he did, burying himself in her body as deeply as he could, as if he could truly lose himself in her.

Then they were moving together. She matched his rhythm at once, wrapping her legs around his as he gripped the bedsheets, trying to hold himself back. Of all the women he'd ever slept with, he couldn't remember any ever affecting him so powerfully, so completely, as if she were trying to drive him to the very limits of self-control. He gritted his teeth as she writhed against him, gasping until her muscles all seemed to tighten at once and she cried out, clutching at him a second before he found his own release. For a few moments, her body continued to tremble and pulsate beneath his and he rolled quickly on to his back, pulling her with him so that she was cradled on top of his chest, her head resting on his shoulder.

He didn't know how long they lay there, nor

how long it took for him to come back to himself, but when he did, it seemed as if some blinders that had been over his eyes had been lifted. The past was the past. He felt genuinely, absurdly happy, and it was all thanks to Violet. The fact that she still wanted him, despite everything he'd done, everything he *had* been, was enough.

She was asleep in his arms and he drew her closer, tucking her into the crook of his arm. She was his wife and he loved her. He should have told her so, he realised, before they'd made love, though perhaps it could wait until the morning. Maybe he'd find a way to make it special somehow. Maybe he'd take her to the centre of the maze and tell her there. Maybe he'd make love to her there again, too. Now he knew that she wanted him too, his mind was suddenly alive to a whole range of possibilities. The very thought made him wish it were morning already.

He'd tell her he loved her, just as soon as they woke up.

Chapter Seventeen

Violet fluttered her lashes until her eyelids finally opened. She felt cold, or more correctly, one side of her body felt cold. The other side was extremely hot, nestled against Lance's shoulder and enveloped in his body heat. Both of his arms were curled loosely around her, but without any blankets her exposed skin was still covered in goosebumps.

Carefully she moved his arm away and sat up, tugging the coverlet gently up the bed, though it was no comfort. She was hungry, too, she realised. No, not just hungry. Their night-time exertions had left her ravenous. She glanced down at her sleeping husband and smiled. Their night together had been more wonderful and surprising and just *more* than she'd ever imagined, as if once he'd decided to stop living in the past, he'd been determined to make up for lost time. It had hurt a little, but not in any way that she'd minded. Now the soreness between her thighs was a reminder of what had just happened between them and she wouldn't take that back even if she could.

She draped her legs over the side of the bed and wriggled into her dressing gown before quietly opening the door and stealing downstairs. Considering the amount of food provided for supper, there had to be *something* left over. Judging by the darkness, it wasn't dawn yet either so she was unlikely to disturb anyone in the kitchens.

She was halfway across the hall when she heard a faint scraping followed by a heavy click, like the sound of a key turning in a lock and a latch being lifted. Sleepily, she looked over her shoulder, sure that she must have misheard, when she saw the front door swing open. She stopped dead in her tracks. The last of their guests had left just after midnight, the servants had all been given the morning off to recover, and it was unlikely that anyone else would be entering the house at this hour. Anyone who *ought* to be there anyway.

She sucked in a breath, too shocked to call out. There was no time to look for a weapon. No time to do anything but hide, she realised desperately, darting behind one of the armchairs beside the still-smouldering fireplace, and then peering out from around the edge.

A black silhouette in the shape of a man wearing a tiered greatcoat stood framed in the doorway, as if he were reluctant to actually cross the threshold. In the darkness it was impossible to make out any features, although something about him seemed strangely familiar. Was he a burglar? Slowly, she reached around the side of the armchair and slid the poker from its place by the fireside, gripping it tightly in one hand. Surely no one with any good intentions would creep into a house in the dead of night?

The stranger stood in the doorway for what seemed like an eternity, staring straight ahead of him as if he were somehow transfixed. Then at last the draught made the fire flicker and he stepped over the threshold, closing the door softly behind him. Violet watched closely, wondering whether or not to scream. But if she did, then Lance would surely coming rushing to find her and the last thing she wanted was for him to trip on the stairs and hurt himself.

Maybe if she made a run for the servants' quarters instead? There was another staircase at the back of the house. If she could reach it and find Martin, then there was no need to frighten Lance. Silently, she raised herself up on her haunches, ready to run. The stranger was coming closer. She had to move before he reached her, had to…

She let out an audible gasp as he moved into the faint puddle of light thrown by the fire. It was Lance! Except that it couldn't be, her confused brain realised. She'd just left him sleeping upstairs. Which meant that there was only one other person it could be, but he was dead… wasn't he? A shiver raced down her spine. Was it a ghost?

Whatever, or whoever, it was made a movement towards her and she leapt up, wielding the poker above her head like a club.

'Don't come any closer! Get back or I'll scream!'

'Wait!' The ghost raised a hand as if to defend himself and then dropped it again, looking almost as surprised as she was. *'Miss Harper?'*

She lowered the poker uncertainly. The ghost knew her name, her old name at least, although he seemed ignorant of her new identity. Somehow that fact made her less afraid of him. Ghosts were supposed to know everything, weren't they? And surely they walked through doors rather than opened them…

'Arthur?' The truth hit her like a thunderbolt.

For a moment he looked as if he were about to deny it, before he sighed and nodded. 'Yes.'

'But how…what…?' She didn't know which

question to ask first. What was he doing there? Where had he been? And, most of all, why was he entering the house in the middle of the night like some kind of criminal?

'I thought you were a ghost!'

He gave a crooked smile. 'I feel a bit like one. It's strange to be back here again.'

'Everyone thinks that you drowned! They found your boat.'

'Yes.'

'There was a search.'

'I thought there might be.'

'Then how… No, *where* have you been?'

He ran a hand over his face. 'You might not believe me if I told you. I can hardly believe it myself.' He pulled the hand away again suddenly. 'But what are *you* doing here, Miss Harper?'

'I live here.'

His face turned even paler than a ghost's. 'You mean that your father bought the house?'

'No.' She blinked. He was talking as if he knew nothing about the events of the past nine months. 'My father's dead. He died three months ago. Your brother inherited the hall.'

'Lance?' One of his hands shot out and clutched her arm. 'He's alive?'

'Of course.' It was her turn to be shocked again. 'Surely you knew that?'

'I heard that he was shot. I thought…'

'He's not dead. He *was* shot, but he survived.'

'Thank you.' He bent his head with a muffled-sounding sob. 'You don't know what it means to me to hear that.'

'I think maybe I do. I've watched him mourn you as well.' Gently she removed his hand from her arm and moved away. 'Wait here while I go and wake him.'

'Wake him?' Arthur regarded her curiously. 'You mean that you and my brother...'

'We were married two months ago.' She couldn't help bursting into a smile at the words.

'But...you and Lance?' He looked incredulous. 'Forgive me, miss, that is, Mrs Amberton, but I'd hoped to find my brother alive. I never expected to find him married as well.'

'It was a surprise for everyone, us included, but between my father's will and your father's hopes for the estate...'

His expression shifted from incredulity to horror. 'You mean that their agreement still stood? I thought that it was only made in relation to me?'

'I believe it was supposed to be just you, but my father's will only mentioned the heir to the Amberton estate and your brother...'

She stopped talking as Arthur began pacing up and down the hallway, dragging his hands through his hair as he went. 'I had no idea. Believe me, I never imagined the two of you would have to go through with the marriage.'

'You weren't to know what would happen.'

'No, but I knew that your father was sick a year ago and unlikely to recover.' He looked shamefaced. 'I confess that was part of the reason I left. But I also knew what he thought of my brother, and even if he hadn't, I would never have expected Lance to go through with it. I thought that with me gone, that would have been an end to the whole business.' He stopped pacing for a moment. 'I've been so selfish. I'm sorry.'

'There's no need. I'm happy.'

'With *Lance*?' He sounded stunned and she laughed.

'Very. So you can stop being sorry for that at least.'

'Violet?'

The sound of Lance's voice calling out from the landing above made them both start in surprise. She looked up to find him already leaning over the banister, candle in hand, though in the near-darkness she supposed it was impossible for him to see who she was speaking to. All he'd be able to tell was that it was a man. Ridiculously enough, she almost felt guilty.

'Lance?' She moved quickly across to the staircase. 'You'd better come down.'

'Who is it?'

'Come and see.' She repressed a smile, part of her tempted to tell him straight away to break the tension, but it wasn't her place to tell.

'Lance?' Arthur moved out of the shadows as he reached the bottom of the stairs. 'It's good to see you again, Little Brother.'

There was a heavy silence as Lance halted abruptly, standing so still that for a few moments it looked as if he'd stopped breathing. Then both brothers moved at the same time, flinging their arms around each other in a fierce, bearlike embrace.

Violet felt a lump in her throat and stepped to one side, unwilling to intrude upon the moment, although it was impossible not to be moved by the poignancy of the scene. Lance's expression held so many emotions she could hardly name them all. Surprise, relief, joy...yes, even joy. Her heart glowed to see it.

'Let me look at you!' Lance stepped back finally, though he kept hold of Arthur's shoulders, clasping tight as if he were afraid to let go. 'You're alive! How is it possible?'

'It's a long story. As I've just been telling your wife.'

They both turned to look at her then and she smiled, sharing their happiness. It was strange, looking at two versions of the same face, and yet despite the obvious physical similarities, the differences between them were more exaggerated now than before. Arthur in particular looked like a whole different man, with cropped hair, tanned skin, and shoulders that seemed to have doubled in size during his absence. He looked as if he'd spent the whole of the past nine months out of doors. A stranger might not even have noticed that he and Lance were twins.

'Come and sit.' She gestured towards the hearth and then reached for the coal scuttle, adding a few nuggets to the fire before stoking it back into life. 'Tell us everything.'

'Yes.' Lance drew his brother towards one of the armchairs and then settled himself in the other, grasping hold of her hand and drawing her on to the chair-arm beside him as he did so. 'What happened to you?'

'I'm not entirely sure. I think I must have run mad for a while.' Arthur's gaze moved between them with open curiosity. 'What must you think of me, Miss Harper? After the way I behaved towards you in the past, you must hate me. I was trying to prove something to my father, but I was unforgivably rude. You were as much a victim as I was, but I treated you atrociously. I'm sorry.'

'You didn't want to marry me.' She said it matter-of-factly.

'No, but believe me, it had nothing to do with you. I never meant to insult you.'

'It's all right. You didn't know me. We didn't know each other. I won't deny that it hurt at the time, but you were unhappy. Anyone with eyes could see that.'

'I suppose I was, though at the time I simply felt trapped.'

'Is that why you ran away?'

'Yes, though I'd no intention of doing so, I swear. I went sailing that day without knowing what I was going to do. All I remember is sitting on the prow, thinking about the future, about the life my father had planned for me, knowing that I didn't have the strength to fight him. The next thing I knew I was in the water, except that it didn't seem like me either. I didn't feel anything, not the cold, not the shock, nothing. It was like I just stopped thinking and jumped.'

'So you weren't trying to drown yourself?' Lance's voice sounded unsteady.

'No.' Arthur shook his head. 'I didn't have a plan. I just knew that I didn't want to think any more. So I swam and swam and kept on swimming. I felt the currents take me and I didn't fight them. It sounds ridiculous now, but I thought I might find an answer if I just kept going. Luckily a fishing boat found me before I froze to death. They were on their way back to Aberdeen and I asked if they would take me with them. I didn't have any money, of course, but the skipper was a kind man. He probably thought I was on the run from the law, but he said I could work off the cost of my passage if I wanted. So I did and I enjoyed it. It made a refreshing change to have a purpose, a task to do. I've always been good on the water and it turns out that I'm good with my hands, too. The crew must have known I was a gentleman, but I proved myself with hard work, and after a while they accepted me. When we got back to Aberdeen I asked if I could stay on board. The skipper offered me a pittance to try to dissuade me, but I accepted.'

'Let me get this straight...' Lance leaned forward slightly. 'Are you saying that all these months, you've been *fishing*?'

'Improbable as it sounds, yes.' Arthur looked towards her ruefully. 'So you see, I'm no ghost, Miss Harper. I've simply been in hiding. Which is another way of saying I've been a coward.'

'You were desperate.' She got up from the chair-arm and crouched beside him. 'There's a difference.'

'Wait.' Lance put up a hand. 'What about Father?'

Arthur's expression became pained. 'I didn't know. It's easy to avoid news when you're at sea and I didn't want to know what was happening. I assumed that things would just work themselves out without me, that you and he would be reconciled...' He dropped his gaze. 'I didn't know about his death. I didn't know anything until we made port at Newcastle yesterday and even then it happened by accident. I was sitting outside a tavern on the quayside when I overheard the landlord telling a story about a family near Whitby. The father had been a viscount, he said, who'd died in the same week one of his sons drowned and the other was shot overseas. He told it like some kind of morality tale, though I've no idea what the moral was. It was the first I'd heard about any of it and it was like my eyes suddenly opened again, as if I'd been asleep and dreaming for the past few months. I asked him what had happened to the other son, but he didn't know, so I came back here as quickly as I could. I know I shouldn't have broken in during the night, but I couldn't wait another moment. It was bad enough hearing what happened to Father. I've been so afraid of learning the worst about you, too.'

'Come.' Violet stood up, trying to break the sombre mood. 'You must be exhausted if you've been travelling since yesterday. I'll get a room ready. Are you hungry?'

'Wait!' Arthur put out a hand to stop her. 'No one else should know that I'm here. Now especially.'

'Don't be ridiculous.' Lance started out of his

chair. 'We ought to wake up the whole house and celebrate.'

'No.' Arthur's voice had an imperative tone she'd never heard there before. 'As far as everyone else is concerned, I drowned that day.'

'What? No, Arthur, you're back.'

'It's too late. If I come back, then there'll be repercussions for all of us. What's done is done. We ought to just leave things as they are.'

'But this is all yours. The house and estate are your birthright. You're the—' Lance stopped mid-sentence, his eyes turning towards her with a look of anguish.

'What?' Violet felt a tendril of foreboding tickle the back of her neck. 'He's the what?'

'The heir.' Her husband's lips seemed to have turned white suddenly. 'Arthur's the heir.'

For a few moments, Lance felt as though time had stopped and all three of them were held suspended, unsure of what to do next, the implications of his words echoing loudly in the air between them. There were so many emotions coursing through him that he wasn't sure which was dominant, only he was aware of a strong undercurrent of panic.

Arthur was the heir. Arthur was alive. Which had been astonishing and incredible and wonderful all at the same time, yet the panic was still threatening to overwhelm him. The realisation brought with it a stab of guilt. How could he feel panic now of all times? The brother he loved, that he'd thought he'd lost, was alive. That was a cause for celebration, not panic. He ought to be jumping with joy, but instead all he could think of was Violet.

She'd been supposed to marry the heir. That was what his father had wanted, what her father's will itself had stated. Now that Arthur had returned, all of it would be called back into question. There would be lawyers and courts and precedents and rival claimants all clamouring over her inheritance. Would she lose the money after all? Did he care? The thought brought him up short. No, he didn't give a damn about the money. He wanted it for the estate, that much was still true, but if it came to a choice between Violet and her inheritance then there was no choice. He wanted her.

But what could he offer her in return? On his own he was just a disgraced former soldier. If he hadn't deserved her before, then he certainly didn't deserve her now. She deserved to keep her fortune and her freedom, too, to be mistress of Amberton Castle, but with a better man at her side—Arthur.

He felt an ache in his chest as if his heart were really breaking in two. Maybe this was his real test, the way for him finally to make amends. This was the pain he deserved. After last night, however, he had a feeling she wouldn't just accept that, not unless he made her—unless he pushed her away. If he could bring himself to do it.

'You can't just leave again, Arthur.' He forced himself to speak calmly.

'I can now that I know you're all right.'

'So that you can pretend to be dead again? I won't take your inheritance.'

'You're not taking, I'm giving it to you. If I stay away for seven years, then it'll be yours anyway. I don't have to be gone for ever.'

'No.' He held Arthur's gaze, his own intractable. 'I'll go to the authorities and tell them you're still alive if you try to leave again. Father wanted you to run the estate. He wanted you to be his heir.'

'Why do you think I ran away?'

'He wanted you to marry Violet, too.'

'It's too late for...'

'No, it's not.'

'What?'

It was Violet who spoke this time and he turned reluctantly to face her.

'We can get a divorce.'

'On what grounds?' She looked as though he'd

just threatened to push her down the stairs and his heart twisted.

'Deceit. You can say that you were misled, that you were tricked into marrying me when the rightful heir was still alive.'

'I'll say no such thing!'

'You have to. Otherwise, your inheritance might be forfeit.'

He heard her draw a sharp intake of breath. 'My inheritance?'

'Yes.' The look of hurt and betrayal on her face made him feel sick, but he kept going. 'You married the wrong man. I'm not the heir.'

Her eyelids flickered. 'So you want me to put you aside and then…what?'

He clenched his jaw, forcing himself to utter the worst. 'Then the two of you can marry. It's what both our fathers wanted, what ought to have happened in the first place. It might be the only way to secure the money.'

There was a heavy silence before she spoke again, her voice sounding almost unnaturally, eerily calm.

'In that case, I'll return to Whitby in the morning.'

'What?' Arthur's face was aghast. 'Have the pair of you gone mad? This is ridiculous.'

'It's the best thing for everyone. I don't want to be the heir, Arthur.' He limped slowly towards the drawing room, pausing briefly in the doorway before slamming the door shut behind him. 'I never wanted it and especially not like this!'

Chapter Eighteen

'How about some shortbread, dear?' Ianthe's aunt held out a plate of biscuits with a sympathetic smile. 'Things always seem better after a little sugar, I find.'

'No, thank you, Sophoria. I'm not hungry.'

Violet felt as though she were in some kind of trance. In all honesty, she probably was hungry. She hadn't eaten anything since supper at the ball and it was almost mid-morning. If she was, however, she didn't feel it. She wasn't sure she could *feel* anything any more. Her whole body seemed to be numb.

'As you wish.' Sophoria sighed and took a seat next to her on the sofa. 'But are you quite certain that everything's over between you and your husband, dear?'

'Of course she is!' Ianthe stopped pacing the length of the parlour long enough to answer for her. 'She's left him, hasn't she?'

'Yes, but she wouldn't be the first woman to run away from her husband and then regret it, would she, dear?'

'Aunt!'

Sophoria shrugged placidly. 'It wasn't a criticism. All I'm saying is that women leave their husbands for all sorts of reasons. Some are quite right to do so and some do it because of a misunderstanding.'

'If you're referring to what happened between Robert and me, then this is a completely different situation and you know it.'

'Do I, dear? It seems to me that every situation is different. We should never presume to know what goes on between a married couple.'

'Maybe not, but I know that Violet's left hers for a good reason. He was a reprobate from the start. I can't believe I was actually starting to like him.'

'I've always been rather partial to a reprobate myself. They make life interesting.'

'Be serious, Aunt.'

'I am. Everyone's tastes are different and I'm afraid you may be letting your prejudices colour your judgement a little.'

'What prejudices?'

'Against, shall we say, a certain type of man. Lance Amberton may have been a reprobate in the past, but from what I've heard he was simply young and foolish. Hardly on a level with Charles Lester.'

Ianthe's hands fell to her hips. 'How can you even mention that man's name?'

'Because I'm afraid you may be confusing one with the other.'

'Lance Amberton's reputation is appalling!'

'*Was* appalling, dear. People can change.'

Violet twisted her head towards the parlour window, looking out over the promenade and past the edge of the cliff to the foam-flecked sea beyond. *Had* Lance really changed? She'd thought that he had. The night before she would have answered that question with certainty, whereas now...

Now she knew that Ianthe was right. He was as much of a reprobate as he'd ever been, only she'd deluded herself into thinking the opposite, into thinking he might truly care for her—into believing that someone she loved might actually love her back. But all he wanted—all he'd *ever* wanted—was her father's fortune to save his family estate. He hadn't lied to her—not exactly. He hadn't needed to when she'd done such a good job of deceiving herself—but she'd only ever been a means to an end. He might have taken her to bed, too, but only after she'd as good as thrown herself at him. After *she'd* actually released him from his seven-year promise! No matter how wonderful it had felt at the time, it hadn't meant anything to him, not really, and she'd been the worst kind of fool, letting her heart be broken by a fortune hunter, just as her father had said it would be.

At least she hadn't told him she loved him.

She closed her eyes, trying to bury the pain, still as fresh as when he'd told her they ought to get a divorce. She could hardly believe that happiness could turn so quickly to despair. Everything that had happened since she'd woken up in his arms in the early hours felt like a bad dream. The remainder of the night and the morning too, although since she hadn't gone back to bed, the two had merged into one. All she'd wanted to do was get away from Amberton Castle as quickly and quietly as possible, preferably without running into Lance again.

So she'd dressed and packed and then sat by her chamber window, watching the lightening sky and waiting until she heard sounds of activity downstairs before picking up her carpet bag and making her way down to the hall, calmly demanding that one of the stable hands take her back to Whitby.

On arrival, she'd gone straight to Ianthe's house, interrupting her and Robert at breakfast. They'd sat and listened in stunned silence as she'd told them about Arthur's return, calmly concluding with the fact that her marriage was over. Only the arrival of Sophoria on her weekly shopping trip had jolted them back to reality. Robert had tactfully excused himself while Ianthe and her aunt had set themselves the task of comforting her. She appreciated the effort, even if she knew it was hopeless—although at the moment they only seemed to be arguing.

'People don't change that much, Aunt.' Ianthe's hands were still braced on her hips.

'I disagree. You should never expect anyone to change, but that doesn't mean that they won't sometimes do it by themselves. You said that Robert likes him.'

'What does it matter who likes him?' Violet interrupted finally. 'He wants a divorce so that I can marry his brother. That's all there is to say.'

'Oh, dear, I'd forgotten that part.' Sophoria patted her hand kindly. 'What did he say exactly?'

'Just that it would be best for everyone if we got a divorce and I married Arthur instead.'

'What did he mean, *best*?'

'I don't know. He just said that his brother was the rightful heir and that we all ought to do what our fathers wanted in the first place. He's worried about losing my inheritance and thinks that my marrying Arthur is the safest way to protect it.'

'But Mr Rowlinson told you the money was safe.'

'Yes, but Lance doesn't know that, not yet.' Fortunately, she added silently, or she might never have known the truth about him...

'And what did Arthur have to say about the idea of you marrying him?'

'He said that Lance must be mad.'

'Yes...' Sophoria tapped her chin thoughtfully '... I have to agree it does sound that way, but then, it was the middle of the night and he'd had a shock. His brother's sudden reappearance must have been extremely disorientating.'

'He was happy to see him.'

'Yes, but it must have thrown his own position into some confusion. People say strange things under those sorts of circumstances.'

'What are you talking about, Aunt?' Ianthe came to a standstill in front of them.

'It just seems a rather extreme reaction to me. Not to mention an ill-thought-out one. I doubt Violet would be legally permitted to marry Arthur when she's already been married to his brother. Even with a divorce, it might not be allowed.'

'What does it matter?' Violet pressed her fingertips to her forehead. 'I've no intention of marrying Arthur and he doesn't care for me either. He doesn't even want his inheritance. He wanted to leave again without anyone else ever knowing he was alive, but Lance said he'd go to the authorities if he tried to run away.'

'But that sounds rather honourable to me, dear.' Sophoria folded her hands decisively in her lap. 'However, all in all, I'm afraid I have to agree with Mr Arthur Amberton and say that your husband has taken leave of his senses.'

'That's not helpful.' Ianthe gave her aunt a pointed look.

'I'm sure it was only temporary. When he comes back to his senses…'

'No!' Violet clasped her hands together fiercely. 'It doesn't matter why he said it! He still said it. He wants a divorce and now so do I. I should never have married him in the first place.'

'Then why did you, dear?'

'Because we had an agreement, or at least we did until I broke it. Now it's all ruined.'

'You know you can stay here for as long as you want.' Ianthe put a comforting hand on her shoulder.

'Thank you, but there'll be a terrible scandal. I can't stay. I need to go somewhere new and start again, maybe set up my own establishment.'

'Where?'

Violet looked back out of the window at the sea. Where *would* she go? Perhaps she should take a leaf out of Arthur Amberton's book and board a ship for some foreign clime, but even as she thought it, the answer became obvious. There was only one place she really wanted to go, the only other place where she might be welcome.

'York. I'll go and find my family.'

'Ow!' Lance growled as someone wrenched back the drawing-room curtains and a shaft of piercing yellow sunlight fell across his chair, startling him back to consciousness.

'Good morning to you, too, Little Brother.' Arthur loomed over him, wearing a distinctly unsympathetic expression. 'Ready to talk yet?'

'Shut the curtains!' Lance glared ferociously. The pain in his head made every movement an effort, but the bright light was even worse. He felt as if there were a myriad tiny swords stabbing into his skull.

'Not until you tell me what the hell you think you're playing at.'

'I'm trying to sleep and I don't want to talk.'

'That's what you said last night—or this morning, I suppose. You told me to mind my own business, or words to that effect anyway.'

'The statement stands.'

Arthur folded his arms. 'Do I have to pummel the truth out of you like when we were boys?'

'I always beat you at fighting.'

'Most of the time, yes, but right now I'd say I have the advantage. What on earth have you done to yourself? You look green.'

'I feel it.' The pain in his head felt like ten ordinary hangovers put together. He hadn't even drunk *that* much. 'I must be getting old.'

'Most people get older and wiser. Apparently you're the exception.'

Lance peered through his fingers at his brother and scowled. 'Is this why you came back to Yorkshire, to insult me?'

'No. I came back to find out if you were still alive, although from the look of things I should have stayed away.'

'Don't say that.' He felt a pang of regret for his bad temper. 'You don't know how wonderful it is to see you again.'

'Which is why you've drunk yourself into a stupor, I suppose?'

'That's not the reason.'

'Then tell me what is. I presume her name starts with a *V.*'

'I'm trying to do the right thing, if you must know. It's just not easy.'

Arthur unfolded his arms and took a seat opposite. 'So explain to me how telling your wife to get a divorce so that I can marry her and have all her money is the right thing? For one thing, it sounds rather sordid. For another, I doubt it would be allowed. In the eyes of the law, she's my sister now.'

'We should still try.'

'Why?'

'Because I have to give it all up, Arthur. I don't deserve any of it, Violet especially. I need to put things right, the way they ought to have been, the way Father wanted them.'

'That's another thing.' Arthur sounded exasperated. 'Since when did you care so much about what Father wanted?'

'I do now.'

'Why?'

'I just do!' Lance tried to jump to his feet and then dropped back again as pain seared through his leg and shot up his spine.

'I'm not leaving until you tell me, Little Brother.'

He leaned forward, hanging his head. 'Because Father was right about *me*. He said I was a reprobate and he was right. I've spent my life being selfish and reckless and thoughtless. I've hurt people. If Violet stays with me, I'll probably hurt her, too. I can't take that risk.'

'You're too hard on yourself, Lance.'

'No, I haven't been hard enough. That's why I have to do this now. I married Violet because she was part of Father's plan for this place, but she was supposed to marry you. Everything I have now was supposed to be yours. Now that you're back it should be yours again. You can run the estate and be a better husband than I can. If Father was right about me, then he was right about that, too.'

'He wasn't right about you. I know you better than anyone, Lance. I know why you behaved the way you did.'

'Don't make excuses for me. I was a bad son from the start.'

'Not from the start. Only since Mother died. You were grieving.'

'It still doesn't excuse anything. I missed her so much, but her death wasn't Father's fault. I knew that deep down, but I still blamed him. It was unfair of me.'

'Maybe he deserved to be blamed. Not for that, but for the way he treated us afterwards. He shut himself away in his room and barely spoke to us, not for days or weeks, but for years. He was grieving, too, in his own way, but he never helped us come to terms with her loss. If you were a bad son, then he was a bad father as well.'

'I still should have reached out to him.'

'You did. Every time you argued with him, you were reaching out. So was he every time he argued back. Only the pair of you were too stubborn to admit what you were doing. I should have banged your heads together a long time ago.'

'I thought you said you didn't come here to insult me?'

'I'd rather insult you than watch you wallow in self-pity.'

'Then what about what I did to you? I failed you, too, Arthur. I should have come back when you asked me to.'

'How could you? You were halfway across the world and a captain in the army. I wanted you to come home, I admit that, but it wasn't your job to save me. I shouldn't have asked. I should have stood up for myself instead of running away, but I knew Father would never budge.'

'I still should have tried to do something. Then you wouldn't have run away and he wouldn't have collapsed.'

'Or maybe he would have anyway. But what happened to him is on my conscience, not yours. It was because of the shock that *I* gave him. I won't let you take the blame for it.'

'I never even tried to be a good son.'

'Well, I did and look where it got me.'

'Did he ever speak of me after I went to Canada?' Lance looked up hopefully.

'Just once.' Arthur heaved a sigh. 'After you left, he shut himself away even more. So did I, mainly to avoid his ranting, but I found him one evening, in that very chair as it happens. He was holding two miniature portraits, the ones Mother commissioned of us when we were boys. He wasn't angry, he was just sorry—for all of it— and we talked. He'd been drinking, of course, but we really talked, about Mother, and you and me, and the future. It was incredible. For those few hours I thought that everything was going to be all right.'

'Then what happened?'

'The next morning he'd forgotten about it. Either that or he pretended to. When I mentioned it at breakfast he looked at me as if I'd gone mad. So I went sailing.'

'I'm sorry, Arthur.'

'So am I. You know, despite everything, I think he really did love us and Mother as much as he was able.'

'You think that he loved us?' Lance felt a tightness in his throat.

'Yes. He could just never show it. He never disinherited you, did he? But he could never back down either. And once he got an idea in his head...'

'Are you making a point?'

'I'm trying to. And I'm not going to marry the woman you love.'

'Why not?' Lance bristled indignantly. 'She's worth a thousand of Lydia Webster.'

'I know that.' Arthur's voice sounded pained. 'I knew that before I ran away.'

'You did? How?'

'It doesn't matter. Suffice to say I found the truth out the hard way, but it's all right. I barely think of her now.'

'I'm still sorry I told you the way I did. I should have been subtler.'

'That was never your style, Little Brother.'

'At least it means you're free to marry Violet.'

'Oh, stop being so pig-headed.' Arthur stretched out a foot to kick his good leg. 'She's your wife!'

'Barely.'

'Meaning what?'

'Meaning we only went to bed once.' Lance cleared his throat self-consciously. 'Last night, in fact.'

Arthur's eyebrows arched upwards. 'She said you've been married for two months.'

'We have.'

'But you only just took her to bed?'

'Yes.'

'Don't you find her attractive?'

'Of course I do! But she's not like all the others. She's different. And I made her a promise. I wasn't going to touch her for seven years, only... things changed. I changed. Last night, I told her everything about my past. I told her the worst things about myself and she didn't hate me. She said she didn't want to wait seven years and neither did I. For the first time since I was shot, I thought that maybe I could move on from the past and be happy again.'

'And were you? Happy, that is, before I arrived?'

'Yes, but that doesn't mean I'm not happy to see you, too.'

'I know that, but let me get this clear. You were happy. She was happy. You slept together. But now you want her to get a divorce and marry me?'

'It's not about what I *want*.'

'Just stop and think for a moment, Lance. Father wasn't right about you and fulfilling his wishes now won't fix the past. It'll only ruin the future and make all three of us unhappy.'

'She deserves somebody better.'

'She deserves somebody who loves her—and don't pretend that you don't. I said so before and you didn't deny it.'

Lance drew in a long breath and then released it through his teeth. 'What if I *do* love her? I just as good as told her I didn't. I made her think it was all about the money.'

'Which is why you need to go upstairs and tell her how you really feel. Right now, before she goes back to Whitby and starts divorce proceedings. Don't make the same mistake Father did, keeping your feelings to yourself. You won't help anyone by turning into him. Tell her how you feel and get on with your life. Do it for me, if you won't for yourself.'

'What do you mean?'

'I mean that I enjoyed my life at sea. It's what I want, or something like it anyway. I've no intention of staying here, birthright or not, and I'm certainly not going to be bullied into marrying anyone. I might not have stood up to Father, but I *can* stand up to you.'

Lance climbed to his feet, facing his brother head-on. Arthur looked different, he realised— bigger, stronger and more resolute. For the first time in their lives, he made him feel like the younger brother.

'I still won't take your inheritance. The house is yours.'

'Then look after it for me.'

'Arthur…'

'No. You didn't do the last thing I asked of you. If you truly want to make amends, then you can do this instead. Look after the house and estate for me. Call yourself a steward if you like, but for pity's sake, go and apologise to your wife.'

The sound of a gasp, followed by a distinctly unladylike exclamation of astonishment, made them both turn around. Mrs Gargrave was standing in the drawing-room doorway, looking between them with an expression of abject horror.

'I'm not a ghost!' Arthur raised his hands quickly.

'You're alive?'

'Indeed I am, Mrs Gargrave. It's good to see you again.'

'Yes…' The housekeeper raised a hand to her head as if she were struggling to remember something important. 'I…came to tell you… about Mrs Amberton…'

'What about her?' Lance's heart gave a painful lurch.

'One of the grooms just came back from Whitby… She asked to be taken there first thing.'

'She's *gone*?'

'Yes.' Mrs Gargrave's eyes settled on Arthur again before her whole body started to teeter unsteadily and then tumble to one side. Both brothers sprang forward, catching her a moment before she hit the floor.

'I seem to be having a bad effect on women today.' Arthur made a face. 'They either run away or faint.'

'Can you deal with this?' Lance gave him a questioning look.

'Of course.' Arthur grabbed hold of his shoulder and then pushed him away. 'Go and find your wife. Tell her you're sorry and that you love her. Tell her to come home. Just don't come back without her.'

Chapter Nineteen

'What do you mean, she's already gone?'

Lance felt as though Ianthe Felstone had just punched him hard in the stomach. Not that he would have been entirely surprised if she had. She looked very much as if she wanted to. She'd looked as if she hadn't wanted to admit him to her house either, only Robert had intervened, letting him in when he'd turned up unannounced, hungover and distinctly the worse for wear on their doorstep. After Mrs Gargrave had fainted, he'd pulled on the first clothes he could find and charged straight out of the house, riding full tilt to Whitby without even waiting for Martin.

'I mean that she's already gone.' Ianthe jutted her chin out angrily. 'She left an hour ago.'

'Where did she go?'

'What does it matter if you want a divorce?'

'I *want* to talk to her.'

'Well, she doesn't want to talk to you, not any more. She doesn't want to be anywhere near you.'

'Mrs Felstone.' Lance ran a hand through his hair, wishing he'd made slightly more effort to look respectable. 'It was a mistake to mention a divorce. In my defence, I was in shock at my brother's return, but I was still a fool and I know it. I also know that I'm one of the most worthless rogues Whitby's ever produced, but I love Violet. I don't want a divorce. If you tell me where she is, I promise I'll never hurt her again.'

'Ianthe.' Robert put a hand on his wife's shoulder and her expression wavered.

'All right, but this is your absolute last chance. If you do anything to upset her again—'

'Then you can push me off Whitby pier yourself. I'll even jump if you tell me to. Now, please, tell me where she is.'

'She's gone to York.'

'York? On her own?'

'Yes, Mr Rowlinson found out where her aunt lives and, no, my Aunt Sophoria went with her.'

'Do you have the address?'

Ianthe sighed and walked across to a bureau, coming back with a slip of paper. 'Here.'

'What train did she catch?'

'The ten o'clock.' Robert spoke this time. 'There's another soon if you hurry.'

'I'll run if I have to.' He was already limping towards the door. 'Thank you.'

The journey inland felt interminable and not just because every burst of the whistle made his head feel as though there were a swarm of bees living inside it. Lance stared out of the window, willing the miles away as the train steamed through the moors, stopping at what seemed to be every station in existence, before entering the flatter expanse of the Vale of York and finally rolling into the city itself. He jumped down from the carriage before the locomotive had even come to a halt, earning himself a remonstrative whistle from the guard, as well as a warning twinge in his leg. He ignored both. All he wanted was to find Violet and make things right again.

If he could make things right again. His stomach clenched at the *if.* He didn't want to think about that.

'Captain Amberton?'

A small figure blocked his way as he reached the end of the platform, bringing him to a surprised halt as he looked down into the bright, sparkling eyes of a white-haired woman swathed almost entirely in pink lace, wearing what appeared to be an Elizabethan-style ruff around her neck.

'Ma'am?' He tipped his hat enquiringly.

'Oh, it is you.' The vision in pink beamed. 'I only saw you once before in person, but some faces are memorable. I'm Sophoria Gibbs.'

'Ianthe's aunt?' He lifted an eyebrow dubiously. It was hard to imagine a greater contrast to the niece.

'The very same and delighted to meet you, although I suppose you're far more interested in seeing your wife. Come along, then.'

She didn't wait for him to offer his arm, tucking her hand into his elbow and leading him determinedly towards the station exit.

'I don't understand.' Lance peered down at her. 'Were you waiting for me?'

'Oh, yes, dear. I found out when the next train was due and came back to find you. I told Violet I was going to the tearoom, but it was only a tiny white lie since I did have a cup of tea while I waited. Of course, she has no idea that you're coming, but then, she thinks you don't want her.' She reached over and patted his arm as if they were old friends. 'But I knew otherwise.'

'You did?'

'Of course!' The old woman nodded vigorously. 'I'm starting to think I'm far more romantic than any of you young people.'

'But where is she?'

'Up there.' She stopped just outside the station, gesturing up at the tall, grey line of the city walls. 'She didn't feel quite ready to visit her aunt yet so we had some lunch, or at least I did, and then took a walk. I think she's feeling a little lost, dear. Why don't you go up there and find her?'

'Thank you.' He scooped her hand up and kissed the back of it. 'Sophoria. That's a beautiful name. May I call you it?'

'I absolutely insist upon it, dear.'

'Then if I can persuade my wife to come back with me, I promise to name our first daughter after you.'

'Well, in that case you *must* succeed. Now, there's a staircase over there. Do you think you can manage it?'

'Nothing's going to stop me.'

'That's the spirit, dear.' The small face nodded approvingly. 'I should think so, too.'

Violet leaned against one of the stone embrasures of the medieval town wall, looking out over the slated rooftops of the city to the horizon beyond. It was all so horribly ironic. She'd wanted to visit York for almost as long as she could remember, ever since she'd flicked through the pages of her mother's old picture book, and yet now she was here, all she could do was look back the way that she'd come, towards the moors, towards Amberton Castle and Lance.

She had her aunt's address in her bag, but she seemed unable to advance another step in the direction of her house, as if doing so would be a final admission that her marriage was over and she was moving on. Would Lance know that she'd left by now? Would he be relieved or would he only care about the money? Either way, it didn't matter. She'd made the decision to leave and she wouldn't go back, not to a husband who didn't love her.

'Violet?'

She tensed at the sound of his voice, though she didn't turn around. For a moment she thought she was imagining things, yet deep down she knew that she wasn't. She could sense him behind her, could tell by the way that her heart leapt first and then started to thud erratically against her ribcage. She took a few deep breaths, trying to calm down, at least enough to hear herself think over the sound of her body's increasingly frantic reaction. He'd come after her! And yet she already knew that he wasn't there for *her*. Just like the first time she'd run away, he'd only come after her for the money. He'd made his feelings about that perfectly clear that morning. He was probably only there to persuade her to come back and marry his brother—to tell her that it was for the *best*.

She ran her hands over the wall, smoothing

her fingers over the cold, hard stone. The city walls had stood for over seven hundred years and the Roman walls beneath were even older. For a fleeting moment, she wished she could turn to stone herself. A statue couldn't hear, couldn't feel, couldn't be hurt. She kept her face fixed straight ahead. Statues couldn't see either, and if she turned to look at him, she was afraid she might be hurt even more.

'How did you find me?' She was surprised at how expressionless her voice sounded.

'Your friend Ianthe decided to give me a last chance and her aunt claims to have been expecting me. She was in the station, waiting.'

'She's a romantic. What are you really doing here, Lance?'

'I was worried about you.'

She gave a cynical half-smile. 'My father always said he was worried about me. That's why he kept me shut up from the world. Maybe he was right about me getting hurt, but I still wanted my freedom. I wanted it from him and now I want it from you, too. If you've only come because you're worried, then you can turn around and leave. I can take care of myself.'

'I know.' His shadow fell over hers. 'I also know that you're perfectly capable of standing on your own two feet, of doing everything your father never let you, but the problem is, I'm not. I'm not capable of standing on my own any more. I'm a mess on my own. I was a mess before I married you, and I'm a mess again now. I can't be without you, Violet.'

'You said you wanted a divorce.'

'I say a lot of stupid things. When I saw Arthur, I panicked. I was so happy to see him again, but when I thought about what it might mean for us…'

'For my inheritance?'

'Hang your inheritance! I don't give a damn about the money! I've been a fool. I thought I was doing the right thing by letting you go, but I've never been good at doing the right thing and I can't start now, not if it means losing you. But you were right last night, I'm not the man I was. You've changed me. You've *made* me a better man and I'll spend the rest of my life being good and honourable and everything else I ought to be, if you'll only forgive me. I didn't mean what I said, Violet.'

Her heart lifted. He hadn't meant it, he didn't want a divorce, yet the memory of the words still hurt. She braced a hand against the wall, holding herself steady.

'You know, when my father died, I felt like I'd finally been let out of prison. I didn't want any man to control me ever again. I wanted to find out who I was instead. I married you because you offered me the freedom to find out, but somehow I gave you control anyway. I gave you the power to hurt me because I was happy with you. I didn't want to go travelling again because I started to feel like I had a home, a real home of my own at last. I didn't feel small and powerless and trapped any more. Even though our marriage was all based on the money, it felt like it was becoming more than that. Last night felt like more than that.'

'It *was* more than that. Yes, I married you for the money, but it was the best mistake I ever made, the right decision for all the wrong reasons. And if we lose it all now, I don't care. The estate won't collapse, nor will the mine. It'll take us longer to make a profit, but we'll succeed eventually. As for the house, it's supposed to look like a castle. A few more crumbling walls won't hurt.' He rested his hand on the stone next to hers. 'I know you like them this way.'

She moved her fingers slightly towards his. 'You remember that?'

'You were coming here the first time you ran away from me—how could I forget that? You said your mother had a picture book of York.'

'Now I know why. She was born here.'

'Ianthe said you were coming to find your aunt.'

'Yes.' She reached her little finger out and

brushed it gently against his hand. 'I was planning to go straight to her house, but... I can't seem to move.'

'Why?' His voice sounded faintly husky.

'Because I feel trapped again. When you said we should get a divorce it made everything I'd felt seem like a lie, as if the person I'd become was a lie, too.' She turned around at last, pressing her back against the wall to look at him. 'I don't want it all to have been a lie.'

'None of it was a lie, Violet, I swear it. *You're* not a lie. You're the woman I love.'

'You love me?' She felt breathless suddenly.

'Yes. I should have told you last night. I love you so much that I'll walk the whole length of these walls on my bad leg if it'll prove it to you.'

'It's two miles.'

'Then it might take me a day or two.' He took a step closer towards her. 'I don't expect you to say you love me back. Just come home with me, Violet. Please.'

'No.' She shook her head and his face fell. 'I need to find my aunt, to find out why she kept away all these years.'

'If that's what you want.' His voice sounded strained. 'I want you to be happy, Violet.'

'Thank you.' She hesitated for another moment and then reached out, clasping his hands in the way he'd held hers on the promenade just before their wedding. 'But after that, I'd like you to take me home.'

'You do?'

'Yes.' Her heart clenched at the hopeful look on his face. 'On condition that you never try to do the right thing ever again, not without checking with me first. You're not very good at it.'

'I know.' Amber eyes lit up with laughter.

'As for my inheritance...'

His expression turned fierce again. 'I told you, I don't care about the blasted money! Your father's cousin's neighbour's cat is welcome to it, for all I care!'

'No, they're not. The other claimant rejected the will. The money's already mine—*ours*. If we *were* to get a divorce, it would probably be all yours.'

'I would never...'

'Then you're stuck with me.' She smiled, releasing his hands to fling her arms around him. 'Or you'll have to think of a good reason to divorce me because I won't do it. I love you, too, Captain Lancelot Amberton, and I don't want a divorce, not ever!'

Epilogue

'It's a beautiful morning. Come and see.' Violet opened their bedroom window and gazed out at the moors.

'I like the view from here.' Lance threw an arm behind his head and lounged back against the bedhead. 'Though I'd prefer it without the dressing gown. Why do you ever bother putting that thing on when you know I'm only going to take it off you again?'

'Because I don't want to horrify the gardeners if they look up.' She turned and gazed around their new chamber with satisfaction. 'I like this new room. I like this wing of the house, too. It really is a fresh start. I wonder why we never thought to simply choose a bedroom of our own together before.'

'Mrs Gargrave's indomitable will.'

'She calmed quite considerably when I told her we'd be closer to the nursery.' She peered at him coyly from under her lashes. 'When the time comes for producing an heir, that is.'

Amber eyes flashed appreciatively. 'You can't say we're not putting the effort in. You've worn me out.'

'I've worn *you* out?'

'Yes.' He stretched both arms above his head and yawned. 'For a small woman, you have a surprising amount of energy, not to mention imagination. I think I might have injured my back this time. I may have to lie here all day to recover.'

'What about the mine?'

He opened his arms out towards her. 'What's the point of having a bad leg if you can't use it as an excuse to sleep in once in a while? Now come back to bed and nurse me.'

'You're incorrigible.'

'You *were* warned.'

'Repeatedly. Why do you think I tried to run away?'

'Twice.' He grinned. 'Am I such a beast?'

'Yes, but you're *my* beast.'

She clambered on to the bed, nestling against his shoulder and rubbing her cheek gently against his chest. He felt warm and solid and temptingly snug. Maybe they could lie there for a bit longer... But it was a beautiful day outside, perfect for the purpose she had in mind.

'Are you enjoying your third month of marriage, Mrs Amberton?' He dipped his head to press a kiss into her hair.

'I got more sleep during the first two…' she stroked a hand over his stomach '…not that I'm complaining.'

'It's your fault for being so damned irresistible.'

'That's not what you said before we were married. You said you could wait seven years.'

'Don't remind me,' he groaned. 'Two months was long enough. I would never have made it to a year with my sanity intact.'

'Then it's lucky you didn't have to wait so long after all.'

She sighed as his lips rubbed across her throat and then started to move downwards, surrendering herself briefly to the feeling, just as she had twice the night before and once already that morning. But this time, she admonished herself, she wasn't going to surrender, not completely. She had her own plans for the day. After that, however…

She slid out from beside him, spinning around to straddle his thighs and drop a kiss on to his chest, before jumping quickly off the bed. 'But you *do* need to wait until tonight. Come on!'

'Tease.' Lance heaved himself up behind her.

'It's the only way I know to motivate you.' She laughed gleefully. 'Come on. There's something I want to show you outside. It's a surprise.'

They dressed and wandered out of the house and across the lawns, arms around each other's waists. The gardens were in full bloom, a riotous mixture of colour and sweet scents all vying for supremacy in the summer sunshine.

'Here we are.' She stopped at the entrance to the maze.

'My surprise is in there?'

'Yes!' She grabbed his hand, pulling him down a long corridor and around a series of bends.

'You know where you're going, I suppose?' He followed after her obediently.

'I'm starting to find my way around.'

She stopped when they reached the centre, gesturing towards the rose arbour in the corner. Between her and Martin they'd restored and repainted the wood, trimmed the rose bushes and trailed them delicately around the frame. 'It looked so sad and neglected before.'

'It was.' Lance looked sombre for a moment. 'This was one of my mother's favourite places.'

She squeezed his hand. 'Now we can sit here together.'

'Yes.' His voice cracked slightly. 'Thank you, Violet.'

'You gave me her sitting room. I wanted to give you something of hers as well.'

'You've given me more than I ever deserved. I never imagined that I could be this happy.'

'Me neither.' She sighed. 'This place really is like a fairy tale. I can't wait to show Aunt Caroline when she comes to visit.'

'Why don't you invite her for a house party this summer? And your uncle Ben and all your new cousins, too.'

'You wouldn't mind?'

'Why would I? It would save us all traipsing back and forth to York every weekend.' He squeezed her hand back. 'I told you they'd love you.'

'So you did. It was just hard to believe back then.'

'You've come a long way. We both have.'

'I still can't believe that my father refused to let them visit me.'

She frowned and he tugged her against him. 'Maybe he wanted to keep you all to himself. I'm starting to understand the impulse. But that's all in the past now. A wise woman once told me that some things are best left there.'

'You're right.' She wrapped her arms around

him gratefully. 'What about Arthur? Will he mind a house party?'

His expression wavered. 'I think Arthur has his own plans.'

'He still wants to go back to sea?'

'I doubt that it would be possible any more. Now his secret's out, he'd have a job finding a skipper willing to employ a viscount. But he's still determined to leave.'

'Then you have to let him.'

'I know. I only hope he finds someone to make him as happy as I am.'

'Who would have thought it, a timid mouse and a reprobate?'

'A kitten and a beast?'

'Violet and Lance.' She lifted her head up to kiss him lightly, and then not so lightly, on the lips. 'Who will Arthur find, I wonder?'

* * * * *

MILLS & BOON

Coming next month

A NIGHT OF SECRET SURRENDER
Sophia James

'I remember you told me once that you wanted to be a writer.' Shay said.

Celeste breathed out and stood, moving towards the window and looking across the city rooftops.

'You are probably the only person in the world who knows this about me.'

'I kept the story you wrote. The one you gifted me for my eighteenth birthday.'

'A tale of two sisters. One good and one evil. I used to imagine myself as the commendable sister, the one whose life ran along the path of righteousness, but now...' She stopped and placed her palm on the glass. When she took it off the frosted warmth of skin left a mark into which she wrote her initials. C.V.F. Celeste Victoria Fournier. Another thing he remembered about her, the two sides of her heritage.

'I panicked today. I have never done that before and it worries me, because if it happens again it will be too dangerous for the both of us and I would not want...'

He stood and took her hand and the same sense of shock he had felt last night seared through him again.

'The dangers are there anyway, Celeste, crouching and close, no matter what we try to do to lessen them.'

She was soft and unresisting as he drew her in, the